MYRINE GOES THROUGH THE QUANTUM DOOR

By
Amouré Kleu

Available as an ebook

ISBN   979-8-9919072-3-1 (paperback)

ISBN   979-8-3024593-5-0 (hardcover)

Copyright © 2024 by Amouré Kleu

All Rights Reserved. No part of this publication may be reproduced, distributed, or transmitted in any form or by any means, including photocopying, recording, or other electronic or mechanical methods without the prior written permission of the publisher. For permission requests, solicit the publisher via the address below.

No part of this book may be used or reproduced in any manner for the purpose of training artificial intelligence technologies or systems, and will be included in all new titles and any backlist titles that are reprinted. 18 Oct 2024

Publify Publishing

Lampasas, TX 76550

contact@publifypublishing.com

DEDICATION

To my support group, Chris and Suzanne Styles – without your unfailing support, this would not have happened.

To Alan, thank you for your support.

And last, but not the least, thank you Amanda Armstrong and Publify Publishing for making my dream come true.

CONTENTS

BEFORE 1
CHAPTER 1 6
CHAPTER 2 17
CHAPTER 3 26
CHAPTER 4 35
CHAPTER 5 46
CHAPTER 6 57
CHAPTER 7 64
CHAPTER 8 73
CHAPTER 9 80
CHAPTER 10 87
CHAPTER 11 100
CHAPTER 12 111
CHAPTER 13 124
CHAPTER 14 132
CHAPTER 15 144
CHAPTER 16 155
CHAPTER 17 166
CHAPTER 18 179
CHAPTER 19 190

CHAPTER 20	199
CHAPTER 21	209
CHAPTER 22	220
CHAPTER 23	232
CHAPTER 24	240
About the Author	249

BEFORE

Mute, her bare feet frozen to the cement bathroom floor, three-year-old Myrine stood between her parents. Her hands fisted in her mother's toweling robe. Above her head, the argument escalated. Fear held her captive in the palm of its hand.

'I told you I don't want her. I *never* wanted her.'

'Stephanie please! You can go back to Uni and finish your degree. My mother will look after M…'

'Noah. Your precious mother can have her! Myrine even looks like her. If it was not because I birthed her, I would have sworn she is your mother's daughter.'

'She is our daughter; you cannot just give her…'

'And you and your mother stopped me from having an abortion. She is your daughter.'

'What do I tell my mother? She will…'

'You can tell her I found her creating fire balls. She is a danger to us and herself. Your magical mother can deal with that.'

Myrine fisted her hands tighter in the folds of her mother's robe and closed her eyes. Lava hot tears spilled over her cheeks. Sudden pain seared her scalp. Her eyes flew open. She stared at her mother's sharp nosed, twisted face. Her breath hitched, and her hands loosened its grip. Her mother shoved her away, and she fell into her father's knees.

Eighteen months followed, in which Myrine stayed with her grandmother at Silken Oak, the Adelstein family wine estate in the Blue Mountains. Her parents moved to Sydney and her father visited sporadically, bearing gifts. Myrine became her grandmother's shadow.

When Myrine turned five, Stephanie had finished her law degree, and accompanied Noah when he visited his mother and Myrine on their respective birthdays. Despite Myrine's best efforts, bearing cut flowers from the rose gardens on those occasions.

No matter how hard she tried, she never pleased her mother. All she received for her efforts were snide comments. She stopped telling her father or grandmother about it. There were never any witnesses and when Myrine told her father, Stephanie ridiculed Myrine and made her out to be a liar.

When it became clear she would never return to her mother and father, Myrine's grandmother legally adopted her. Her grandmother noticed Myrine's supernatural magical powers. Encouraging Myrine, Grandma taught her the importance of controlling her powers.

'You must take care, darling child. Control your powers. It is not good if your powers control you.'

Wise beyond her age, Myrine absorbed all the knowledge in physical and theoretical lessons Grandma imparted to her. Myrine's energy was boundless, and Grandma enlisted her trusted companion, Aedric's help to train Myrine in combining martial arts with her supernatural powers. He was also a specialist in numerology calculations and imparted his vast knowledge to Myrine.

Myrine's date of birth, 21 September 1994, was numerically in sync with the Infinity Symbol, its sum total being eight. It foretold that she would be taking over from Grandma as Light Force Leader on Earth when she turned eighteen.

Despite her mother's vituperous objections, at age six, Grandma enrolled Myrine at St Katherine's School for the Gifted in Katoomba. By age fourteen, Myrine had fully developed her supernatural powers. Grandma thought it was the right time to share the history and importance of the Adelstein female Light Force members.

'You are very special, my child. I spoke with Aedric, and we are going to veer in a bit of a different direction with your training.'

'But I love my training with both of you.'

'You will continue your training, dearest. We are simply going to have you combine your supernatural powers with your martial arts training.

'Why?'

'From your numerology reading that Aedric had done, you will be a superior Light Force. So, if you had to combine your martial art skills with your magical supernatural abilities, it would better prepare you for your future.'

A bubble of excitement set Myrine afloat. Then her mind raced ahead, and she could not get a fix on what it all meant. A tendril of anxiety uncurled in her stomach. Her training changed course, and she learnt to combine her supernatural magical abilities with her martial arts. She overcame her anxiety and threw herself heart and soul into her new training.

The morning of her sixteenth birthday, Grandma told her she would travel to Tsaonin when she turned eighteen. There they would inaugurate her as the next Light Force Leader of Earth.

'Do I have to take over from you so early?'

'My child. I am not getting any younger, and I never had a daughter to take my place. I want you to start the journey of your future whilst I can still be there to mentor you.'

Myrine see-sawed between panic and pride. Her final thought when she got ready for her sixteenth birthday dinner with Grandma,

Myrine Goes Through the Quantum Door

Aedric and her parents was: - *maybe now mother would love and accept me.*

Her parents arrived for her birthday dinner. Myrine hardly tasted the food. She had decided, without telling a soul, to share the news of her upcoming inauguration in two years' time. Ignoring her gut instinct, she blurted out her news as they were about to have desert.

'What?! Are you insane, old woman? Are you disinheriting Noah of his birthright?'

'Myrine passed all the tests and the Universal Light Force Leader agreed she is to take over from me as the leader here on Earth when she turns eighteen.'

'I cannot believe my ears. Noah, can you believe this?'

'The Adelstein's rights to lead the Light Forces on Earth are handed down from the eldest female to the next eldest female in line. As far as I am aware, my only child is male, and it therefore falls to his daughter, who bears the Adelstein name and is the next female in line.'

'What would a stupid eighteen-year-old know about the responsibilities of a leader?'

'You may not have noticed, but Myrine is very mature for her age and has proven that she is capable of …'

'The Light Forces' days are numbered. A new era is dawning, and the Dark Forces will soon rule Earth.'

'And you and your Dark Forces don't have the Infinity Charm…'

'Myrine is my daughter and shall return home with us now. Noah, get the Infinity Charm from your mother and bring it to me.'

Horrified that her mother was a Dark Force member, Myrine stared daggers at her mother. For the first time in her life, Myrine acknowledged that which always lurked in her subconscious. Her mother did not love her. She only wanted her now so she could use her for her own gain.

Myrine stood up and stepped back from the table. She saw Grandma fingering the Infinity Charm hanging around her neck and immobilize her father. Myrine felt the whisper of movement to her left. She teleported herself a meter backwards, evading her mother. The last vestiges of her self-control snapped, and she threw a fireball. Off-kilter, it skimmed close to Grandma and landed in the fireplace, setting the dry wood ablaze. Aedric knocked Stephanie off balance and Grandma whipped a rope out of thin air, binding Stephanie's wrists.

'Aedric. Put them in their car and drive them off the premises. Remove the gate control from Noah, as well as any keys of the house and the winery. It will be in the car's console.'

The next day, the Sheriff arrived and served Grandma with a court application in which her mother requested the court to order that Myrine be returned to her care. A harrowing eighteen months followed. The court finally ordered that Myrine's adoption by Grandma was legal and to remain in place. On the court steps, after the order was granted, Stephanie turned to Myrine.

'This is not the end.'

CHAPTER 1

Myrine shuffled around on the solid Ironwood chair in Aedric's dining room. Aedric, a talented numerologist, and ex Special Forces, arrived a month after Myrine came to live with Grandma at Silken Oak. Besides being Grandma's right-hand man, he was also Myrine's extra mural tutor. He taught her how to refine some of her supernatural powers and combine it successfully with martial arts. Schooled her in numerology. Over the years, she came to think of him as her surrogate father.

Myrine looked at the questionnaire, then at the wall clock. It had to be completed on time. She straightened her back and rotated her shoulders. This would be her last test with Aedric, before she was due to travel through the Quantum Door on her eighteenth birthday. In two week's time.

Since her nightmare dream last night, she worried about the numerology calculations Aedric had done. It would have to be absolute, or she would find herself portal hopping through the five hostile Dark Force planes between Earth and Tsaonin. She tried to regain her focus on the questionnaire. Her mind refused to co-operate. There must be a way she could convince Grandma to delay their intended travel.

She pulled her chair closer to the table, banishing the goblins of fear. A lock of copper red hair fell over her eyes. She tucked it behind her right ear, picked up the pencil, and opened the questionnaire. The front door opened and Myrine heard Aedric's familiar footsteps approach.

'Any problems with the questions?'

'No. Just making sure I understand the question correctly before I answer.'

'Are you sure?'

Myrine bent forward and ticked off the answer to the first question in section one, then half-smiled at Aedric.

'I leave you to it, then. Keep your eye on the time.'

Aedric disappeared down the passage towards his study and she returned her full attention to the questionnaire. Getting the answers wrong or handing in an incomplete questionnaire wouldn't carry any favour with Grandma.

Myrine read through the first section, ticking off the answers. A thrill fizzed through her. If the whole test was like this, she would be done in no time, and she could focus on how to twist Grandma's arm. She turned the page to the second section. It was not beyond Aedric to lay a trap by asking the same question in two different ways. Putting her pencil down, she pulled on her left earlobe. She was not allowed an eraser to correct her answers. She swallowed, eased the page back and double checked her previous answers. All were correct.

Myrine put her elbows on the table, dropped her head into her hands, and took a deep breath. She turned the page to the second section. This time, she traced every question with her right index finger, read through it, and mouthed the answers. And there it was. The hidden trick. In the second last question of section two. *Got you.* She picked up her pencil, re-read each question and ticked off the answers.

Myrine sat back in the chair and rolled the pencil between her palms. She glanced at the wall clock. Fifteen minutes to go. She turned the page. The bold heading of the last section – **The Quantum Door** - leapt off the page. Butterfly wings quivered behind her navel. She bit down on her lower lip.

An onslaught of images from the dream of the night before, assaulted her. The grotesque image of the half man, half Goanna-like creature chasing her loomed. Apprehension blossomed full force in her stomach and sent a gas bubble galloping through her intestines.

Her hand shook as she answered the questions on what to do if one entered the Quantum Door at the wrong time.

'Use unstable portals,' she whispered, and ticked off the last answer. She shut the questionnaire, shuddered, and put the pencil down. She clamped her damp hands between her knees. Aedric's footsteps sounded in the passage. Myrine swung herself sideways on the chair.

'I finished the questionnaire.'

'That's good. You have done it on time. I'll make us a cuppa and we can go through it.'

'I would rather..'

But Aedric had already disappeared into the kitchen. She stood up, walked halfway to the kitchen. Stopped. Walked back to her chair and sat down. Myrine could not remember ever being this apprehensive.

Grandma taught her that intuition was the highest form of knowledge and never to be ignored. She would understand when Myrine explained about the warning from her nightmare. All she needed was some time alone with Grandma. Without Aedric present.

She had to convince Aedric to let her go earlier than usual. The wall clock chimed. The kettle whistled. If she could avoid staying with Aedric whilst he marked the questionnaire, there would be enough time for her to see Grandma alone before dinner at six. From experience, she knew that any hope for her request to be considered, she needed Grandma's undivided attention.

Aedric appeared with two steaming cups of peppermint tea and set down one in front of Myrine. He walked around the table and settled in a chair opposite her. She studied his face as he pulled the questionnaire towards himself and flicked it open, going straight to the second section. He looked at the bottom of the page and rubbed the side of his nose with his thumb. Aedric looked at her, a smile crinkling the corners of his mouth.

'Aah. You caught me out this time?'

Myrine grinned, lifted her chin and looked him square in the eye.

'Yip.'

She watched Aedric pushing the questionnaire aside. Their ritual was to first have their tea. Now would be the moment to distract him. She picked up her cup, brought the rim to her lips, and took a large sip. The tea scalded her tongue. Myrine ignored the pain and forced herself to swallow. She suppressed a yelp and rolled her tongue across her numb palate. Her hand shook. She clattered the cup onto its saucer. Hot tea splattered. She jumped up, ran to the kitchen, and grabbed a tea towel.

'Myrine? What is wrong?'

Myrine ignored Aedric and wiped the table.

'Myrine?'

She fumbled the soiled tea cloth into a damp ball and looked at Aedric. His thick black eyebrows two question marks above his eyes. Her eyes skittered away. Maybe there was a way she could convince Aedric that the upcoming travel through the Quantum Door must be delayed.

'Aedric..'

Myrine swallowed the squeak and cleared her throat. She scuffed her feet. Heat suffused her neck and spread to her cheeks. She checked the time on the wall clock. Looked at Aedric, watching her. His arms folded across his chest. She put down the bundled tea cloth, put her hands behind her back, and crossed her fingers.

'What is bothering you?'

Myrine licked her lips.

'Have you ever encountered problems when you travelled through the Quantum Door?'

'I always travelled through it at the correct time and date, in line with my numerology calculations.'

Myrine mentally kicked herself. Opening the door to a lecture would not help her. She loved him dearly, but his unwillingness to even consider the possibility of a miscalculation rubbed salt into her raw nerves. Biting the inside of her cheek, she stood and let his words wash over her. Interrupting him was not an option. It would only make him repeat what he had already said.

Her mind drifted. From her studies with Grandma, she knew if she travelled through the Quantum Door at the wrong time, she would have to brave the treacherous portals linking the five universal planes between Earth and Tsaonin. Worse, the Dark Forces ruled those planes.

'Myrine. Do you understand?'

Time to pretend she had been listening. She displayed what she hoped was a convincing smile and nodded her head.

'I know you have prepared everything with the utmost care. I know neither you nor Grandma would allow me to come to any harm, but…'

'Your Grandma will be with you.'

'I know. But what if something goes wrong?'

'Your Grandma is experienced in travelling through the Quantum Door. She has done so on many occasions.'

'But what if your numerology calculations are wrong?'

'Numbers don't lie. The only time it could be wrong is if you have changed your name, which you have not. The calculations, which were done in accordance with your date of birth and your registered birth names, show you are to travel through the Quantum Door on your birthday two weeks from now.'

'A rule is not a rule unless there is an exception to it, Aedric! What if..'

'Why are you afraid of going through the Quantum Door?'

'I..'

No. He would write off her nightmare as a nervous reaction to the upcoming travel.

'Your Grandma and I have triple checked the calculations and each time it showed the same time and date. It is very much like the astral travelling you have done so many times.'

'Something could go wrong.'

'Nothing will go wrong. You will be fine. You have been fully trained. Now stop fretting. There is nothing to fear.'

'Not everything in life can be based on numbers, Aedric! You cannot always be right.'

She should have known Aedric, the perfectionist, would insist on the correctness of his numerology calculations. She was glad she stopped herself from bringing up her nightmare. He would either disregard it or lecture her. She has known him long enough to know it was more likely to be the latter.

A sudden gust dragged a protesting tree branch across the window. Myrine's gaze jerked to the window. A cloud had gauze-wrapped the sun and dialed its brightness down to a cold and dirty dishwater grey. The wall clock struck four.

The number of deaths in Chinese. The Chinese tradition considered it an inauspicious number, homophonous to death. Omen after omen. Myrine rubbed the back of her neck, bent down, dragged her school bag from under the table and put it on the chair.

'We still have to go through your answers.'

She looked at Aedric's stern face and, lifting her chin, she held his stare.

'I prefer we discuss it with Grandma present at dinner. I would like to leave now. There seems to be a storm brewing.'

Aedric looked out the window, pushed back his chair and nodded.

'We can do that. She always likes me to go through it with her, anyway. You want me to run you over to the main house?'

Myrine looked down. She wanted to speak to Grandma without him present. They would just join forces and try to reassure her. She would not get a word in edgeways.

'No. I prefer walking home. The exercise will help clear my head. If I leave now, I will make it home before the rain.'

Myrine lifted her school bag and struggled one strap over her shoulder.

'Leave your bag. I will bring it with me when I come over for dinner later.'

She slipped the strap off her shoulder and walked round to Aedric. She pecked him on his whiskery cheek. Half-hearted, she allowed him to pull her into a hug.

'You will be fine, child. I have checked the numbers countless times.'

Myrine stepped back.

'I am not so sure. You have not always been right.'

She saw his cheeks redden. It was a low blow to remind him of the one and only mistake he made that nearly landed him and Grandma in serious trouble. Without another word, she turned and rushed out the front door.

Standing on the top step, she eyed the dark grey sky. Pulling her hoodie tighter around her shoulders, she stepped onto the footpath. Her sneakers crunched through the Silken Oak leaves, littering the footpath. Their musky odour swirled up around her and tickled her nose. Taking a tissue out of her pocket, she sneezed into it.

Myrine crumpled the tissue into a ball and squashed it back into her hoodie's pocket. She checked her watch. The walk would take about twenty minutes, leaving her with barely enough time to speak with Grandma before dinner. She set off for the main house. The wind had picked up its pace to a low howl. It carried the promise of rain on its breath. The weather was ominously similar to that at the beginning of her dream.

Myrine hastened through the woods. Exiting the woods, she reached the last stretch where hedges grew on either side of the footpath. She stopped and gulped some air. Behind her, a tree branch creaked. Her scalp prickled. Her back hollowed. She glanced over her shoulder. Tree branches rustled and swayed. With a rifle-shot crack, a tree branch fell on the footpath. She staggered back, tripped over a loose shoelace, and landed with a painful thud.

Myrine knew she was allowing her imagination to play tricks on her mind. She re-tied her shoelaces, got up, and dusted the seat of her pants. She set off with a determined power walk towards the main house. She was sure there was a warning to be heeded, hidden in her dream.

Myrine rounded the second last bend of the footpath. She half-registered a dark image stationary in the middle of the footpath. The Goanna turned its head and fixed her with a dead-eye reptilian stare. Her feet stuttered to a stop. The Goanna flicked out its forked tongue. The vision of the creature in her dream jumped into her head.

Time slowed. A steel band cinched around her windpipe. Her heart started beating a fierce tattoo against its rib cage prison. Her pulse leapt in synchronization, and trip-hammered in her ears. All sound around

Myrine was muted. Goosebumps raised on her forearms, pinching her skin.

She knew she could enter the Goanna's mind and move it off the path and gathered her energy. About to enter the Goanna's mind, a vision of the fierce goanna-like creature rearing up neutralised her. Her confidence flagged. She could not afford to get stuck for an hour like she did during one of her practices with Aedric.

With her eyes glued to the Goanna on the footpath, she crouched, and no longer presented as being taller than the hedge. They stared at each other. An eternity passed. The Goanna dropped its head, swaggered off the path, and disappeared under the hedge.

Her eyes on the spot where the Goanna had disappeared, Myrine eased a step forward. The underbrush rustled. Goanna's were not confrontational but it would still be better to stay clear of it. If cornered, it would retaliate with a nasty tail-swipe. She shuffled forward. At the spot where the Goanna had disappeared, she stopped and scanned the ground below the hedge.

On the screen of Myrine's mind, an obstinate clip from her nightmarish dream replayed the scene of the large goanna-like creature, ready to attack. Now if that was not a bad Omen….

Ensured the Goanna had moved on, Myrine straightened up. She rubbed the small of her back. Sodden with sweat, her shirt clung to her back. She looked up. The sky was now filled with pregnant purple and slate grey clouds. From the woods behind her, a Noisy Miner shrieked its eerie alarm call.

A tremor piano-fingered up her spine. She snapped a look over her shoulder. There have always been Noisy Miners in these woods. But the feeling of impending doom kept nibbling at her. Is it just a bird or is it another warning? She started running towards the main house.

Rounding the last bend, the main house came into view. Above the roof, two angry thunder clouds collided. A phosphorus bolt of lightning cascaded over the dark house. Thunder rumbled, clearing its throat.

How odd. Grandma always switched the lights on. Her feet slowed. She pursed her lips. Myrine could not remember ever coming home to a dark house. The back door, her usual option of entry, did not feel right. She contemplated the dark house. Warning bells clanged.

Myrine slid behind the Silken Oak tree, standing sentry near the back door. She could slip in the front door that was hardly used, but never locked. She peeked around the tree trunk and squinted at the house. The outdoor light above the back door flicked on. Myrine jerked her head back and molded herself to the tree trunk.

She heard the familiar squeak of the screen door. The loud jangle of an unfamiliar mobile ringtone sprung into the air. Her ears went on high alert. She recognised the shrill voice of her mother's secretary, Serilda. In that instant, it confirmed something sinister was afoot. Neither that woman nor her mother, both Dark Force members, were allowed here. They were banned from Silken Oak Estate since the court case.

How on earth had Serilda gained entry to the estate? And into the house!? What happened to Grandma's security settings that kept the Dark Forces out?

Myrine's nostrils flared. She gripped the rough tree trunk and leaned sideways. It was Serilda, standing framed in the backdoor. Her mobile to her ear. Myrine took a silent step sideways, and another one forward. Her ears strained, she followed snatches of Serilda's side of the conversation.

'No, she is not here. ……………Yes, I have checked the entire house. ………… She is probably still at Aedric's cottage. …… Ok. I will go there now.'

The ice-icy hand of unease caressed the back of Myrine's neck as she deduced that the only person who would normally be at Aedric's cottage at this time of day was she herself. She knew she could overpower Serilda.

But. What if Serilda was not the only Dark Force on the property? Myrine squelched her angry impulse and retreated into the shadow of the tree. It would be foolish to show herself before she knew what was happening.

Myrine watched Serilda disappear around the corner of the house. She sent an urgent telepathic warning to Aedric. A car alarm blipped, followed by a car door slamming shut. Following the sound of the car's tyres crunching over the loose gravel of the driveway, Myrine forced herself to wait until it completely faded.

She stepped out from behind the tree trunk and scrutinized the house. The only light was that of the outside backdoor light. In the garden, the solar security lights one by one ghosted to life.

She sent out a tentative telepathic enquiry to Grandma and waited. It remained unanswered.

CHAPTER 2

Myrine rushed to the back door. She teetered to a stop at the bottom step. Behind her, a gust shook the sentry oak's branches and crackled through its leaves. Her back hollowed, and a shudder rippled through her. She glanced over her shoulder. No one in sight. This was the wrong time to give in to panic. She looked back at the door.

A raindrop plopped-splashed on her crown. She looked up. Pregnant purple-blue clouds, Pac-man swallowed the few remaining cotton-candy clouds. Errant raindrops splotched around her. Thunder cleared its throat. She pinched her nose, swallowed a sneeze, and crept up the two steps. She squeezed the screen door's handle down, opened it a crack, and wriggled into the opening. The screen door settled against her back. She opened the backdoor halfway and peered into the silent gloom. Holding her breath, she braced a hand against the screen door and stepped forward. She turned, eased the screen door shut and silently closed the backdoor.

She flattened her palms against the back door and leaned back. Pulsatile silence sung in her ears. A vein triple-pulsed below her jawline. She counted to thirty in her head. Her heartbeat slowed and her ears cleared. Her sight adjusted to the gloom, and she did a detailed sweep of the open-plan kitchen and dining room. A feather of unease tickled her tailbone. The absence of Grandma's usual dinner preparations screamed at her. An enormous crack of thunder sliced through the silence. A few heavy raindrops landed on the roof. Within a split-second, it escalated into a full-on drumming session.

Pushing away from the back door and, under cover of the noise, she moved deeper into the semi-darkness. A billion-candle powered streak of lightning crackled through the open blinds of the kitchen window. Her right foot snagged on the heavy base of a kitchen counter stool. She wobbled. The chair tilted. She snatched it, righted it, and set it back under the counter. She ignored the throb in her big toe, rocked onto the balls of her feet and inched towards the living room. Eyes on the doorway to the living room, she missed the sliver of light sneaking through the tiny crack of the unlatched door leading from the kitchen to the herb cellar. Dark blobs of familiar yet unfamiliar furniture dotted the living room.

Myrine turned and went up the staircase. She stepped over the loose riser on the last step and hesitated on the landing. The rain had stopped. Above her, a roof truss released a static creak. A nervous tick sprung to life in her right eyelid. She could not afford to get trapped upstairs in the house. She approached the first room on her right and eased open the half-closed door. The desk lamp threw a mellow circle on the green leather desktop. Languid dust motes drifted up and down its light beams. Grandma's reading glasses lay askance on an open book. The top desk drawer was misaligned.

Stepping up to the desk, Myrine eased the drawer open. Her fingers found the spring catch in the back panel and unlatched it. It was empty. Panic ripped a hole in her gut. One hand pressed to her breastbone, the other, white knuckled on the desktop, she dry-swallowed. The key to Grandma's safe, where she kept the Infinity Charm, was gone.

Myrine snuck out of the study, down the empty corridor, past all the rooms, and into Grandma's bedroom. She hovered in the doorjamb and sniffed at the air. An unfamiliar perfume tainted it. Satisfied that the room was empty, she went to the walk-in robe. She pushed aside the clothing hangers, sunk to her haunches and lifted the fake floorboard. The safe door was open. The safe empty.

Myrine willed herself to her feet. She, now more than ever before, had to keep her wits about her. Even if her mother had the Infinity Charm, she still needed Myrine to unlock its powers on her eighteenth birthday. She rushed out of the room. A quick check-over of the spare bedroom had shown it to be undisturbed.

She walked into her own bedroom. Bunny sat silent sentry against her bed pillows. Her mind in turmoil, she picked up Bunny and hugged him to her chest. Walking to the open window, she unconsciously rubbed his one threadbare ear. There was no movement in the gardens below.

Putting Bunny back, she picked up her Mag-Lite mini pocket torch from the bedside table and switched it on. Taking care to keep the beam below the windowsill level, she closed the bedroom door and walked into her walk-in robe. She set down the torch on its tail cap on top of the chest of drawers. She rummaged through her clothes. Grabbing a pair of all-weather pants, shirt, and hoodie, she changed into it. From her shoe rack, she grabbed a sturdy pair of water-proof walking shoes at the back of her shoe cupboard and pulled it on. She unhooked her personalised utility belt from the belt rack and tied it around her waist. It was better to be over prepared rather than under.

Myrine studied her shadow-face in the full-length mirror behind the door as she re-tied her ponytail. She wondered if the stranger staring back at her had what it takes to go up against her mother and the Dark Forces. It worried her that she would most likely have to rely on her supernatural powers. She should have been less obstinate and more proactive in developing them during training with Grandma and Aedric. It was no use wasting time on wishful thinking. Myrine straightened her shoulders and lifted her chin. There was only one more room left to check. The herb cellar. She flicked off the torch, stuck it in her belt, and left her room.

On her way to the stairs, passing the study door, a flicker of movement caught the corner of Myrine's eye. She halted, reversed her steps, and stopped at the study door. The large security screen on the wall opposite the desk had come alive. Stunned, she watched as the automatic gates to the estate opened. Her mother's midnight-black Range Rover entered. It confirmed her suspicion that the Dark Forces were behind whatever was taking place. Myrine counted what looked like three male passengers in the car.

A premonitory tremor fluttered. Her mother was here to make good on her threat to take Myrine and the Infinity charm from Grandma's protective custody and hand her over to Surneal, the Universal Dark Force leader. She flashed back to her terrified three-year-old self when Dad delivered her to Grandma. Fast forward to the present, Dad once again supported her mother during the recent court case to overturn her formal adoption by Grandma.

Then, yesterday, he popped in for a peace-making visit. She slapped her forehead. Her missing gate control since yesterday. Dad must have taken it. A wave of misery washed through her. She should have told Grandma it was missing.

Myrine watched the screen until her mother's car took the right-hand fork towards Aedric's cottage. She hurried out of the study and bounded down the stairs. Breathless, she reached the herb cellar door and wrenched it open. Bright light from below spilled over the stairs. Myrine cocked her head. Not a sound. She pushed the door closed without clicking it shut. Taking hold of the banister and slide-walked down the staircase. She jumped over the last two steps. Glass crunched under her feet.

Myrine rocked to a stop and frowned at the mess. She skirted the glass shards and eased deeper into the cellar. At the back, Grandma sat in a chair behind her work bench, duct tape over her mouth. Grandma's eyes fluttered open. Mute, they stared at each other. Myrine surged forward and sank to her knees in front of Grandma. She recoiled.

Grandma's wrists were encircled by a black magic witch's ladder knot. No wonder Grandma did not respond to her messages.

Myrine struggled to her feet. She bit down on her lower lip and removed the duct tape. She rested her forehead against Grandma's.

'I need your guidance to undo the witch's ladder knot. Mother is on the premises, and we need to get out of here now.'

'This witch's ladder knot curtails all my powers. It is time you learn to trust in yourself and follow your inner guidance.'

'I am not sure I …..'

'Stop it Myrine. Look at me. You have every ability I have and more. Now is not the time to re-debate this worn-out issue.'

Myrine straightened up and scanned through her eidetic memory. She hunkered down and started unraveling the knot strand by strand. Despite the cool cellar air, sweat streamed down her back and dampened her armpits. More than once, she had to rub her palms on her pants. The last strand of the witch's ladder knot unraveled, Myrine stood up and helped Grandma up. They hugged each other in a tight embrace.

'I am so sorry; I think Dad took my gate control yesterday and….'

'Don't worry about that now. All is not lost.'

'The safe… the Infinity Charm…'

'I have it. We have little time. Come with me.'

She trailed behind Grandma to the hidden chamber in the side wall. When the wall panel opened, Myrine was immediately drawn to the shimmery backpack inside the chamber.

'Wait child. Let me explain first.'

Myrine put her hands in front of her and interlaced her fingers. She sponged up the rapid-fire delivery of information.

Myrine Goes Through the Quantum Door | 21

'Take off your watch and put this one on. This is your Quantum watch. It will show the exact time you must go through the Quantum Door to land in Tsaonin. Once there, go to the Pagoda of Tsaonin and ask for an audience with Aerwyna.'

'You are not coming with me?'

'I have to stay to delay them so you can get to the Quantum Door safely. Take off your hoodie and turn around so I can put your backpack on.'

Conflicted, Myrine took off her hoodie, turned around and slipped her arms through the backpack's shoulder straps.

'Put your hoodie back on.'

The backpack immediately became invisible as its feather weight settled against her back. Myrine turned around and reached for Grandma's hands.

'Please come with me.'

'Myrine. They have come for you and the Infinity Charm. Surneal is on his way. They will focus on me to get you to surrender yourself. If Surneal has you and the Infinity Charm, he will have the power to unseat the Light Force Universal Ruler in Tsaonin.'

'I am scared I might make a mistake. I had a nightmare last night and in it I went through the Quantum Door at the wrong time and…..'

'I set this watch to show you the correct time to enter the Quantum Door, taking you directly to Tsaonin.'

'And if something happens and I enter at the wrong time?'

'You will have two weeks Earth time to get to Tsaonin. The time on this watch will calibrate with Earth time and tell you how much time you have to travel through the plane portals to get to Tsaonin.'

'I have never been on any of the planes. What if I cannot find the portals?'

'You passed your studies on all the planes at 100%. All the knowledge you need is up here.'

'I will be alone and without protection.'

'You will never be alone. Your spirit guides will all be with you. You have your supernatural powers…'

'But what if…'

'No more buts.'

Myrine drew back from Grandma. Uninvited tears filled her eyes. She clenched her jaw and balled her hands.

'Come now. Come now. Your mother and her cohorts will soon be back here. We have to hurry.'

Myrine opened her right hand and allowed Grandma to guide her palm to the side-pocket of the backpack. The charm vibrated under their hands.

'This is your destiny, as the eldest female Adelstein after me. It is the only way we can save Earth from the ruling of the Dark Forces. In two weeks from now, its power will transfer to you. Keep it safe until then.'

She dropped her head on Grandma's shoulder.

'I am just too scared.'

'Rather scared than overconfident. It will keep you alert.'

Her palm on the side-pocket, Myrine followed Grandma to the workbench. She watched Grandma take two vials of colourless liquid and mix it.

'Before I drink this, I need you to promise me you will leave and go through the Quantum Door.'

Myrine shook her head.

'Say it aloud.'

'I promise.'

'Now remember. You cannot use the Infinity Charm before your eighteenth birthday, and it has to remain hidden at all times until then. Especially from the Dark Forces. You understand how to use the backpack.'

'Yes, Grandma.'

'This potion will put me in a deep coma for two weeks.'

'Wait! Are you sure mother won't harm you? She hates you with a vengeance.'

'She needs me alive until she has you and the Infinity Charm in her possession. Until then, I am safe.'

'She won't find me.'

'You made a promise.'

'I meant before I reach the Quantum Door in the winery, and I will go through it as promised.'

'I am going to sit down now and take this potion. It will put me in a coma, and I won't be able to communicate with you telepathically. It will only alert the Dark Forces of your whereabouts. You must re-tie the witch's ladder knot around my hands. It will not harm me. You have broken its power. We just need it to look as if it was never removed.'

Myrine walked around the workbench and hugged Grandma. Grandma sunk into the chair.

'The potion will work within twenty seconds. When you have re-tied me, clear away the vials and leave immediately.'

'I will. I love you.'

'I love you too, my darling child.'

Myrine kept her gaze on Grandma's emerald green eyes, so much like her own, until they closed. She picked up the witch's knot. She concentrated and conjured the picture of how it looked, concentrated her kinetic power, and watched it re-fasten itself.

Myrine cast about for the duct tape and found it under the workbench. She stood up too soon and caught the back of her head on the edge of the workbench. She stumbled onto her feet. Black and white starbursts exploded behind her eyelids. She touched the back of her head. There was no blood, just a hellish lump.

She turned back to Grandma, smoothed the duct tape over mouth, taking care not to obstruct her airflow. Placing her right-hand index and middle finger on Grandma's neck, she checked Grandma's pulse. It was slow, but steady. Myrine pushed a stray ribbon of silver-white hair behind Grandma's ear. She picked up the glass vials from the workbench, turned and went to the basin in the back corner. After rinsing them, she secreted it in the secret wall chamber and rolled the wall panel shut.

If only she told Grandma about her missing gate control last night. She shut her eyes tight and recited the Ho'oponopono prayer. I love you. I'm sorry. Please forgive me. Thank you. Her vibrational energy settled. She turned, marched to the stairs, and gripped the banister. Halfway to the top, a vibration tremored through the floorboards above. One of the upper stairwell walls creaked.

CHAPTER 3

Two steps from the top, Myrine heard the tell-tale squeak of the kitchen's screen door. She teetered to a stop. Her grip tightened around the banister. If that was Serilda, she could incapacitate her with little effort, but only if she was alone. She crept up the last two steps, flattened her left hand against the cellar door and inched the opening a tad wider. After a moment's hesitation, she upped her concentration of rod receptors, lowering her cone receptors and enabled her cat-like night vision.

She squinted at the dark silhouette detaching itself from the backdoor. It looked like a female but seemed to be taller than Serilda. It would be best not to take any chances. To save Grandma and the Earth from the Dark Forces, she had to reach the Quantum Door on time, and go to Tsaonin as promised.

She stood stock-still and tracked the figure moving towards the lighter shadows near the kitchen window. Her overly tight calf muscles quivered. There was something familiar in the sinuous way it moved. The figure stopped short of the kitchen window, turned its back to Myrine and faced the wall. Myrine gnashed her teeth and rotated her stiff neck without taking her eyes off the figure. The fluorescent kitchen light snapped on. The sudden brilliance scorched Myrine's eyeballs.

Blinded, she stumbled back behind the cellar door, closed her eyes, and pressed her palms over her eye sockets, shutting down her cat-like night vision. Her heart thundered. Her pulse trampled her eardrums. Fail and Grandma would die, and the evil Dark Forces would rule Earth.

How was she going to find out who it was without being seen? She dropped her hands, fisted them at her sides, and blinked. There had to be a way out of this. But first, she needed to find out who was in the kitchen. The sharp noise of the kitchen blinds being drawn closed sliced through her tattered nerves. At least in the cellar she could be safe in her old hiding spot, which only Grandma knew about, but then again, if it was Serilda....

Myrine sank down in a low crouch and peeked around the bottom half of the door into the bright kitchen. She craned her neck and searched the kitchen floor at the far end near the window. Her stomach laminated itself to her spine.

Dragonscats!

There was only one woman who wore black court shoes like that. Her mother. Shock waves raced through every part of her body. The only option now was to reach the secret chamber behind the panel before mother saw her. Myrine scampered down the stairs, barely avoiding the crushed glass, and raced to the panel covering the secret chamber. Her numbed fingers fumbled and scrabble-searched over the panel for the invisible indentation. *Where is it!?*

Got you. She pushed it with her index finger and stood back. She fisted her right hand and shoved the first two knuckles into the indent, giving it an almighty push. *Why won't it move?* She frowned at the stubborn panel, trying to work out what was wrong. *Of course, the spell.* She needed to incant the spell, the one she'd concocted at age twelve. Then the panel would open.

Above, the cellar door crashed open and banged against the wall. A demonic draft tumbled into the basement. Myrine clasped the back of her neck and hazarded a quick look at the stairs. She knew she had mere seconds before her mother would reach the bottom of the stairs and see her. If caught, her mother would hand her over to the Universal Dark Force leader, Surneal, who had the power to turn the Infinity Charm's powers to the Dark Forces. Her promise to Grandma to take the Infinity Charm to Tsaonin to save Earth from the Dark Forces would fail. Worse! They would kill Grandma and every Light Force member refusing to convert to a Dark Force member. With renewed determination, Myrine turned to the panel and pressed her palm over the indentation.

Magicae cogo te aperire, Myrine murmured. Faint, sapphire blue chain links sprung to life on the indentation. It started unlocking. The panel had barely whooshed open when Myrine hunched her shoulders and reverse-squished herself into the tight alcove. A stair creaked and Myrine looked up at the elongated shadow sliding down the stairs. *Almost there.* She hooked the middle finger of her left hand into the inner locking ring and pulled it towards herself.

As it reached halfway, the panel snagged on the hem of her left pant leg. Her finger slipped halfway out of the ring. *Oh no, no, no.* She wiggled her finger deeper into the ring, and hanging on for dear life, she arched forward, jiggling the stuck hem. It refused to budge. Her heart roared in her ears and a rivulet of salted sweat snaked down her temple, pooling in the outer corner of her right eye. She hated that her mother had the power to unnerve her to this extent. The scars left by her mother's recent evil attempt to regain custody of her, only to get access to the Infinity Charm and its powers, were still raw. She swiped away the sweat with her right hand and sniff-swallowed.

Stay calm, Myrine. Tear the pants if you have to. Measured steps crunched through the glass on the cellar floor. She let go of the locking ring, gripped her pant leg in both hands, ripped it free, and closed the panel. *Dragonscats. That was too close.* The pummel of her heart slowed from frantic to a Tick-Tock pace. She inhaled a breath of stale air, shut her eyes, and conjured pictures of green meadows filled with colourful flowers. Imagining their sweet fragrance, she took a deep breath through her nose, forcing the air into her core before breathing out slowly through her mouth. Her nerves somewhat settled.

Hopefully, mother did not stay too long, and she could still leave and get to the Quantum Door in time. Hands splayed on the floor, Myrine force-twisted her legs underneath her. Her shins protested against the arctic-cold flagstone floor. She rested her bum on her heels and wiped her nose on the cuff of her hoodie. The space was tighter than she could remember from the last time she hid in here. Well, it was five years ago. No wonder it felt tight.

Rising to her knees, she opened the spy hole cover she had last opened when she was twelve. She last used it during a game of hide and seek with Grandma. Grandma could not find her. This time, it was not a game. She rested her forehead against the panel and lined up her right eye to the spyhole. Through the distorted tunnel view, she saw her mother towering over Grandma. The skin on Myrine's face drum-tightened and drew her jaw into a clench.

If her mother so much as touched a hair on Grandma's head, she would kill her. Her gaze roved over her mother's sharp facial features. A faint smirk pulled her mother's thin lips into a pencil line below her straight, narrow-tipped nose. Not a hair was out of place in her severe midnight black bob. Myrine watched her mother lifting one of Grandma's eyelids with her bony, red-taloned finger. Thin penciled eyebrows furrowing, she straightened up. Hands on her hips, her mother scrutinized the cellar, then turned back to face Grandma.

'I wonder, Grace, if you think playing silly little games will delay the inevitable? Surneal's forces have infiltrated all the planes between Earth and Tsaonin and are ruling over most of them. You can think again if you think your insipid little Myrine can save you and Earth from us. We are stronger than ever before. Your time as the Ruler of Earth is over. In fact, the time of the Light Forces ruling the Universe is over.'

Stephanie's voice had risen with each clipped sentence and spittle foamed in the corner of her mouth. She leaned forward and hissed, 'Why not give up the pretense of being unconscious, you stupid old cow?'

Myrine's concentration fluttered between her mother's one-sided tirade and trying to form a plan of attack. Her eyes flicked to her wrist. She checked the illuminated dial of her Quantum watch. If she combined those of her supernatural powers, which were already fully developed, she could incapacitate her mother. Then she would get to the Quantum Door in the Winery on time.

If nothing else, her mother's speech confirmed the direness of the situation Grandma had shared earlier. She knew she had no choice but to fulfill her promise to Grandma. At least, her mother's conceited speech forewarned her about the Dark Forces on the planes between Earth and Tsaonin. The sound of a sharp slap jerked Myrine's attention back to her mother, and she watched her mother deliver another slap to Grandma's cheek. Grandma's red-cheeked face lolled to the side.

Fury bared its teeth and blazed through her. Through a red haze, she saw her mother grab the water pitcher off the workbench and pour the contents over Grandma's head.

'I have to stop her. Grandma is defenseless and if she suffered an injury, she could die whilst in her self-induced coma. Maybe I could combine the strongest of my developed supernatural powers with my martial arts training. She also does not know I am here, giving me the extra element of surprise. I can do it if I control my fear and allow my supernatural powers to flow naturally.'

Flame sharp blood icicles pin pricked Myrine's veins. Her heart somersaulted. She licked her dry lips and reached for the locking ring. Curling her left middle finger through its cold metal ring. Taking utmost care, turning it slowly, she released the lock. She slid the panel open one quarter of the way. With her right hand, she gripped the side of the panel's frame. Adrenaline strummed up and down the bowstrings of her tight nerves.

She strained forward. Her mother's back was turned as she rummaged through the bottled herbs. Myrine assessed the distance between them. A fleeting thought. *Mother did not have supernatural powers, nor was she gifted, but.* She would just have to play it by ear. She could use her fully developed kinetic power. Her sudden appearance would certainly cause an element of surprise and would be to her benefit. Following an immediate physical attack, she stood a good chance. Or did she?

What if mother received some powers as an advance payment for delivering me and the Infinity Charm? Time to find out what the woman was capable of. She concentrated and opened the clairsentience pocket in her mind. If she kept the enquiring tendril moderate, her mother may not detect the invasion of her mind-enquiring tendril. Readying herself to release the tendril, the Infinity Charm, secreted in the magic backpack, delivered a fierce shock to her side.

Myrine rubbed her side and remembered Grandma saying the Infinity Charm would warn her of an imminent danger before she entered the Quantum Door. She also instructed her to heed its warning. Once through the Quantum Door though, it would deactivate until Myrine turned eighteen.

On the wall behind Grandma, her mother's shadow moved. *Dragonscats, she is on the move.* Myrine withdrew into the secret chamber and slid the panel shut. Hopefully, she had not been seen. She peered through the spyhole. Her mother was walking towards the panel, a frown on her face and her mobile against her ear. Myrine activated her enhanced hearing.

'Have you found her? ….. I see. Have you made sure Aedric's hands are tied so he cannot use them. ……. Yes. That is a good idea. He could help us. …… No. I will phone Noah myself. ……….. I will be there in the next ten minutes unless I find the little bitch. I have a feeling she is hiding somewhere.'

Myrine shrunk back from the spyhole, crossed her arms over her chest, and stuck her damp palms into her armpits. She clamped her forearms down, pressing her hands deeper into her armpits. Afraid to breathe, she took shallow breaths through her nose. Outside, dull footsteps thumped closer. Myrine curbed the pressing need to check her watch. How long has it been now? Could she make it to the Quantum Door in time?

The footsteps halted in front of the closed panel. Myrine's whole body was petrified. What if her father knew about this hiding place and told her mother? Lucky for her, she enchanted the lock. Unless one knew where to look, the indentation is near invisible.

The panel vibrated. Dust thickened the air. Myrine covered her nose with her forearm and breathed through her mouth. Her scorched windpipe tightened.

'Myrine! Come out!'

The panel shook under an onslaught of kicks and slaps. Myrine remained silent. A tense sliver of time passed. The pushing against the panel came to an abrupt halt.

'I will find you, Myrine. I will find you wherever you are. Your useless grandmother will give you up to save her own skin.'

Not in a trillion years would that ever happen. A mobile phone rang. Her mother answered. Who was her mother talking to? Frustrated, Myrine re-opened the spy hole and looked out. Her mother stood with her back to the panel, her mobile clutched to her ear. At least there was no one else here to worry about. Myrine laid her right ear against the panel and concentrated.

'I want you to come here right away,' she heard her mother instruct the person on the other end, before ending the call. Myrine turned her eye back to the spyhole. Her eyes burnt into her mother's back as she walked away and stopped next to Grandma's chair. Thank goodness her mother was no longer standing at the panel. Her heart performed a somersault of Olympic proportions as her mother bent over Grandma. *Please, please, don't hurt her.*

She should have ignored the Infinity Charm's earlier warning, and maybe she would have been able to incapacitate her mother. In her gut, she knew if she tried now, it would be a disaster of epic proportions. Hot tears welled and lay unspent on her bottom eyelids. She could not remember ever feeling this helpless in her life. She watched her mother pull open Grandma's eyelids before leaning back and folding her arms across her chest.

There must be something she could do with one of her supernatural powers. Inspiration struck. She thought of Grandma's words of encouragement during one of their sessions last week. She only had to believe in herself to make it possible. *Come on Myrine, you can do this.* She closed her eyes, went deep within herself, and centered her core. With great care, she formed a thought and planted it in her mother's mind. Myrine opened her eyes and looked through the spyhole. A frown formed on her mother's forehead. Her mother did not move away. Anxiety opened its cavernous mouth in the pit of Myrine's stomach. *Why is she still standing there? Why did it not work!!*

Myrine re-formed the thought and pushed it harder into her mother's mind. Her mother looked at her watch, wheeled around and stomped towards the stairs. *Yesss.* Myrine's temples throbbed as she held the thought in place with every ounce of energy she had left. Her mother started climbing up the stairs. She had to keep it in place until her mother had left the cellar. Myrine waited for her mother to disappear up the stairs. Three beats later, she opened the panel and hovered in the opening.

It was hard to know whether it was safe to leave. She tried to engage her enhanced hearing, but her low energy levels interfered and all she could hear was a low vibrational buzz of angry bees. She should have practiced her supernatural skills more, then her energy levels would not have been sapped so quickly. From experience, she knew she only needed a minute to recover from this particular exercise. Frustrated, she counted off the seconds in her head.

Mother was unlikely to come back right now. Hopefully, she left the house and went to Aedric's cottage as per her earlier telephone conversation. Myrine knew she would have to take a chance, because when mother dear returned, it would surely be with reinforcements. She crawled out of her hiding spot onto the herb cellar floor and closed the panel behind her.

Straightening her cramped legs, she hobbled over to Grandma and checked her breathing. She held a finger under Grandma's nose. Grandma was alive, even though it did not seem like it. Wrestling with the limp body, Myrine moved it into a more comfortable position. After an awkward hug, she dropped a featherlight kiss on Grandma's forehead.

Myrine knew a daunting task awaited her. She closed her eyes and pinched her eyebrows with her thumb and middle finger. Her treacherous mind returned to the nightmarish images of her dream. Unable to stop herself, Myrine envisaged images of unstable portals guarded by ogreish phantoms that roamed the five planets between Earth and Tsaonin. The Infinity Charm buzzed against her side and jolted her back to reality. She looked at Grandma.

I so wish you could come with me, but I will keep my promise.

She turned and walked to the stairwell.

CHAPTER 4

Myrine turned and raced up the stairs. The brightly lit kitchen was empty. She crab-walked to the kitchen window and lifted one of the blind's slats and peeked out. The featureless faces of the bollard security lights stood sentry around the garden. Mist-skirts swirled around their grounded poles. Tree branches swayed, flicking variegated shadows-patterns across the grass.

At least the rain had stopped. Satisfied that no one was about in the immediate vicinity, Myrine dropped the slat. She had a gut feeling she was going to need her supernatural powers en route to the Quantum Door. Her physical abilities were far beyond what one would expect from a slip of a girl. On its own, it would not be enough to overpower her mother's Dark Force peons.

At least after the intensive training sessions with Aedric earlier in the year, some of her self-confidence had returned. 'Your powers are like muscles. Your performance will improve, and you will lose less and less energy the more regularly you use it. If you want total control, practice.' Still, those powers she feared using were underdeveloped. If only she had been less stubborn during her practice sessions.

Myrine turned to the back door. Frightful images depicting unstable portals guarded by ogreish phantoms popped into her mind. The enormity of having to go through the Quantum Door on her own hit her. She squeezed her eyes shut and circle-rubbed the lids with her palms. Her mother's confirmation that the Dark Forces have taken control of the planes between Earth and Tsaonin had given her fair warning of what to expect if she went through the Quantum Door at the wrong time. How to deal with it, though, was another story.

Sighing, she opened her eyes and checked her Quantum watch. If she had enough time, she could stop at Aedric's cottage on the way to the Quantum Door in the winery. Maybe he would go with her. She straightened her sleeve over her watch and reached for the back door handle.

Loud footsteps thundered on the floor above. Myrine's whole body marionette jerked to attention. She spun around and looked up. She knew it could not be her mother. The footsteps were far too heavy. Her mother must have let in one of her male guards to search the house. The Infinity Charm vibrated a warning against her side. *I better get out of here before whoever it was came downstairs.* With her intimate knowledge of the property, her chances of surviving discovery would be ten times better outside.

Myrine's heart fluttered. Keeping her eyes on the dark living area, she blind-searched for the back door handle behind her. A loud crash reverberated through the ceiling. Her fingers touched the handle. She swung around, grabbed it in both hands. She inched the door open. Bracing herself, she curled her right hand around the squeaky screen door's handle and slowly pushed it down. A faint click. The latch released.

Myrine inched the screen door open far enough to squeeze through. She reached for the doorjamb with her left hand and steadied herself. Inching the screen door wider, she twisted at the waist and lifted her right foot.

A tremendous crash followed by a thunderous expletive sounded from upstairs. Myrine's hand slipped off the door handle. She stumbled. The screen screeched open. Banged against the outer wall. Halfway through the door opening, the screen door bounced back, delivering a nasty thump to Myrine's right shoulder. She faltered. Her left foot caught on the threshold. She teetered down the backdoor steps and sprawled onto the grass, landing in the square of light spilling from the open study window above.

Myrine rolled out of the light, scrambled to her feet, and headed for the deep shadows beyond the security lights. At the edge of the grass, she barely avoided a bandicoot hole and scooted into the bed of tall shrubs. She pulled the cap of her hoodie over her head, ignored the thorns plucking at her clothes, and wriggled through the shrubbery.

On the other side of the wall of shrubbery, she stood up. Through a break in the shrubs, she squinted at the house. Framed in the study window stood a huge indistinctive shadow-figure. She shrunk back from its searching gaze. The balled-up cluster of nerves in the pit of Myrine's stomach coiled and uncoiled.

She shifted sideways and looked towards the footpath leading to the Winery. Her hand drifted to the Infinity Charm. *Maybe I should stay off the footpath until I reach the copse. There would be fewer chances of bumping into other Dark Force peons searching for me.* Careful not to get tangled in the underbrush, her senses on high alert, Myrine squirreled along in the shadows of the hedge separating the lawn from the footpath. She reached the area where the copse started and stopped. She had two choices. Go on the footpath through the copse or go around it.

According to her Quantum watch, not much time had passed since she got out of the house. *I would reach the Quantum Door with ten minutes to spare. If I kept to the left edge of the footpath through the copse, I could step into the trees and hide if someone came along. That would leave twenty minutes spare to check on Aedric.*

Myrine shuffled into a large opening in the hedge. She craned forward and peeked up and down the deserted footpath. Breaking from the cover of the hedge, Myrine dashed down the open five meters of footpath and entered the copse. Crossing over to the left, she proceeded at a half run, half walk. Near the end of the copse, a subtle disturbance stirred the air. She stopped in her tracks.

It must be one of my mother's Dark Force peons searching for me. She grabbed a sturdy stick from the side of the footpath. Swung it onto her right shoulder in a soft ball baton-style grip and stepped off the footpath. Mouse still, she kept her eyes trained on the footpath. A powerful white halogen orb bobbed in the distance, punching the darkness into a bruised grey as it came closer. Myrine picked up the slight footfalls of two sets of footsteps. One she could deal with, but it was not worth the risk taking on two.

She rolled onto the balls of her feet and hastened deeper into the copse. Tucked sideways behind the slim trunk of a sapling, she watched the footpath. Two shadow figures came into view. The sounds of their low conversation murmured through the air.

Myrine leaned further forward and strained her ears. One was definitely Serilda. There is no mistaking that screechy voice. Something in the male's baritone seemed familiar. As they drew abreast of her hiding place, they stopped. The male studied the ground before he turned to Serilda, displaying his prominent hook nose in silhouette. *That is detective Teivel.* Myrine had heard rumours that the highly trained ex-detective from Sydney had certain black magic powers which aided him during his checkered career. His abrupt retirement a few months ago had led to much speculation in the Sydney Morning Herald. A tendril of doom spidered up her spine.

Teivel swung the torch light and its beam zoomed over the trees. Myrine jerked her head back. The beam missed her by bare centimeters. A brush-turkey roosting nearby took an awkward flight. The beam swung in its direction. Teivel took a step in Myrine's direction.

Any hope of remaining undetected depended on whether she could deflect Teivel before he stepped into the woods. She closed her eyes and concentrated. Sensing a family of Tiger Quoll marsupials in a nearby tree, she used her kinetic power and rattled the branch on which the biggest male perched. His whiskers twitched. She rattled the branch again. In a blur of brown spotted fur, he scampered down the tree trunk and emerged in front of Teivel and Serilda. He turned tail and scurried into the undergrowth.

'It is only an animal.'

'I am not so sure about that. Something unsettled him.'

'Maybe the torchlight you are swinging over the trees had something to do with it?'

Teivel snorted and carried on sweeping his torchlight across the trees. Myrine sank to her knees. Dug deep and released a blast of energy. The branches under the rest of the family of Tiger Quoll rattled. They scampered down the tree, scattered in different directions, and crashed through the underbrush. Teivel stepped into the underbrush and swept his torchlight over it.

'We have to get to the main house for you to interrogate the old woman…'

'Yes', Teivel grunted, playing a wide arc of light over the underbrush before he stepped back onto the footpath.

'Let's go then. Burton is on his way with the dogs and will meet us at the house. The dogs will sniff her out soon enough.'

Myrine listened to their footsteps as it faded away. She swallowed the bitter bile that had filled her mouth. *I have to get to the Quantum Door before the dogs get here.*

She did not fear the dogs. She could control them. But they could still give her away.

Myrine bent her knees slightly. Ungluing her left foot, she placed it heel down first, and placed it slightly to the left in front of her. She rolled her weight forward until her foot was flattened securely on the ground. Her balance secured on her left foot, she raised her right foot to the back of her left knee before swinging it out at a right angle, securing the heel in front of her left foot, and rolled her weight forward onto it. She repeated the tai-chi silent walk process and reached the footpath seven steps later.

A furtive glance along the footpath toward the main house assured her no one lurked. She stepped back onto the footpath. It was clear. She ran full tilt down the path, pulling to a stop at the edge of the copse. A side stitch stabbed her under the lower edge of her ribcage. She slumped forward and grabbed at it with both hands and squeezed. The pain receded to a dull throb. She straightened bit by bit and looked about. Now to cross unnoticed over the open bit of lawn to the footpath on the other side of Aedric's cottage that led to the Winery.

Her mother's car standing parked in front of Aedric's cottage arrested her attention. Aedric knew where the Quantum Door was. *Dragonscats.* A chill rippled through her. The skin on her face tightened.

Maybe I could.... A sudden thunderclap rocked through her core. Her head snapped up. She eyed the starless sky. Unrestrained, lightning played zap and went seeking behind the thick blanket of clouds. *No. Bad idea. If mother and her peons are still there, it means Aedric has not told them where the Quantum Door was.*

She glanced over her shoulder at the exit from the woods. Satisfied no one lurked in the shadows, she sprinted across the short stretch of lawn and hunkered down behind a large terracotta pot housing a rosemary bush. The palms of her hands resting on the rim of the pot, she swiveled on her haunches to the side to get a better look at the front door of Aedric's cottage. *Perhaps she could.....*

The front door of the cottage flew open. A bloodied and unsteady Aedric appeared between two Dark Force guards. They dragged him down the steps. Her mother followed close behind with two more guards. *What the dragonscats!* A chorus of cicadas erupted full blast in her ears. Anger bubbled up and threatened to conbobble her senses. She semi-rose from her cover. The Infinity Charm delivered a painful zap to her side.

She sunk back to her haunches. Hot tears filled her bottom eyelids. *If only I did not tell her on my sixteenth birthday that I was going to be the next bearer of the Infinity Charm when I turn eighteen, this would not have happened.* She bit down on her lower lip. Looking back, she wondered how she could ever have thought she could win over her mother. *There is no time for this now.*

Myrine sensed Aedric's desperation as the guards marched him to the car. Creating a volume of static interference around the Dark Forces, she sent a telepathic message to Aedric.

'I'm here. They have not caught me. Is there anything I can do to help you?'

'No, no, no. Go to the Quantum Door. Now. I am taking them to the unstable portal in the stable. Go. Save us.'

Aedric's words sent shockwaves through Myrine. The guards loaded Aedric into the backseat of her mother's car, got into the back seat and sat on either side of him. Her mother stood at the bottom step of the cottage. Heads together, her mother and the other two guards conferred in whispers. Myrine engaged her enhanced hearing, but the conversation had ended. *Dragonscats. It could have helped if she knew what they were planning.* Her mother got into her car and the two guards set off along the footpath towards the Winery. *Did your mother know about the Winery?*

Myrine was sure that what unfolded tonight had been a well-planned attack. Whether or not she wanted to admit it, her father's role in stealing the keys showed his direct involvement in taking an action against his own mother and daughter. *If she had just told Grandma about the missing key, this might have been prevented.* Despite Grandma's diction that everything happened for a reason, she remained unconvinced that there was any good reason that this happened.

The car door slammed. Myrine ducked, bumping her head against the rim of the terracotta pot. The car engine roared, gravel squelched, and its headlights arced over the pot, missing Myrine by centimeters.

She remained mouse still and watched the taillights disappear down the driveway. Breaking at the three-way intersection, it took off towards the stables.

Myrine got up and teleported herself twice and got to within three meters of the two guards walking to the Winery. Staying alert, she followed them at a safe distance. She would have to refrain from using any of her supernatural powers or she would not have enough energy if she faced any obstacles at the Winery. Thank goodness the sky remained darkened with clouds, rendering her shadow trail invisible.

The weasel faced guard lit a cigarette and blew the smoke out the corner of his mouth. A foul vapour sailed over his shoulder, and Myrine started breathing through her mouth. Moments later, the walkie-talkie on the pock faced guard's belt crackled. The guards stopped. Pock face put his phone on speaker. Myrine snuck closer to the guards.

'We are on our way, mate.'

'There is nothing and no-one here. I am tired of standing around. You were supposed to relieve me twenty minutes ago.'

'Boss lady ordered us to stay and interrogate the old bloke. He reckons the girl has gone to the stable.'

'The stable?'

'Yeah. He was going on about the correct portal door being in the stable.'

'The girl's old man seemed to think it was here in the Winery.'

'Yeah. The Boss lady reckoned we must cover both. She also has guards checking all the footpaths and the dogs will be here soon.'

Weasel face crushed his cigarette under his heel and the guards started off in tandem towards the Winery. Myrine followed. The guards had stun guns hooked on their belts. She could disable pock face first. He was more blubber than muscle. Then she could use his stun gun on weasel face. Before she could form a complete plan of attack, the guards reached the back of the Winery and split up.

They each took a side path approaching the Winery from the left and right. She checked her Quantum watch. Seventeen minutes should be enough time to get into the Winery and enter the Quantum Door. She cast about. The best way would be to cut across the lawns and move from tree trunk to tree trunk until I reach the front of the Winery. She stepped off the footpath, judged the distance to the nearest tree, and ran for it. A shout emanated from the footpath. Her pulse fluttered. She dove to the grass and leopard crawled behind the tree and lay motionless.

A torch beam strobed wildly across the grass and stopped centimeters short of the tree. A sprig of grass uncurled, tickled her nose. Her eyes on the torch beam, she wriggled her top lip from side to side. It felt like eons before the beam moved away. Dragonscats, that was much too close for comfort. She leopard crawled to the next tree trunk, got up and peered around it. Better use my night vision and check for obstacles to that tree trunk over there. She suppressed the urge to check her watch, gave the surroundings another once over and moved to the next tree and from there, she zig zagged from tree trunk to tree trunk until she found herself behind the tree closest to the Winery door.

A sudden thunderclap marionette-jerked her nerves and red-hot sparks flared in her fingertips. The guard in front of the Winery must be the one the other two spoke to. Myrine steadied her nerves and pushed a hypnotic suggestion into the guard's mind, and he strolled away from the front door. Myrine waited until he was halfway to the far side corner, rushed to the front door and stumbled over an inert body. Her hand shot out, and she steadied herself against the front door. Her link with the Dark Force guard shattered.

The Dark Force guard turned around, jangling a bunch of keys, and walked back towards her and the Winery's front door. She had no choice but to use more of her energy to avert the guard. She sent a blast of energy to the tree where she stood moments ago, rattling the branches. The guard stopped, his thick brow furrowing into a conjoined caterpillar, and he took a few steps towards the tree, his back to Myrine. The other two guards appeared around the corner.

'James, did you know there is a window with a broken latch at the back of the Winery?'

'No, but there is no one inside. I checked.'

The guard in front of Myrine turned and walked towards the others. Myrine gripped the door handle and turned it. Soundless, it opened. *At last, something* was *in my favour.* She slipped inside and turned to close it. A car roared up the driveway. Its lights washed over the door and spilled a wedge of light stretching into the Winery. Myrine jumped into the shadow of the door and pushed it shut. She scurried to the last row of wine barrels covering the Quantum Door. As usual, the barrels were empty, creating a façade. She checked her Quantum watch. Three minutes to go. She stood at the ready, her feet on the springboard step she had to use to jump into the correct door as it opened.

The Winery door flew open and slammed against the wall. Her mind numb, she lurched forward, her eyes locked on her father, stepping closer and closer to her and the Quantum Door.

'Myrine, please come to me, darling. Your Grandmother needs you. Come with me. We can sort this out.'

The pain of her father's past betrayals reeled through her. Her heart spasmed. Her lower lip trembled. She bit down hard, and copper-blood filled her mouth. She swallowed. *No, I cannot let him stop me. No more mind games. Enough is enough.* She straightened and faced him.

'You liar! You would do anything for your dear wife. She is an evil woman.'

'She is not evil. She is your mother.'

'Yeah, so she forced you to get rid of me and you gave me to your mother. And now that I have something she wants, …..'

Her father grabbed at her. She twisted away and ripped her hoodie's sleeve out of his hand. Her momentum sent her blundering against the Quantum Door, and it hissed open. She teetered on the edge. Her hands missed the doorframe, and she fell into the spinning wheel of doors opening and closing.

The last thing she saw was her mother's face appearing over her father's shoulder, her eyes stabbing blades of hatred at her.

CHAPTER 5

Meanwhile, in Betwonium…

18-year-old Rollandario snuck through the side door of the castle wall facing the river. Sketchpad clutched tightly under his arm, he sprint-slipped down the embankment, found his feet at the bottom and raced alongside the river. He only had an hour until sundown.

He reached his outlook. Pastel-coloured weed-daisies sprinkled in the grass. He admired their graceful dip-dance in the afternoon breeze. Carefully, he stepped through them and sunk down on a flat rock at the edge of a thicket. The rainbow above the waterfall announced the portal was open.

Opening his sketchpad to a blank page, he drew a rough sketch of the guard points around the portal. If he could find a way past the day guards, he could leave Betwonium. Sundown, the portal shuts. Maybe there was a way to open it at night. A cloud passed in front of the sun. Rollandario shuddered. How long could he hide his enmity of the Dark Forces? He yearned to join the Light Forces.

Picking a blade of grass, he chewed on it. His Adelstein blood, even though only three quarters, overshadowed his one quarter Betwoniumite blood inherited from his father's side. The magnetic pull towards Tsaonin has become ever stronger since his eighteenth birthday a month ago. With it, he had to acknowledge that he fitted neither into his mother's nor his father's expectations of him.

Last week his pitiful defiance, washing the black dye from his natural Adelstein copper-red hair, had his mother strap him to the table in the mind-control room for three hours. He was lucky his father was away, or he would have ended up on Dr Dreckonium's table.

Every morning, he checked his whole body. The only visible Betwoniumite features were his thick purple-white spotted tongue and his one lizard eye in screaming contrast with his other emerald green eye. Born with it, he had no choice but to make his peace with it. Thankfully, no scales had grown anywhere, as happened with the other Betwoniumite young adult males his age. His hand closed around the small tubular bottle secreted deep in his pants pocket. It must be the potion. Secretly made from the recipe in his mother's book of potions.

He flexed his fingers. A tiny flame alighted on his left hand's index finger. He grinned. His well-hidden magical power was growing stronger. Yes, yes, yes. His practising every day was paying off. He could now light it with a mere thought. His thickened tongue stuck out of the corner of his mouth. He looked at the flame. There had to be a way he could use it to his advantage. Maybe he could throw it into the underbrush and ignite a fire.

Heavy footsteps crunched in the bushes behind him. Rollandario quickly retracted the flame. He could smell his father's mould-dust smell before he saw him. His stomach fish flopped.

Rollandario jumped up. His breath became sharp, shallow bursts. Facing the thicket, he waited. He fisted his shaky hands. His anxious mind squirrelled in search of a reasonable excuse. No one was allowed in the exit portal's vicinity without permission. It included him, the son of the ruler of the Betwonium army.

The bushes parted. Beldarius stomped through the daisies and stopped within a step of his son. Rollandario noted he had morphed into his natural lizard-like form. Healed battle scars roped Beldarius' left arm. Raised ridges of smaller scars punctuated his chest and stomach. Rollandario gazed at the raised pulsating vein in the middle of his father's forehead. It did not bode well. He reversed a step. His father's cold black stare froze him. He dropped his eyes, dry swallowed and bowed his head.

'Rollandario!'

'Father.'

'What are you doing here?!'

'Father, I...'

'Speak up, boy.'

The hiss in his father's voice rolled Rollandario's nerves into an even tighter knot. He looked down at the trampled daisies. His eyes fell on his sketchpad lying next to the rock. One eye on his father, he bent down and stretched a hand towards it. His left-hand fingers gripped a corner.

'Is that what I think it is?'

Inwardly, Rollandario cringed. A tremor raced up his spine. He picked up the sketchpad and held it at his side. With a speed belying his size, his father ripped it out of his hand. *If his father found the page with the sketch of the setup around the portal, he was doomed.* Rollandario chanted under his breath, imploring his good luck fairy to protect him. After glancing at the first two pages, his father closed the sketchpad. Rollandario inhaled deeply. Beldarius flung the sketchpad at Rollandario, who half caught it as it hit him in the chest.

'Still wasting your time on useless things. You should practise your weaponry skills. Not waste time on that nonsense. Taking over from me as the Ruler of the Betwonium army, you need to be a worthy soldier. Not a misfit drawing pictures of flowers.'

'I am worthy. Not everyone has to be like you.'

Watching the change in his father's face and posture, Rollandario wished he could grab the words back and swallow them. The vein in his father's forehead bulged and pulsed, his lizard-claw hands opened and closed. Beldarius' upper body elongated, and he stretched forward towards Rollandario. Rollandario stumbled back. Cleared his throat.

'I ..'

Rollandario was unprepared for the vicious slap against the side of his face. His neck cricked. By some miracle, he kept his balance and kept his tight grip on his sketchpad. Pain flared where a claw scratched his cheek. Angry tears burnt in his eyes.

'Go pack your bags. You are leaving in the morning with the training squad.'

The next morning, loath to go down to the breakfast room, Rollandario sat on his bed, his backpack on the floor next to him. Thoughts of the week ahead had sent him from panic to worry and back to panic. He knew the only thing that saved him from something worse than verbal bullying was the fact that he was the ruler of the army's son.

He wondered if that would save him this time. For all he knew, his father had arranged a severe punishment for his indiscretion the day before. He pressed his hands to his temples. He should have known better than to talk back.

The dong-dong-dong of a high-priority incoming message through the Quantum Slipstream pulsing louder with each dong, boom-pulsed through the castle. Rollandario grabbed his backpack, flew down the stairs, and sat in his appointed chair as his mother and father entered the breakfast room.

He watched Faeyet, his mother's sly fosterling slave, creeping up to the kitchen doorway. *Eavesdropping at every opportunity. Conniving little bitch.* She had morphed into her blue-eyed strawberry-blonde slave girl look. Required by his mother, of course. He was very sure it gave his mother great pleasure to have an Adelstein lookalike as a slave. But for his intimate knowledge of the real Faeyet, the Schemer, he could have felt sorry for her.

His mother walked to the full-sized wall-screen and switched it on with her thumbprint. Surneal's message unscrolled, followed by a photograph of Myrine Adelstein. Copper red hair and emerald green eyes, she was the epitome of an Adelstein. The message conveyed that Myrine was in possession of the Earth Light Force Ruler's Infinity Charm. But for the whispered conversations between his parents he had overheard two days ago, he would have believed the story circulating that Myrine had stolen the Infinity charm. So typical of the Dark Forces to askew the truth and twist it to suit their own purposes.

He leaned his elbows on the table. From under his lashes, he watched his mother and father. Heads bent together. Their voices a low hum. His mind found a life of its own, jumping from one incomplete scenario to another.

He wondered if his father was aware of his mother's intention to leave Betwonium and join Surneal's inner circle as head witch, where there was no place for his father. A ripple of unease stirred in the nether regions of his stomach. Divorces were not allowed in Betwonium.

Something about the furtive meetings between Beldarius and Faeyet led him to believe that his father was on to it and using Faeyet as a spy. Then there was the conversation he overheard between Faeyet and his mother, when she promised Faeyet her freedom once she leaves. Knowing Faeyet, she is probably playing the two against each other, hoping to secure her freedom, irrespective of which one comes out on top.

In his gut he knew neither of his parents would allow a fosterling slave its freedom, ever. He had no intention of hanging around until the outcome. He had seen enough horror outcomes of betrayals within betrayals on this planet. If he could get to Myrine first, then…

His thought stuttered to a stop as Faeyet was instructed to go to the incoming portal, waylay Myrine and lead her down the mountain. And into the forest where Beldarius will be waiting. His head swivelled to his mother. With an evil smile on her face, Eugenia got up from the table and handed a pouch to his father.

'I will prepare the mind room and have it ready. We will extract every secret there is from that girl.'

His father nodded, scraped back his chair, and rose to his feet. His mother flounced out of the room. Beldarius started for the back door, stopped, and turned.

'Rollandario!'

He startled out of his chair. His feet tangled in the chair legs. Stumbling, he caught the chair and righted it just before it crashed to the floor.

'Father?'

'Get your clumsy arse to the barracks and inform the troop commanders to meet me on the parade ground.'

Rollandario shouldered past Faeyet hovering at the backdoor and took off at a run across the courtyard. For once, he was not relieved at missing the dreaded training. He knew he had to save Myrine but had no inkling as to how to do it.

Two hours later, after his father's briefing, he insinuated himself into his father's platoon going into the forest. They were to stake out the path leading through the forest to the exit portal.

Marching with the others, Rollandario kept his own council. He had yet to come up with a workable plan. There would be no room for failure. Frustration and fear dogged his every step. He missed his father's call for the platoon to halt and bumped into the soldier in front of him.

'Hey dumbo. Watch where you are going.'

'Sorry.'

Rollandario joined the other soldiers, spread out in a semi-circle around his father. Horrified, he watched Beldarius take out the pouch Eugenia gave him and spread a slip-switch knot of powdered brown-grey Cynoglosium over the path. Once on the ground it was hardly noticeable. Taking care not to touch it, the two of the senior platoon officers covered it with loose leaves and forest debris.

Rollandario shuddered. If Myrine stepped into the slip-switch of Cynoglosium, it would immobilise her and she would not be able to use her supernatural powers. From Surneal's message, Rollandario gathered that Myrine was endowed with a myriad of powers and had supernatural skills far beyond the usual. She was destined to be the next Light Force Leader of Earth, which the Dark Forces were to prevent at all costs. The reward for the capture of Myrine and handing her and the Infinity Charm to Surneal, was entry to the Dark Forces coveted inner circle of Surneal.

It was clear to Rollandario that Surneal and the Dark Forces intended to take over the reign on Earth. That would leave only Tsaonin under the rule of the Light Forces. And as sure as there was a sun in the sky, Tsaonin will be the final destination of the Dark Forces. Dread reared its nauseous head in the pit of Rollandario's stomach. The thought of the Dark Forces ruling the Universe was beyond horrendous.

Instinctively Rollandario knew he had to save Myrine and help her get to Tsaonin. He knew that it would simultaneously save him from a future as a Dark Force member as envisaged by his parents. He hated the anarchy spread by the Dark Forces. *Oh, what he would give to live in peace and harmony!*

Beldarius' shouted orders for the troops to spread out around the trap and hide in the trees and underbrush, interrupting Rollandario's thoughts. The troops sunk into the undergrowth, beneath the giant redwood trees, until they were all hidden, including from themselves. Rollandario popped his head above the undergrowth. Seeing no movement, he took a chance and slunk towards the entrance into the woods. Halfway there, a rough hand gripped his upper arm.

'And where do you think you are going?'

'I… I am looking for a suitable spot from which I can watch the path to alert my father.'

Rollandario looked at Dr Dreckonium who kept pace with him. He dropped the idea of going all the way to the entrance into the woods. He scanned the ground to the side of the footpath and found a hollow one meter from the footpath. To his greatest irritation, Dreckonium sat down on a flat stone next to the hollow.

'I heard the girl is highly trained in martial arts and can use it in combination with her supernatural powers.'

'Yes, but…'

Rollandario did not take up the invitation to speak. He kept his gaze on Dreckonium, whilst the doctor looked him up and down.

'I don't think a little whippet like you would stand a chance against her skills.'

Rollandario felt his ears burn. It surprised him that it did not release a glow in the dark. Maybe he should use this moment to pump Dr Dreckonium for information about Myrine. The egotistical old fart is a known braggart, and it should be easy.

'So, what sort of supernatural powers does the girl have?'

'Aahh. Why the interest?'

'Just asking. Wondering why everyone seems to take such great measures of caution in preparing to capture a girl.'

'Well. Surneal will not be charmed if she escapes again. She is a wily one. She already escaped capture on Earth. Lucky for Surneal, she missed the opening in the Quantum Door leading to Tsaonin and landed here.'

'But if we don't capture her, she could still go to Tsaonin, right?'

'True. But she would have to travel through each and every one of the next four planes between us and Tsaonin.'

'There is no portal direct to Tsaonin except from Earth?'

'There used to be. Surneal, when he took over the planes between Earth and Tsaonin, sealed all the portals that had a Quantum Door directly to Tsaonin. Those he employed to seal them were never seen again.'

Despite the sticky humidity, a cold shiver cascaded through Rollandario. He did not know that the exit portal did not lead directly to Tsaonin. His shoulders sagged. How much of the circulated stories about the other planes were true or not, he did not know. All he knew was that it would be a treacherous journey from plane to plane between. All ruled by the Dark Forces.

A rustle shocked him out of his thoughts. He jerked his head sideways. Dr Dreckonium was taking a little bag from his one pocket. Putting it on the ground at his feet, he took a blowpipe with a fitted arrow from the other.

'I must commend you, Rollandario. This is a perfect spot to lie in ambush of the girl.'

'What is in the pouch?'

'My secret sleep recipe. From the little bag, he took a pot and held it up. It was glowing a purple-red in the dark.'

'You can't use that. You killed Cerendus with it!'

'The trick, my dear boy, is to use a tiny bit and it will render her unconscious for long enough to tie her with the slip-switch powdered with Cynoglosium. Then take her to your mother. Oh, and your mother had no further use for Cerendus.'

A furball of sour vomit hissed into Rollandario's throat, gagging him. He turned his head sideways, leaned forward opening his mouth wide and tried to silence his gasps for air. Cerendus was the closest to a friend he had ever had in his miserable life. A heavy hand fell on his shoulder.

'Anything the matter boy?'

'No. Probably just my allergic reaction to some of the ferns in the undergrowth.'

Rollandario stood up and rotated his shoulders, breathing deeply. The acid in his throat eased somewhat. He sat back down. He felt Dreckonium's stare boring into him and turned his head. Malevolence glittered in the black eyes staring at him, but he refused to look away. Dreckonium started preparing his blowpipe.

'So what is the plan for Myrine once she has been captured?'

Dreckonium put the blowpipe down and rubbed his long fingered bony hands together. A gleeful smile on his thin lips, he slapped his hands together and leaned towards Rollandario. It took great effort for Rollandario not to turn from Dreckonium's sour breath.

'Your little cousin Myrine, your mother's niece, is going to be an Adelstein turned into a Dark Force. After that, when she unlocks the Infinity Charm when she turns eighteen in a few week's time, it would be used by her as instructed by Surneal. And then....'

Dreckonium smacked his thin lips. A speck of spittle gathered in the corner of his mouth. His tongue snaked out and he licked at it. Rollandario bit his tongue, refusing to ask another question. He followed Dreckonium's gaze to the footpath. There was nothing.

'And then!'

Rollandario jumped at the sudden boom of Dreckonium's voice in his ear.

'The Infinity Charm will be under her spell as a fully-fledged Dark Force Member. She will be sent back to Earth. With your mother as her personal advisor. She will rule as the new generation Dark Force leader.

Her grandmother will be kept alive long enough to watch her beloved granddaughter unseat the Light Forces on Earth.'

'But does the Infinity Charm not belong to the Light Forces?'

'Oh no, no, no. The Infinity Charm belongs to the Adelsteins. Myrine has it with her as she is to be its next controller when she turns eighteen. And turning her into a Dark Force member before her birthday is imperative.'

'What if Myrine is not turned into a Dark Force member?'

'Perish the thought. She will become a Dark Force member. It does not matter what her numerology number is. Every number in numerology has a dark side to it. Surneal will be here tomorrow to personally oversee her induction.'

Unease unfolded in the pit of Rollandario's stomach and teetered all the way up to his heart, clutching it in a cold steel grip.

If only he could find a way to save Myrine from Surneal and the Dark Forces.

CHAPTER 6

Myrine's head spun. Her nostrils flared at the gamy stink clogging the air. Taking rapid breaths through her mouth, she engaged her night vision and probed the semi-dark surrounds. *I must have landed in some kind of underground cave.* The only movement, unsettled dust particles.

Her heart trip-hammered. She put her right hand over it. She knew she was not in Tsaonin. That portal opened in a meadow next to the Crystal Castle. It meant her only option was to find her way out of whichever plane she had landed on.

Having left Earth, the Infinity Charm in Myrine's magic backpack disconnected from her Grandmother. It became silent. It would remain silent and unable to forewarn Myrine of any danger. It could only be reactivated once Myrine turned eighteen or if she returned to Earth before then, it would recalibrate itself with its current mistress, Grace. Myrine's Grandma.

If she had landed in Tsaonin though, she would have been under the protection of Aerwyna, Light Force Ruler of the Universe. Having fallen through the wrong door left Myrine with only her instincts, supernatural powers, martial arts training, and the use of the magical backpack Grandma gave her. Myrine shoved the morose thoughts away. Ignoring the complaints in her tailbone, she rolled over onto all fours. If she wanted to save Grandma and Earth, she dared not go back to Earth.

Myrine stood up and dusted her gritty hands. She closed her eyes and concentrated. There was a slight breeze. She licked her right index finger and held it above her head. Now to find the opening from which it came. She settled her backpack back into position. With the aid of her night vision she walked to the nearest rock wall.

Using the wall as a guide she started up a slight incline. The breeze became stronger. In the distance, a murky lighter grey spot appeared. The cavern walls narrowed. She turned sideways and shuffle-stepped towards the light.

Reaching the light, the narrow cavern tunnel opened into another chamber. Light streamed into the chamber from a chest-high opening ahead of her. She breathed a sigh of relief, let go of the wall and started for the opening.

From the corner of her eye she caught a slight movement. She whipped to her left. Her breath whooshed out in an involuntary squeak. Instinctive, she exuded a bubble of see through ectoplasm around herself. The cavern was dark enough for the ectoplasm to be visible. The abominable creature reached out with its impossibly long coarse-haired arm. With one of its six yellow-horned nails it prodded the ectoplasm bubble. Myrine jumped backwards. Two silver-ball eyes on stalks popped up from its head. Dropping its arms, it gorilla-stepped closer.

A quick glance over her shoulder confirmed she was too far from the exit to drop her ectoplasm bubble-shield and get out. She looked back at the creature and realised it had taken another step towards her. Behind it, the wall seemed to move. More silver-ball eyes appeared. Three more creatures stepped forward.

With no time to formulate a real plan, she took two huge step-jumps backwards and retracted the ectoplasm bubble. Stretching her arms forward, palms upturned, she spell-casted two tennis ball sized fireballs and kept it hovering above each palm. A collective snarl ensued from the creatures. Their stalk eyes retracted, disappeared from sight.

They hunkered down and crept towards her on all fours. So, they don't like fire or is it the light of the fire?

Myrine let fly the one fireball, exploding it in front of the closest creature. It reared up and scuffled away from the fire. The moment the fireball fizzled out; it was back in position. Myrine threw the second fireball and turned her palms towards the fireball. A wall of flame erupted and danced between her and the creatures.

Keeping the firewall going, Myrine turned sideways and scissor-stepped towards the exit, her head swinging between the firewall and the exit. She gauged the distance. Dropped the firewall and hauled herself through the exit. A horned claw reached out, raked the sole of her left boot. She delivered a vicious kick at it with her right foot. With a howl, it fell away. She pulled her legs through the exit and rolled away from it. Bright midday sunlight engulfed her. Erratic black dots danced at the back of her eyes. She shivered in the sudden heat and blinked her watery eyes.

Frustrated grunts and screeches rose from the cavern below. Myrine jumped up. Eyes on the exit she moved further away and dusted herself whilst waiting for her eyes to adjust. The creatures had quieted down. None appeared in the exit, confirming her erstwhile thoughts that it probably did not like light.

Turning a full circle, Myrine took in the unfamiliar vista. She was halfway down a humongous mountain. The cavern exit was set in a steep precipice that stretched to the sky. A few meters in front of her the edge of the mountain fell away. She walked to a boulder balanced on the edge, took off her hoodie and slipped off the magical backpack.

Following Grandma's instructions, she envisioned compact binoculars. Myrine unzipped the backpack and took it out. Drawing from the knowledge of her studies with Grandma about portals, she searched for signs of a lake, dam, or river. She found the tell-tale signs of a portal shimmer first. Eventually she caught sight of a river disappearing behind a thick forest in the far distance.

Myrine found a faint and narrow goat trail, strewn with gravel. She walked back to the boulder, put the binoculars into the backpack and fished out a lightweight sleeveless jacket. From the side pocket of her magical backpack, she took the magic water bottle and drank her fill. The bottle replaced its own contents as soon as she put it back in the backpack's side pocket. Once she had shrugged on her backpack, she donned the sleeveless jacket over it. Satisfied that it hid the backpack, keeping it invisible as instructed by Grandma, she tied her own hoodie around her waist and started along the winding path down the mountain.

It took all her concentration not to slip on the treacherous trail. Soon her fringe became plastered to her forehead. Her feet felt too big for her boots and her dampened shirt clung to her back. She knew sweat was the body's way of cooling itself, but she hated the icky sticky feeling.

She could teleport down the mountain, but it would drain the last bit of her energy. It would be better to rebuild her energy in case she needed one or more of her supernatural powers once she was off the mountain.

If only she had listened to Aedric and practiced more diligently, her energy would not be sapped so quickly. Well, it is too late now. That is water under the bridge. At least her physical training stood her in good stead. Now that she is using her supernatural powers, her energy levels would decrease less and less over time.

Ahead, the path disappeared around yet another boulder. She stood for a moment and looked at the sun's downward tract in the sky. Her progress was too slow. She needed to move at a better pace. She walked around the boulder. On the other side, a straw haired young female stood in the middle of the path. Myrine stopped and planted her feet a ruler width apart. Something was off. The eyes were too round. The ears high up her head. And why would she be wearing a dress?

'You must be Myrine, right?'

'And you are?'

'Faeyet.'

Myrine frowned and cocked her head sideways. She squinted at Faeyet. She needed to get information out of Faeyet without divulging her ignorance of her whereabouts. It was imperative to confirm which plane she was on.

'You are on Betwonium. We have been expecting you. I am here to accompany you to the castle.'

Myrine blanked her mind, hid her thought processes, and looked at her feet. She would have to be careful with her thoughts. It seemed Faeyet could read her mind. It would be better to keep her thought protection mind-shield up.

'I don't have time to visit the castle. I am ..'

'On your way to Tsaonin. We know. But first you need to refresh yourself.'

The thought of a decent shower sent a shiver of anticipation through Myrine. Her stomach growled at the thought of a plate of nourishing food. She realised that with the time difference between Earth and Betwonium, the second of the seven planes, she had not eaten in more than a day.

Then it hit her. Dragonscats. Betwonium. It is ruled by the Dark Forces and this 'person' she is speaking to must be a Fosterling. From her studies with Grandma, Myrine knew that Fosterlings, the original inhabitants of Betwonium, were accomplished shape shifters. Most of them were forced to work as slaves for the Betwoniumites, who now ruled this plane. She would have to be careful, this one seems to be searching for information.

In that instant Myrine followed her gut instinct and decided to play dumb. Not alluding to her knowledge, she herself might be able to gather some information. She thanked her lucky stars that only herself,

Grandma and Aedric knew about her studies of the other planes under Grandma's private tuition. A tiny win. Her mother did not know and could not share this information with the Dark Forces.

At least, thanks to Faeyet's chattering, she now knew where she was, and she had an inkling of where the one and only outgoing portal was. Usually there would be several, but the Betwoniumites had obliterated all but one to stop the Fosterlings fleeing the plane.

'Whose castle are we going to?'

'Beldarius. The Ruler of the Army has graciously invited you to be his guest.'

That English. Maybe she learned the language from reading age-old novels. It seemed her only choice would be to follow Faeyet down the mountain. Once they were on level ground, she would find a way to get rid of her and find the exit portal. By then her energy levels would have built up enough strength for her to use more than one of her supernatural magical powers. And combine it with her martial arts training.

'Oh. Okay. Let's go then.'

On the way down, watching Faeyet walking with an uncommon ease for a person in a wide skirted dress. Faeyet chattered all the way down the mountain in her sing-song voice, hardly ever requiring a response. Except…

'I hear you have supernatural powers.'

'Not really.'

Myrine stopped in time to avoid bumping into Faeyet who now stood blocking the narrow path and faced her. A frown creased her marbled forehead. For the first time Myrine noticed how closely Faeyet resembled the Adelstein looks.

'Not really? What does that mean?'

'Two years ago, I made a mistake. There was a sort of accident that frightened me, and I stopped using my supernatural powers. My energy levels dropped.'

'But you have not lost your supernatural powers. If you practice, your energy will restore.'

'Yes, but it takes time and lots of practice.'

Well, that was close enough to the truth if this creature had any information from Earth. She wondered what Faeyet was capable of, besides shape shifting. She had a strong gut feeling it would be in her own best interests to hide the extent of her supernatural powers. Rather save her energy, to use it later to her best advantage.

'So how did you escape the Fosterling guards in the cave in which the portal from Earth opens?'

Irritated, Myrine pulled her Mag-Lite torch from her utility belt and showed it to Faeyet.

'I switched this on to see where I was. They did not like the light. So, I kept it shining in their eyes and got out.'

'Oh. Lucky you had that.'

Faeyet turned around. That was close. She stuck the torch back in her belt and followed Faeyet, who was already a few meters ahead of her. Surefooted and fast in skirts. *I would need to keep my wits about me with this one.* From the buzz in her veins, she knew her energy levels were at full capacity.

She had only two earth weeks to get to Tsaonin. And even if time was much slower on the planes between Earth and Tsaonin, Myrine was loath to waste unnecessary time.

The more Myrine thought of going to the castle, the harder her gut protested.

CHAPTER 7

Myrine searched her eidetic memories for more details about Betwonium. Grandma had ensured she kept up to date with the history and current status of all the planes in the Universe. She scowled at the back of Faeyet's head. Every time a response to Faeyet was required, she lost her train of thought and had to start over again. She wished there was a way to shut her up without causing a confrontation.

'Eugenia, Beldarius' wife, ….'

That's it. All the puzzle pieces fell into place. Eugenia, her disgraced aunt, and Grandma's cousin. Kicked out of Tsaonin, when Grandma caught her with the ageless Surneal, Dark Force Leader of the Universe. Their plans to take over Tsaonin, thwarted. Eugenia, stripped of her Adelstein powers, was banished to Betwonium. Rumour had it that with the help of Surneal, she had become a powerful black magic witch.

Dragonscats. She had to get away from Faeyet. One thing was clear: she had to avoid the castle at all costs. Ahead of her, Faeyet carried on chattering, slipping in a question here and there. Myrine deflected it with vague answers.

Dusk had fallen as they reached the foot of the mountain. The portal's shimmer, which was created by the sun's rays, was no longer visible. Myrine engaged her enhanced hearing and picked up the distant sound of a river. About a hundred meters in the distance lay a vast forest.

'What are you looking for?'

'Thought I heard a river. Is there one near here?'

'Yes. It runs through the forest. Around the castle to the exit portal on the other side of it.'

Myrine followed Faeyet's gestures as she explained about the river.

'There is an easy pathway through the forest, which leads to the castle.'

'Why don't we follow the river? I need to get to the exit portal.'

'The exit portal only opens during the day. The river is treacherous. From the castle, there is an easy way to get to the exit portal.'

Myrine frowned, caught Faeyet's raised eyebrows and blanked her face. Outgoing portals were always open. She decided not to let on what she knew about portals. Rather not alert Faeyet. It would only serve to be bombarded with another torrent of questions. Going with Faeyet to the castle where Eugenia was sure to be waiting would not be a good idea at all.

'Well. Once I get to the exit portal, I could wait until morning when it opens.'

'It is too dangerous. You will be safe at the castle and can rest there until morning.'

'What dangers?'

'Too much to explain. Let's go.'

Myrine allowed Faeyet to grab her wrist and pull her along across the open clearing towards the forest. It would be easier to lose Faeyet once they were in the forest. At the entrance to the forest, Myrine shook her wrist out of Faeyet's hand. Ahead of them, fireflies swarmed and sparkled, hanging together from tree branches, lighting a well-trodden pathway.

Intent on the sounds of the river becoming louder, Myrine hardly noticed the light show. The sound of the river came from the left of the path. Myrine stopped, sunk down on one knee and fiddled with a bootlace, whilst she committed the spot to memory. From under her eyelashes, she saw Faeyet marching back and forth across the width of the path.

'Come on. Dinner will be waiting for us.'

'Just need to fasten my bootlaces.'

Myrine got up. A few meters ahead, the pathway narrowed and disappeared around a bend. Despite the humidity, there was a chill in the air. Untying her hoodie from around her waist, Myrine put it on, over the sleeveless vest covering her magic backpack. Her throat burned, but she dared not take her water bottle from the backpack's side pocket. She worked up some spit, swallowed and stepped forward. Faeyet remained at her side.

The path narrowed to a single person lane. Myrine stopped.

'You know the way. I'll follow you.'

'Stay close.'

'I will.'

The now winding path became steeper. The undergrowth denser, encroaching on the footpath. Myrine concentrated and kept her arcane power of suggestion focused on Faeyet. Her spirits buoyed when the manipulation succeeded after two minutes. Faeyet stopped looking back.

Myrine slowed. The distance between her and Faeyet grew. Faeyet disappeared around the next bend. Not knowing when another opportunity will present itself or how far they still have to go, Myrine stepped into the undergrowth. She was now on the opposite side of where the river was running.

Once Faeyet noticed she was no longer behind her, she was sure to search the side going to the river first. Keeping her eyes on the pathway, Myrine sidled a little deeper into the undergrowth. She stopped behind a broad tree trunk and waited.

A split second later, a horse nickered. Faeyet screamed. A tremendous commotion ensued on the footpath ahead. Unbeknownst to Myrine, the Cynoglosium trap meant for her had ensnared Faeyet. Under cover of the noise, Myrine turned on her heel and crashed deeper into the undergrowth. She hunkered down at the base of a large tree. She peered through the undergrowth but could not see the footpath. She crept forward until she could see the footpath and settled behind a waist high clump of undergrowth. The commotion died down. Breaking the few seconds of silence, several pairs of footsteps thundered closer.

A humongous man in a black uniform, a copper insignia with a red devil's head on his jacket's left breast, came into view. She surmised from Faeyet's chatterings that this was Beldarius. He held Faeyet, who had shifted back into her fosterling self, by the scruff of her neck. His troops followed in his wake. They came to a stop near where Myrine stepped off the path. Myrine held her breath. If she moved now, they would hear her. She shallow breathed through her mouth. Waited and watched.

Faeyet wriggled out of Beldarius' grip. Land on all fours and snuffled at the ground. Then rose to her back legs, a six-fingered hand pointing to the footpath.

'Here. You see. Here. That is her footsteps.'

Beldarius called four of his troops forward. Myrine heard him instructing them to check the underbrush on the side of the footpath. *Oh no, not number four again.* Myrine knew if she stayed where she was, they would discover her. Neither could she physically move for fear of the noise she would make. One guard moved closer to where she entered the underbrush.

Instinctively reacting, she teleported herself two meters deeper into the woods. A shout rose from the footpath. She cringed. Someone started crashing through the underbrush. Using the noise as cover, she turned and blindly propelled herself sideways in the direction Faeyet and she had been walking. Hopefully, they would search towards the entrance of the woods.

Behind her, Beldarius' voice roared an order for all the troops to join the search. It sounded very close. Without stopping, Myrine hazarded a look over her shoulder. She crashed into a rotten tree trunk lying on the ground. She grabbed at it to keep her balance. Clambering over it, her boot slipped on a piece of loose bark, catapulting her headlong into a deep ditch behind it. Myrine pushed herself up from under the age-old bed of rotten leaves.

Standing chest deep in the leaves, she looked up. The rim was at least half a meter above her head. The urge to sneeze overwhelmed her. She pinched her nose shut. Her cheeks swelled up. It would not be safe to get out whilst they were searching for her.

She crawled into the far corner and scooped aside leaves. Burrowing into the hollow, she raked loose leaves over herself up to her neck. She pulled the collar of her hoodie over her nose, holding it in place with her right hand. Neck hunched into her shoulders, she engaged her night vision and monitored the rim. Slow footsteps thundered closer. Myrine shallow breathed through her mouth. At least her clothing was dark.

Above her, the rotten tree trunk shuddered. She glanced at it. The biggest boot Myrine had ever seen rested on it. Bits of bark and dirt rained into the ditch. A grain of dust struck her left eye. She closed it against the burn. A river of tears streamed down her cheek. Her other eye watered up in sympathy. She pressed a thumb knuckle against her sore eye, keeping the right one focused on the edge.

'I smell an earthling.'

A head appeared next to the boots. The neck craned forward. Paralysed, Myrine stared into a disconcerting set of eyes. One emerald green, one lizard black. With a wink of the emerald green eye, the head disappeared.

'There is nothing in the ditch Dad. There are some footsteps going that way. I think we should search closer to the footpath.'

'Rollandario is lying.'

'Faeyet. Rollandario. Enough. Rollandario, you go with troop commander Ignatium. Ignatium, you do not let him out of your sight. Start searching from the entry into the forest Faeyet. Get yourself over here.'

Myrine wondered who Rollandario was. *Was he leading them from me? Why?* Above her, Beldarius sat down, his bulk bulging over the tree trunk. Hesitant footsteps approached.

'Does she know where the exit portal is?'

'Yes.'

'What powers does she have?'

'I don't think she really has any.'

'You think? Or do you know?'

'I asked, and she said she did not have any.'

'Gmph. That would be the day that the future Light Force Leader of Earth has no powers. Has she got the Infinity Charm?'

'I don't know.'

A sharp animal hiss. An acrid odour drifted over the ditch. The smell of scorched flesh. A plaintive wail.

'Please. I am sorry. She won't get far. I will help you find her.'

'You had better find her. And find her soon or you will join your ancestors.'

Myrine suppressed her empathic feelings for Faeyet. That little bitch was going to lead her into a trap. The tree trunk creaked. Myrine watched as Beldarius, his back to the ditch, stretched to his full humongous height. Faeyet dangled from his left hand. He moved away, and they disappeared from sight. An ominous quiet had settled in their wake.

To stay where she was would be inviting discovery. Myrine rose slowly. The leaves rustled and fell away. She stood on her tiptoes, but still could not see over the rim of the ditch. One step at a time, she crunched, waited, crunched to the side where the tree trunk lay. At its root plate, a thick root drooped over the edge. Gripping it, she pulled herself up and swung an arm over the top of the ditch. She clutched a handful of little roots. Her boots scrabbling for purchase, she heaved herself out of the ditch.

She scooted around the root plate. No sign of any movement. She stood up, took her water bottle from her backpack, and took a large swallow. She wet the cuff of her hoodie and bathed her scratchy eye before wiping her face and neck.

If she went back to the footpath, she could follow it back to where she heard the river, then cross over to the river's side. It would be faster than trying to navigate the unknown woods. The only trick would be to avoid the returning search party. She had noted earlier that they did not pussyfoot. It should be easy enough to duck into hiding, should she hear them. Hopefully, they were no longer near the exit where they were instructed to start their search.

Myrine tai chi walked back to the footpath. Her hips rotating, she slightly bent her knees. Swinging out one foot at a slight angle, placing its heel down, she rolled her weight forward onto the ball of her foot. Securing her balance, she lifted the other foot, repeating the process, moving from tree trunk to tree trunk. Waiting behind each and surveying the way ahead before moving to the next tree trunk.

Close to the footpath, two troops appeared, walking back from the entrance to the woods. Her muscles tensed. Her breath quickened. She froze, her weight balanced on her right foot, her left foot toes to the ground ready to push into a lift. She eased her weight back onto her left foot and sunk to her haunches.

Neither one looked in her direction as they passed within a meter of her. She assembled her trembling limbs and stood her feet a ruler measure apart. Were they the last of the search party or are there more? Before she could decide what to do, Beldarius' voice thundered from the right.

'Have you found her?'

In unison, the two troops confirmed in the negative.

'She will try to go to the exit portal. We will camp here where the signs showed she entered the woods. Ignatium, go station yourself halfway between here and the forest entrance. You, Fernitium, go to the other side of the camp and position yourself between the camp and the portal exit.'

The two troops left to take up their positions as ordered. Myrine remained where she was and watched. Beldarius spread the rest of the troops in a wide catch net, across the footpath.

Myrine recognised that the set up entrapped her within the vicinity of Beldarius' tented camp. He was not a person to trifle with. She did not know the woods, nor could she afford to hang around until daylight.

She knew the more she used her supernatural powers, the stronger it would become, and so her energy levels would strengthen and hold longer. An idea developed at the back of her mind. Myrine waited for the camp to settle down into slumber before she made her move. *I may just as well take a catnap myself.* She crawled under a large tree fern, sat down at its base, and set her body clock for one hour.

One hour later, she startled awake. It took a moment for her to realise where she was. A quick drink from her water bottle, and she crept to the edge of the footpath. To her right, the camp lay in silence. To the left, the river beckoned. It was now or never.

Powering up her kinetic energy, she raised a slight disturbance in the woods to the right of the camp, which was midway between the two sentries. It was a bit close for comfort, but she needed them both to run towards it. Both would want the prize Beldarius offered earlier to the one who captured her. She counted on their greed, overriding their common sense.

Both troops rushed towards the disturbance. *Some things never change.* Without looking back, Myrine hopped onto the path and sprinted to the exit. She nearly missed the entry leading to the river she had noticed upon entering the woods with Faeyet.

Myrine wiggled through an opening where she heard the river. The dense underbrush slowed her down. Near the riverbank, a curtain of sinuous hanging vines barred her way. On the other side of the vines lay a stark sandy riverbank.

She took her spyderco knife from her utility belt. The vines hissed. A thick vine detached itself and snaked towards her. Myrine nimbly sidestepped it. It embedded itself in the ground behind her. In front of her, the vines pulsed and hissed. Another muscled vine snaked forward. At the last moment, Myrine stepped to her left. It embedded itself in the ground to her right. More vines detached and moved. Each time, she avoided capture. Before long, she was caged in by them.

Dragonscats! Surrounded, she turned in a slow circle. Her right thumb found the round hole at the base of her knife and she flicked it open.

A loud hiss from the circle of vines. They snaked closer.

CHAPTER 8

Turning, Myrine fervently looked around. Noticed a gap in the vines to her right, left by the vines that had moved closer to encircle her. Spyderco in her right hand, she placed her thumb in the thumbhole, ensuring the blade remain steady and open. Feet thirty centimeters apart, distributing her weight evenly, she slid her forty-centimetre Icon steel truncheon from her utility belt with her left hand. Assuming a shield stance, she lifted her left arm holding the truncheon and kept her right arm bent at the elbow waist high. She took a deep breath through her nose and slowly released it through her mouth, settling her chi.

Myrine blurred into motion. Cutting and clubbing, she widened the gap in the wall of vines until it was big enough to dive through. She brought her arms together above her head. Pushed forward with her legs and performed a gymnastic dive forward roll. She landed on the sandy riverbank. Behind her, the damaged vines released a terrible sulphurous stink. Gagging, she kept low to the ground under the rising stink and crawled on all fours towards the river.

Having reached the river's edge, she stood up. Here, the air was not as foul. She folded her knife and clipped it onto her belt. Truncheon in hand, she looked back at the vines. They had re-assembled, curling around one another. Walled off the gap between the riverbank and the forest. *At least they did not move towards her. There was no going back now.* She pushed the truncheon through its loop on her belt and dusted her hands against the seat of her pants.

On the opposite side of the fast-flowing river, dragon toothed cliffs rose into the night sky. A bright graveyard moon hung above the cliff rim, in a starless sky. Its rays painted the fleecy clouds around it, a bruised lilac-purple. Part of its rays threw a sheen across the ink black river water.

Bone tired, she kneeled on the sand, took off her hoodie and sleeveless vest. Unslung her backpack. *Grandma said if I formed a clear picture of what I needed, I would find it in my backpack.* Picturing a juicy red apple, she opened her backpack and took one out. She ate it to the core. Magic energy flowed from the apple's juices into her veins.

Scooping a hole in the sand, she buried the core. She rinsed her hands in the river. Wiped her mouth and patted her hands dry on the seat of her pants. With her renewed energy came determination. *She had to get to the exit portal, come what may.*

An idea struck her. She stuck a hand into her open backpack. It was time to find out if she was on the correct path towards the exit portal. She envisioned the item she required and withdrew a magnetometer. Myrine held the compass-like magnetometer in the palm of her right hand. Straightened her arm and raised it chest high. The metal needle vibrated on its axis, then picked up the resonance frequency of the portal and stilled. It pointed directly down the river, in sync with the flow of the water.

She shrugged on her backpack and donned her sleeveless vest, covering it. A slight breeze sprung up, sending sinister whispers across the river water. A shiver piano fingered up and down Myrine's spine. A tendril of wind stroked the hairs on the back of her neck. Involuntarily, her left shoulder jerk pulled up to her earlobe. She rubbed her arms and turned in a full circle. *It was only the wind. Or was it? No. She had to stop jumping at every darned imaginary shadow.* Annoyance stabbed through Myrine. Her lips drawn into a grim line, she put on her hoodie. Zipped it, leaving the hood off her head. Sipping from her never empty water bottle, she trudged alongside the river toward the exit portal's frequency.

Myrine had judged the distance to the exit portal from the magnetometer's reading to be at least a two-hour walk. She slipped the water bottle back into the side pocket of her backpack and settled into an even, not too brisk pace. *It would be better if she conserved her energy. Who knows what next she might encounter?* Her past hours of disciplined physical training with Aedric now stood her in good stead. Without stopping, she looked up at the sky. Noted the position of the moon. Then checked her quantum watch. If she kept up her pace, there would be time to catch a power nap at the exit portal before it opens at sunrise. *If Beldarius and his troops thought she was in the woods,* she reminded herself.

She came up to a weathered pier. Beside it, a rusty tinny lay upside down. Next to it, a splintered oar handle rose from the sand. The other lay half buried in the sand. After a cursory once over, Myrine walked to the edge of the river. The current was flowing fast. She looked back at the tinny. Dismissed the idea to try and use it and carried on walking.

Fifty meters further, she rounded a bend and happened upon a thicket of mangroves. A few hesitant steps into the mangroves, the sand had turned to slush. An eerie hush fell over the mangroves. The only noise, the sucking of the mud as it released a boot at every step she took. She stopped and looked down. Slowly the bubbles were popping around her boots. Myrine was sure that it indicated the presence of quicksand.

She looked about. More bubbles fizzed and popped ahead of her. Worry twisted her intestines into a painful knot. She felt a tug. Looked down again. The sand had crept over the toe box and was steadily sucking her boots in. She wrenched her left foot out of the sand. Her right foot sunk into the muck up to its crown. She put her left foot as far back as she could. Her body wobbled. She grabbed onto a medium sized hardwood mangrove twig with both hands.

Hungry, larger bubbles started popping around her right foot. Using the twig as leverage, her right thigh quivering, she strained and pulled her right foot upwards. At first there was no give. Her stomach dropped. She knew she was pulling too fast. Chin on her chest she kept her gaze on the sand around her right boot, giving her right leg a few seconds of rest.

The sand was slowly creeping up to the tongue of her boot. It covered the first row of laces. With renewed effort, reminding herself to move slowly, she started to pull her right foot. She could cry with relief when it was eventually released with a huge gluck suck. Keeping her hold on the twig, she turned her body. Behind her the sand was hard packed. A squelch made her look back at the sand in front of her. It was undulating towards the hard packed sand.

Using the twig, she swung her body onto the hard packed sand. Landed awkward and lost precious seconds finding her feet. Racing away from the encroaching quicksand, she retraced her steps out of the mangroves. The slush behind her released vicious spits and bubbles. A look over her shoulder confirmed it was following her. She skip-jumped the last two steps out of the mangroves.

She walked backwards, looking at the mangroves. Stopped at a safe distance. The quicksand did not stray past the grove. She stopped and surveyed the area. There was no way through or around the mangroves. Contemplating the river, it was too far to swim. Realising she was losing valuable time, Myrine raced back to the weathered pier. Breathless, she got to the tinny. Head hanging, she leaned against it, rubbing the stitch in her left side. Her breathing returned to near normal. She walked to the buried oar and pulled it out of the sand. It seemed undamaged. She dragged it to the tinny, dropping it on the sand next to it.

The tinny was rusty, but on a closer inspection, there were no holes in the hull. A flicker of hope flared. Myrine combined one of her supernatural sub-powers with her physical strength and heaved the tinny onto its side. Another shove and it was lying on its hull. She dragged it to the water's edge. *Was it her imagination or was the river flowing faster?* She walked back to where she had dropped the one oar on the sand. She looked at the splintered handle of the other oar. Pulled it out of the sand. Stumbling back, landing on her butt, she came up with just a splintered handle. Flung it aside.

Maybe she should have stayed in the forest. A quick glance at her quantum watch. She scowled. Too late. *And this time she might not be so lucky getting through those vines. She would have to take her chances with the tinny.* Sighing, she grabbed the undamaged oar, jogged to the tinny and threw it into the middle of the hull. She pushed the tinny into the river and hauled herself over the side as the water reached her thighs. The tinny wobbled. Myrine gripped the sides and steadied it.

On her knees between the wooden seat in the middle of the tinny and the stern side, she bent forward and dragged the oar towards her. Using the sweep row method she read about once that rowers with one oar used, she steered the tinny towards the current in the middle of the river. *This was not as easy as it looked like on YouTube.*

At the mercy of the undertow, the tinny settled into a sideways drift. Myrine shuffled on her knees to the middle of the tinny. The tinny rocked precariously at every shuffle. Sweat beaded her forehead. After anxious seconds, she had reached the wooden bench. The middle of the tinny was narrow enough for her to reach the water on either side with the oar. She used the oar to more or less keep the tinny on track. Rounding a bend in the river, the mangroves she encountered earlier appeared. Keeping the tinny more or less in the middle of the current, she avoided those that stood trunk deep a third of the way into the river. She could have sworn they were not that far into the river when she had first encountered them.

The river narrowed slightly. Without warning, the current became stronger. For fear of overturning the tinny, Myrine dared not do more than lightly touch the oar to the river's surface. Ahead, too fast for comfort, another blind bend appeared. The river narrowed even more. The oar became slippery in her hands, and it took all her concentration to keep the tinny on track and round the bend. The river bottlenecked, flowing through a rocky passage.

On the right-hand side of the bottleneck, the mangroves had become an impenetrable thicket. White-topped waves foamed against the cliff edge on her left. The tinny bucked and bobbed over and between rock slabs in the river. Dropping the now useless oar to the bottom of the tinny, Myrine sunk to all fours and crawled towards the bow and gripped the edges. Her weight pushed down the tinny's bow and it barely scraped through the bottleneck.

Myrine lifted a hand to wipe wet strands of her hair off her face. The tinny listed sideways. Plunged over a one-meter drop and pitched Myrine into the water. She landed an arm's length from the tinny. Kicking, she propelled herself back to the tinny, grabbed its edge and hauled herself halfway over the side. Water circled around a rip in the tinny's bottom.

Dropping back into the water, Myrine kicked hard against the side of the sinking tinny. In her efforts to avoid being sucked under by the sinking tinny, she landed herself smack in the middle of the current. It took all her effort to tamp down the automatic instinct to fight against the current. At least it was not as strong as before the bottleneck, the river having widened again. With slow sideways strokes, she extricated herself from the current. Treading water, she looked about.

She was between the cliff and the current. In the distance, she could hear the waterfall. *If she dropped over the waterfall, there should be a plunge pool at the bottom of it.* Her adrenaline spike flagged. Her waterlogged boots dragged her legs downwards. The water was frigid. She bicycled in slow motion with her legs, forcing her feet upwards, and started swimming towards the sound of the waterfall. She knew she had to keep moving and find a way out before hypothermia set in.

Maybe when she reached the area before the waterfall's ledge there would be a chance to get out of the river before it plunged over the edge. She wondered if in Betwonium the same applied to rivers and waterfalls as it did on earth. Shallower before it plunged over the edge. *She could only hope.*

Myrine started trickle breathing, swimming slowly alongside the cliff. Here and there she stopped, hanging onto a rocky outcrop, taking a breather, rubbing her arms to keep the circulation going. The cliff was getting lower. She kept vigilant for a spot where she could climb out of the river.

Her mind circled around the possibilities as she forced her tired body onwards. *What if she went over the edge and concussed herself? Worse yet. Broke an ankle. Stop it!*

She forced the nasty little voice in her mind to the back of her head. Dismissed the niggling feeling of impending doom.

It was what it was.

CHAPTER 9

Her waterlogged boots became heavier with every kick. Myrine changed her swimming style to front crawl, using her arms only. If it was not that she would need her boots once she got out of the river, she would have ditched them long ago. About thirty meters further along the river, the waterfall now thunderous, Myrine encountered the rock bed preceding the edge before the waterfall.

Myrine gripped a rocky ledge and pulled her legs under her. Finding purchase in the sludge at the river's bottom with her boots, she stood up. Chest deep in the swirling water, her breath ragged, she leaned against the ledge. The cliff on her left no longer stretched into the sky. It had crumbled into a rubble-wall of varying sized rock boulders. Unhindered by the tall cliff's edge, the silver rays of the butcher's moon skated across the water, skipping over darker sections. Despite the shallow water, the river's flow remained strong. It tried to pull her along as it navigated around the rock ledges, through deeper ponds of water, toward the waterfall's edge. An undercurrent nipped at her ankles.

Myrine judged the distance to the edge of the waterfall to be about twenty odd meters. *It would be a better idea to get out of the river now and go along the top.* A massive splash to the right behind her interrupted her thoughts. She glanced over her shoulder. Three rock ponds behind her to the right, the water seemed to boil. Thunderstruck, she watched as a thick tentacle shot up in a spray of water. It thundered down on the rock ledge in front of it, sending waves bashing against the left river edge near Myrine. The water in the rock pond erupted in a geyser spray. One wave caught Myrine unawares. Thumped her left shoulder against the ledge she was holding onto.

Without taking her eyes off it, Myrine righted herself, ignoring the dull ache in her shoulder. The thick, muscular tentacle rippled. With a wet slurp-suck, its front lifted off the flat rock ledge. Elongating, it snaked through the air. Dipped down into the next pond. The other end lifted out of the water. Followed. Disappeared from sight. The water, two rock ponds from Myrine, started boiling.

With an adrenal burst of energy, Myrine drag-walked herself into the shallower water next to the rock boulders on her left. Battling to keep her balance, she stumbled over slippery pebbles and rocks. She found a decent crevice. With her left hand, she latched onto it. The current dragged her feet sideways. With a strength borne of pure despair, she hung on and walked her feet backwards. Her body righted. With her right boot, she found another crevice. Pushing with her right leg, she gripped the crevice above her with both hands. She brought her left knee out of the water and hauled herself out of the water.

Her arms trembled. Her thighs burned. The muscles in her neck corded. Seconds became eons. Her left hand slipped. Her right hand found a purchase. With an immense effort, she pulled herself onto a flat-topped rock boulder. Found herself one meter above the ground on the other side. Knees bent; she jumped off it. From the other side of the boulder, a frustrated, hungry wail rendered the air. Myrine ran.

One hundred meters further, she came to a halt and looked back at the barren landscape behind her. Nothing followed in her wake. She was near the bottom of a dry slope, sparsely dotted with trees. The roar of the waterfall had stilled to a drone in the distance.

Myrine's adrenaline rush dissipated. Despite the warm windless air, bone clattering shivers rocked her body. She sank down under a tree. Struggled out of her boots and poured the water out. Next, she took off her sodden socks. Wrung them out. Putting them on her boots.

Standing up, she took off her hoodie and sleeveless vest. Hung it on a low branch. Carefully, she took off her waterproofed magic backpack and set it against the tree trunk. Off her back, it immediately became visible to the naked eye. *Exactly what Grandma warned me about. I have to have it on my back at all times.* Myrine cast a furtive look about. Satisfied nothing lurked close by, she took off her shirt and pants and wrung most of the water out of it. Hung it on another tree branch.

Standing in her underwear, she gave her limbs a vigorous rub. Her body relaxed and accepted the warmth of the air. She checked her quantum watch and was surprised to see that there were still one and three-quarter hours until sunrise. She would have to go back to the top of the cliff. Hopefully, the creature she had just escaped was water bound.

She got dressed in her damp pants, shirt, and socks, worming her feet into her boots. Taking her backpack, she settled it on her back and put on her sleeveless vest, covering it. Then tied her hoodie around her waist. Her eyes swept over the moonlit landscape. Barring a few trees dotted here and there, it was barren. No sign of life. *Not enough cover for any of Beldarius' guards to hide either. But then again, they may be hidden somewhere near the waterfall. It would be best to remain vigilant and cautious.*

Spyderco knife at the ready, Myrine willed her obstinate legs into motion. Her body bent forward; she trudged back up the incline towards the rim of the cliff. Stopping every now and then, she did a quick survey of her surroundings. She reached the rim and slowed. The ground plateaued and had turned to shale. Keeping in line with the rocky rim on her left, she moved towards the sound of the waterfall.

Her breath rasping, she reached the spot above the waterfall where it cascaded over the edge in the river. She bent forward, hands gripping her knees, and inhaled a few deep breaths, then straightened. Hands on her hips, she hollowed her back and bent it backwards, holding the position for twenty seconds. Standing upright, she rotated her torso from left to right and back for ten counts, swinging her arms in tandem.

With her hoodie's cuff, Myrine wiped her sticky face and tightened her damp ponytail. Her eyes darted across the river below. An involuntary shudder shook through her. The sinking butcher's moon painted the cliff face down to the waterfall in sinister shades of grey. She licked her dry lips and reached for her water bottle.

Time was nearing moonset. She judged it to be at least an hour and a half before sunrise. Later she would realise that she should have checked her Quantum watch for the correct Betwonium time. She walked to the edge of the rim and looked over it. Three storeys below to the right, the water foamed, churning in rapids, before cascading over the edge into the plunge basin below. The portal would be behind the curtain of water.

Her mind drifted back to the information Faeyet imparted during her chatterings. The guards were supposed to arrive at sunrise. She could dive into the plunge basin. Then again, if it was shallow, it would be taking too great a risk. *Or what if there were more of those tentacle things waiting in there?* She had to find a way to free climb down the cliff.

Myrine settled into a hollow between two rock boulders, her feet hanging over the cliff face. The moonlight was not bright enough to properly inspect the cliff face. She engaged her cat-like night vision and studied the cliff face. Finding what she was looking for, she plotted a route and committed it to memory. She was loath to climb in the dark.

If she started fifteen minutes before sunrise, it would be light enough. She judged it would take roughly half an hour to climb down the cliff to the plateau behind the waterfall. If she was there by sunrise, she should be able to enter the exit portal. Hopefully unhindered.

If only she had practised her supernatural powers instead of being obstinate, she could have used her teleportation skill to teleport straight to the rock plateau behind the waterfall. It was her own fault her energy did not extend beyond teleporting three meters before giving out. *It would be too dicey to teleport from ledge to ledge down this unknown cliff face.*

Myrine squinted at the low-hanging moon. Checked her quantum watch. She had about half an hour to rest before she had to start down the cliff. With a sigh, she unfastened her hoodie from her waist, put it on, and pulled the hood over her head. Leaning her head against the rock, she folded her hands in her lap. Setting her body clock for a thirty-minute power nap, she closed her eyes.

Myrine startled awake. It was strange not to hear the morning squabbles of parrots, each proclaiming the morning to be its own. She rubbed the grit out of her eyes and looked around. The butcher's moon was gone. Dusk had unfolded its light grey blanket and drawn it across the sky. She was late.

She scrambled up, steadied herself against the boulder and looked down the cliff face, falling away below her. No shimmer from the portal yet. Myrine scanned the cliff face where she earlier spotted footholds which would allow her to free climb down to the waterfall. She rolled her shoulders, settled her magical backpack, and zipped her sleeveless vest, making sure it was covered. She decided to keep her hoodie on and zipped that up as well. Turning around, she lowered herself down. Her feet found purchase.

Two-thirds of the way down, the sun's gleaming bald head popped into the sky. She felt its rays lightly stroking across her back. She bit her bottom lip. Increased her speed.

Shuffling sideways on a thin ledge, one hip tight against the cliff's wall, Myrine stopped, niggled by an eerie feeling of watching eyes. She looked down at the waterfall. Behind the water curtain, the portal mouth yawned and started shimmering. No other movement. Inwardly, she shook her head at herself. It must have been her imagination. Using her anxiety to play tricks on her. There was nobody watching her.

No more dawdling! Beldarius' guards could not be far off. She looked down. Her trajectory had taken her away from the plunge basin. She was standing perpendicular to the rock platform behind the waterfall. Too far to try and jump into the plunge basin at the foot of the waterfall. Too far to teleport to the rock plateau. After a final quick look around at the surroundings, she turned back to face the cliff. She resumed her downward free climb.

At least the cliff's face was still in shadow. With her dark clothing, she could only hope that she remained camouflaged long enough to evade detection from the guards when they arrived. A rock crumbled under her left foot. Gravel spewed onto the rocks below, shattering the morning silence. *Dragonscats!* Behind her, out of sight on the opposite side of the waterfall, slight movements swayed the treetops.

Myrine's shoulders tensed. Her forehead against the cliff face, one leg dangling, she froze. She remained mouse still for a few seconds after the last gravel stone had fallen. Her ears strained into the ensuing silence. There was no sound of oncoming boots. She blew out a breath, resumed her climb and picked her next foothold with more care. Not wanting to waste time, she suppressed the inherent want to constantly look over her shoulder. *Come on Myrine. Don't look down. Climb!*

The rush of the waterfall became louder still as she was swallowed by its misty curtain. The cliff's edge changed from dry to slippery. It took all of Myrine's concentration to avoid slipping. She kept wiping her hands against her hoodie's side before moving it towards the next handhold. Wipe grip, wipe grip, she moved her sore hands from one handhold to the next. With every foot hold she scuffled her foot securely into a foothold. Her hands white knuckled, the arches of her feet aching, she resolutely carried on climbing downwards. Time lengthened. Suspended her in a timeless capsule.

Three minutes later, the full sphere of the sun blazed into the sky. Its rays struck the wet cliff face. Blinded Myrine. She turned her head to the west and closed her eyes. Dark spots danced behind her eyelids. A spasm of fear rippled through her. Squinting her eyes, she turned her head back to the cliff face and carried on climbing.

In the woods on the other side of the waterfall, the wart-faced Brunkai controller, Fanisius, switched on a solar powered impulse control strapped to his wrist. Tapping a code into it, he sent the plant-like Brunkai drones into the air. They dislodged from their tree perches.

Their sinuous vine tendrils folded tight against their smooth-haired coconut shaped bodies. Swift and noiseless, they floated into the air. With his twig fingers, Fanisius rolled the black ball in the electric impulse control in small slow circles. The Brunkai formed a tight circle formation above his bristle haired head.

Myrine, her sole concentration on climbing down the cliff. Her only thoughts to reach the exit portal before Beldarius' guards arrived, she remained unaware of the new threat.

Fanisius swayed to the edge of the trees. Stopped. His rheumy eyes fixed on Myrine. Noiseless, he swayed towards the edge of the river on his stumpy legs. The Brunkai followed, remaining in a tight formation above his head. On the cliff above Myrine, Beldarius appeared, right hand in the air, open palm towards Fanisius. At the water's edge, Fanisius splayed root-like toes and wedged his bare feet into the soft riverbank. Beldarius dropped his hand.

Fanisius flicked the ball of the impulse control in an upward motion, pointing a twig finger at Myrine. Five Brunkai broke away and rocketed to Myrine. The remaining two picked Fanisius up by his sinewy twig arms and flew him to Beldarius at the top of the cliff. Together they stood, looking down as the Brunkai reached Myrine.

Against the cliff face, a startled Myrine struggled against the sinuous vines encasing her wrists and ankles. A vine tendril encircled her neck, forcing her head back. The fifth Brunkai released a vapour of acerbic Dragon's breath calment directly over Myrine's face. Her eyes rolled back. Her body sagged.

The four Brunkai, holding Myrine's wrists and ankles, pulled her away from the cliff face.

CHAPTER 10

The Brunkai flew Myrine's compliant body to the top of the cliff, where the two holding her ankles let go of it. The other two holding her wrists lowered her to the ground in front of Beldarius before letting go. Her knees buckled. Chin on her chest, Myrine folded into a heap at Beldarius' feet. Half dazed, her mind racing, she dumbly stared at Beldarius' boots. *Dragonscats. Those are bigger than Aedric's size thirteens! One stomp and I would be history. I had better come up with something really good if I am going to explain my way out of this mess.*

The last bit of the Dragon's breath, calmant the Brunkai had sprayed on her, dissipated. Myrine's body tingled. Her ears cleared and her vision returned. Sensing she was surrounded, she remained inert. Nearby, a cacophonous voice whispered.

'Be careful. Surneal's message warned of her multiple supernatural magic powers.'

From under her eyelashes, Myrine dared a sidelong glance in its direction. Inwardly, she shrunk as her gaze fell upon a hook-nosed devil face. Cloaked in a long black coat, head mirror strapped to its forehead. The voice's owner stood next to Beldarius. Bulging close set black eyes with no irises turned towards her. A thin split-end tongue flicked across his blade thin lips. Myrine snapped her eyes down. Fiery adrenaline spiked nerves needled her cheek bones. Stones crunched. She glanced to her left. Beldarius had stepped closer to her.

Tension stifled the air. Near silent seconds stretched. She could feel Beldarius' eyes crawling over her. Ignoring the yearning to cup her hand around the back of her neck, Myrine snatched a few shallow breaths through her mouth and held her breath. Her inner instinct warned her to remain immobile. In her mind, she heard Aedric's voice. *'Always let your opponent make the first move.'*

'Faeyet has informed me that her so-called supernatural magic powers are not fully developed.'

Slowly, Myrine released her pent-up breath. *At least I convinced the Fosterling.*

'Faeyet is a mere Fosterling. What does she know?'

Myrine tensed.

'Well, there is one way to control her until we deliver her to Eugenia. Did you bring the sporalenium?'

A rustle of clothing. The pop of a bottle cap. *If I created a firewall between myself and them, and held it long enough, I could dive into the plunge basin.* Myrine knew her chances were slim, but if she caught them unawares...

She flattened her palms on the ground next to her thighs and started pushing herself up. An unexpected pain seared through her scalp. Beldarius had grabbed her by her ponytail. He wrenched her to her feet. Turned her towards him and bent down until his eyes were level with hers. It took all Myrine's self-control not to cringe as she noticed his oval-shaped pupils narrowing to a horizontal orange slit in his slurry brown eyes.

A snippet from the book Grandma kept regarding Betwonium raced through her mind. It was said that Betwoniumites were cold-blooded monsters, parading in human form. But, if they attacked, they shape shifted into their giant lizard form. Grateful that Beldarius was in his humanlike form, Myrine swallowed her fear. Despite the heat, an icy shiver trotted down her spine. Beldarius still held her by her ponytail, but now that she stood upright, he was no longer pulling on it. She tipped her head a fraction to the left and looked up at him.

'Can you let go of my ponytail, please?'

Beldarius leaned into her and uttered a hiss. Gave her ponytail a vicious tug. Furiously, Myrine blinked away the hot tears spurting into her eyes. Behind Beldarius, anticipatory titters rose from his troops.

'I can explain why I...'

Another painful tug of her ponytail. Her nose started watering. She raised a hand to wipe it. Her scalp was on fire.

'QUIET!'

Myrine's heart stuttered. She shut her mouth. Beldarius bent further forward. Unable to move away, she had no choice but to allow him to crowd her. She noticed the change in his eyes. His narrowed pupils had become a hardly visible orange slit. Menace blanketed the surrounding air. Instinctively, she knew she had to remain docile, or he would change over to his natural form. Petrified, she lowered her eyes and stared at her feet.

'You will speak when spoken to. Do you understand?'

'Yes.'

She hated that she could not hide the tremble in her whispered reply. A satisfactory grunt from Beldarius. *At least showing weakness seemed to appease him. Typical bully boy.* She repeated the Ho'oponopono prayer in her mind. Her nerves settled somewhat. She would have to wait for an appropriate opportunity to escape.

Beldarius straightened without releasing his grip on Myrine's ponytail. From the corner of her eye, Myrine watched him beckon Dr Dreckonium to his side with his other hand. Intuitively, she knew she had to shut the door in her mind, leading to the whereabouts of the Infinity charm. She barely managed, as Dr Dreckonium's footsteps crunched to a stop next to Beldarius.

'Besides the Infinity Charm, shall I check her for the presence of supernatural powers?'

'Good idea.'

Myrine's heart pumped full throttle, setting the pulse in her jaw throbbing at a frenetic pace. Unable to move her head for fear she would tear every hair out of her scalp, she raised her hands, held her scalp on both sides above her ears and pressed gently. She shut down her supernatural powers.

I know I did not really enjoy having these supernatural powers, but I feel naked without them. It may be the only thing, combined with my martial arts skills, that will get me out of this mess.

Spray bottle in hand, Dr Dreckonium approached her. Stopped in front of her. The head mirror strapped to his forehead bulged. He stepped forward until he was toe to toe with her. Myrine let go of her temples. Before she could cover her face, a rotten orange peel smelling mist wafted over Myrine's face. Beldarius let go of her ponytail. Clutching her throat, she bent forward and gagged. A tiny drool of bitter saliva dribbled over her chin. Her empty stomach heaved. Acid fumes roiled in her throat.

She looked up at Dr Dreckonium through blurry eyes. His head mirror emitted a reddish glow as he moved his head up and down. A shockwave of nerves stapled painful pinholes across her forehead and cheeks. *Is he scanning me? Will he find my backpack?*

'There is nothing on her except a utility belt with what looks like some weapons.'

'Any supernatural powers in evidence?'

'Nah. The information received from both Faeyet and Earth that she refused to use them and they did not develop seems true.'

'Seems? Or definitely?'

'In my experience, if she had any supernatural powers, my infrared millimeter-wave scanner would have found it.'

Myrine straightened up onto her rubbery legs. Wiped the back of her mouth with her hoodie's sleeve cuff. Her gaze skittered from the hook-nosed devil faced Dr Dreckonium to Beldarius. Both were watching her intently. Myrine's skin crawled. Evil pervaded the air.

Something shimmered behind the rough scaly skin on Beldarius' face. His onyx lizard eyes glittered as he held her eyes with his hypnotic, reptilian stare. Her mind reeled as he opened his thin, bloodless lips in a sharp toothed grin.

Her senses reeling, Myrine swallowed back bitter bile. She lowered her eyes. She swallowed back bitter bile. Her only salvation left her magical backpack that was on her back, hidden by her hoodie. But there was no way she could reach it unobserved. She knew she had to keep her backpack hidden at all costs.

Myrine blinked her dry eyes a few times. The ground stopped swaying under her feet. Her vision cleared. Keeping her eyes downcast. She forced herself to stay upright on her rubbery legs. She straightened her hoodie, surreptitiously ensuring her magical backpack was in place. She lifted her head. Her skin crawled as she looked at Beldarius, a sharp toothed grin on his face.

'Faeyet, come here. Take off her utility belt.'

Fearing her backpack would show, Myrine unbuckled her belt, pulled it out of her pants loops, and held it out. Faeyet snatched it from her and handed it to Beldarius. Turning her head from side-to-side, Myrine counted at least twenty men besides Beldarius, Faeyet, Dr Dreckonium and Fanisius.

She gathered that the extra men to those he had in the forest with him must be the day guards guarding the portal. Her gaze travelled to the grotesque, wart-faced Fanisius next to Beldarius. She had read about tree-men, afflicted by a rare genetic condition. Above his head, she recognised the plant-like drones that plucked her off the cliff. There were ten. They hovered in a circle, their tentacles tucked tight against their yellow-green coconut bodies.

Her body stiffened. No amount of martial arts skills were going to save her from this lot. It would only alert them to her physical capabilities. She did not even want to think what could happen if her magical backpack showed. She could not afford to have them find the Infinity Charm. The blonde, humanlike version of Faeyet stepped forward and came to a stop in front of Myrine.

'You have angered the ruler of our Betwonium army by not accepting his gracious invitation to stay overnight at his castle.'

Behind Faeyet, Beldarius snort-grunted in confirmation. Eyeing Faeyet, Myrine debated her answer. Should she call out Beldarius on this bullcrap invitation story? His agenda was clearly to stop her from reaching the portal. Nope. That would not do. Before Myrine could think of an acceptable response, Faeyet continued.

'That was not very polite. It is a rule of Betwonium, that all foreign visitors announce themselves at the ruler of our army, Beldarius', castle. Only once they are cleared will Beldarius grant them permission to travel through this portal.'

Another confirmatory huff from Beldarius. Faeyet's false honeyed voice barely hid her condescending tone.

'For you to get his permission, you have to tell us where the Infinity Charm is. Once it has been found, you can leave.'

Without her supernatural powers, Myrine could not read Beldarius' mind to determine his true intentions. Momentarily, Myrine considered opening the door to her supernatural powers. A glance at Beldarius and Dr Dreckonium as they stood watching her had her reconsider. She firmly kept the door shut. She lifted her chin.

'I don't have time for delays. I have to get to Tsaonin. Grandma needs desperate help. Please permit me to travel through the exit portal immediately.'

Beldarius pushed Faeyet aside and leaned into Myrine's face. The rot on his breath threatened to gag her, and she turned her face away. His next words punched Myrine in the gut.

'You will wait at the castle for Surneal to arrive and tell him where the Infinity Charm is hidden that you brought with you from Earth.'

Myrine blanched. Confirmation of Grandma's statement before she left her in the herb cellar reverberated through her. *The Dark Forces want to control all seven planes in the Universe and to access Tsaonin where our universal ruler lives. To do that, they need control of you. Only you can unlock the Infinity Charm once you turn eighteen.*

She looked at Faeyet's smirking face. Unable to supernaturally cloak her thoughts, Faeyet had been reading her mind. She clenched her jaw and concentrated her thoughts on what she saw around her. Flitting from one object to the next. She turned her eyes back to Beldarius.

'I don't know where it is.'

She tried and failed to hide the tremor in her voice. Unable to hold his gaze, she looked back at Faeyet. A frown of concentration played on Faeyet's forehead. An onslaught of inquisitive tendrils bombarded Myrine's mind. Suppressing her natural instinct to wrench the tendrils away, she gritted her teeth and flooded her mind with pictures of hazy meadows. It was the best she could do without using her powers.

'She does, she does. I nearly found it in her thoughts before she stopped thinking about it. There was also something about a backpack. Maybe she hid it somewhere and the Infinity Charm is in it.'

An ominous silence followed Faeyet's screechy outburst. Myrine half turned to Beldarius but kept an eye on Faeyet. From the corner of her left eye, she noted the earlier shimmer had re-appeared. Much stronger. Undulating in his cheeks. Malevolence pulsed in the air between them. Seconds stretched.

'Where. Is. Your backpack!'

A vapour of near unbearable stench followed every hissed word. Myrine knew her response would have to sound believable. For Faeyet's benefit, she formed a series of images showing her losing the backpack, as she tumbled through the wrong door opening in the Quantum Door, when she left Earth. Unbidden, a glimpse of a thought about the Infinity Charm hidden in it popped up. Myrine's shoulders tightened. Sweat dampened her armpits. With a serious burst of energy, she pushed the image of the infinity Charm from her mind.

'I think I lost it when I fell through the Quantum Door.'

Myrine could see in the look Beldarius gave her, he was calculating and weighing her answer. Then he looked at Faeyet, who was staring at Myrine. With an effort, Myrine willed herself not to look away from Faeyet. Inwardly, she cringed at the ugly expression that crossed Faeyet's face.

'She knows where the Infinity Charm is.'

'Yesss. I think so too.'

Dragonscats. She was dangerous. I had better be careful around her. For that matter, I had better be careful around everyone until I find out what their abilities entailed, so I could circumvent it. So far, only Faeyet showed herself to be a mind reader. All the Betwoniumites will at least be capable of shape shifting.

Beldarius moved, jerking Myrine back to the present. He raised his right hand. Myrine crossed her arms in front of her face and ducked. Losing her footing, her ankle rolled, and she crumpled to her knees. She looked up. A hideous grin on his face, Beldarius half-turned from her and called Fanisius forward. Dr Dreckonium voiced an insulting comment regarding Myrine's alleged abilities. Laughter rippled through the troops. Heat suffused Myrine's face. She climbed to her feet. Her hands fisted at her sides. She glared at Dreckonium.

With a bark of hoarse laughter, Fanisius swayed forward, stopping next to Beldarius. Out of earshot, heads together, they conferred in whispers. Fanisius swayed away from Beldarius. Signalled to the circling Brunkai. Two broke away from the tight circle above his head and shot towards Myrine. Before she could move, they had fastened their tentacles around her wrists.

'Faeyet, go to the castle and tell Eugenia to make the necessary preparations to receive our little guest.'

A high-pitched titter issued from Faeyet. Myrine's head swung to her. She did not like the way Faeyet grinned at her. It was difficult to keep her mind from running amok with wild ideas about the 'preparations'. No need to give Faeyet any insights. She watched Faeyet, morphing into her normal Fosterling self before loping off into the distance, Myrine's utility belt flapping at her side.

At the same time, Beldarius and Dr Dreckonium had walked to his troops and from Beldarius' gestures, it seemed he was giving them instructions of some sort. Myrine took a step in Beldarius' direction. Fanisius swayed and lifted his arms. The Brunkai's grip on Myrine's wrists tightened, and they lifted her a ruler's length off the ground, keeping her in place. Useless, her feet dangled in the air.

Dr Dreckonium took off in the direction Faeyet had disappeared and Beldarius walked back to Myrine. The guards followed in his wake. With Dr Dreckonium out of the way, Myrine thought it was safe to return her supernatural powers to normal. At least her brain was no longer fogged with whatever it was Dreckonium had sprayed on her. A tingle in her veins announced the slow return of her supernatural powers. She balled her hands. From the subconscious 'oops' part of her brain, a warning sounded. She unclenched her hands. Willed herself to relax. Her supernatural powers were not fully activated. Yet.

Myrine blanked her mind and hid her thoughts. *Better safe than sorry. Who knows who else here were mind readers.* Despite a sliver of fear skittering down her spine, she lifted her chin and looked at Beldarius as he approached. His obsidian gaze was hard and expressionless. Her innards tightened into a ball behind her navel. Stopping in front of her,

Beldarius motioned to Fanisius to come closer. The Brunkai lowered Myrine back to the ground and let go of her wrists. She rubbed at the red indentations circling her wrists.

'I did not mean to offend you by not accepting your invitation. I…'

'You will speak when spoken to.'

Myrine bit back a sharp retort. Now was not the time to give free rein to her temper. Nodded. Cast her eyes down. A heavy sigh escaped her. She had to appear compliant at all costs. She should have known by now she could not reason with Beldarius. Unless, of course, she showed him the Infinity Charm.

'You have two choices. You can walk with three of my troops, Fanisius and the Brunkai, as your guards to the castle. Or …'

Beldarius inclined his head. Peered at her. A fleshy tongue tip appeared and flicked over his lower lip, leaving a slug-sheen. He bent forward. Myrine leaned back and let out a breath.

'Or?'

Beldarius stood back and rubbed his chin. His eyes skimmed over Myrine. She suppressed a shiver. Her skin crawled.

'I knock some sense into you and have the Brunkai drag you to my castle.'

Myrine was unsure whether or not she should answer and held her tongue. Beldarius leaned into her, crowding her personal space. His foul breath washed over her.

'Sooooooo. What is it to be?'

Myrine swallowed.

'I will walk.'

'Speak up.'

'I will walk.'

Beldarius beckoned to the group of troops and three came forward.

'These three will be your personal guards. You are to follow their every instruction.'

Myrine nodded. She noted one of them had two different eyes. A stunning emerald green eye and a lizard eye. He seemed out of place. His intense stare was unsettling.

'Rollandario.'

The troop's stare moved away from her to Beldarius.

'Father?'

With a jolt, Myrine recognised his voice. He was the one who called Beldarius away from the ditch last night. A myriad of questions tumbled through her mind. *Maybe an ally? Could she trust him?*

'You follow Ignatium's orders.'

'Yes, Father.'

'Not a toe out of line. You hear me?'

'Yes, Father.'

'See that you deliver her to your mother. The mind room will be ready for the extraction of information concerning the whereabouts of the Infinity Charm.'

Myrine's intestines tightened into a painful ball. *Is he weak or is he scared of Beldarius? I have never heard about a mind room. Must be something new since the last updated notes on Betwonium that Grandma had.*

Myrine's hand strayed to the side where the Infinity Charm lay motionless in the secret pocket of her invisible backpack. Beldarius swung back to her. She jerked her hand away from her side. Fiddled with the knot on her hoodie that was still tied around her waist.

'What are you doing?'

'Untying my hoodie. I want to put it on.'

She dropped her eyes from Beldarius' flat, cold-eyed stare. Trepidation raced through her. Scarcely able to hide the tremor in her hands, she untied her hoodie from her waist. With a show, she shook it out and put it on.

With two guards in front of her and Rollandario behind her, she was marched at a stiff pace along the path. To her right, Fanisius amble-swayed along the Brunkai, following above his head. Beldarius stayed behind with the rest of his troops.

No one said a word. The uncomfortable silence broken only by their discordant footsteps, interspersed with Fanisius' swish-sway steps. Two hours later, they came to a solid rock bridge. It could only be crossed in a single file. They stopped. The guards debated in which order to cross the bridge. In the distance, the castle walls loomed. *Once behind those walls, my chances of escaping would be minimal.* Far beneath them, the river rushed along towards the waterfall.

Myrine took a hesitant step sideways. She peered over the edge at the river below. If she sat and then rolled herself forward, she could dive bomb into it. She lowered herself onto the grassy edge at the base of the bridge.

The burliest of the guards turned. Took a gigantic step and gripped Myrine by the upper arms, pinning them and lifted her to his eye level.

'I hear earthling flesh is quite sweet.'

He brought Myrine closer to his face. His thick purple spotted tongue flicked out. He licked her cheek. Over his shoulder, she saw Ignatium, then Rollandario turn. They raced to the two of them.

'Hey! What are you doing?!

Ignatium forced the thick-necked guard to lower her to the ground. Myrine stumbled into Rollandario, who caught her and held her upright, her back to the other two. He whispered in her ear. She pushed back, looked into his odd-eyed eyes.

Before Myrine could ask the uppermost question leading on from his urgent whisper, Fanisius appeared beside them. Rollandario's hands dropped away from Myrine's shoulders.

CHAPTER 11

Whilst Ignatius berated the thick-necked guard, Myrine stood silently under the watchful eyes of Fanisius. The drones hovering above his head were a constant reminder that it would be impossible to make a getaway with them around. Her shoulders sagged. She looked at her feet. She now more than ever wished she had not been so obstinate in her refusal to practice and develop her supernatural powers to its fullest extent.

Mired in self-pity, Myrine started as a voice spoke in her mind. With Faeyet not around, she did not expect someone in her immediate surroundings to read her mind, never mind communicate telepathically.

'None of them are capable of telepathy, nor can they read minds. It is safe for us to communicate in this manner.'

Recognising Rollandario's voice, Myrine frowned up at him. His mismatched eyes were focused on her.

'Keep your face expressionless or you will alert Fanisius. He is a sensitive.'

Keeping the frown on her face, Myrine turned to Fanisius, who stared at her. His watery eyes querying. Shrugging her shoulders, she turned her back to him and stared into the distance with unseeing eyes.

'And you are prepared to help me get through the portal if I take you with me to Tsaonin? Why?'

Astonished, she listened to Rollandario's rapid fire delivery of information. Rollandario claimed to be her cousin, his mother, the banished Adelstein aunt who joined the Dark Forces. Myrine stopped short of shaking her head. She was unsure whether to believe his claim that he felt drawn towards the Light Forces. He disclosed he hoped to follow his inner calling to join the Light Forces. Head spinning, Myrine remained rooted to the spot. Before she could properly digest the flood of information, footsteps crunched. She turned her head to the bridge. Ignatius was walking back to them. The thick-necked guard, his aura bristling, stood motionless just inside the pillared entrance to the bridge.

Gesticulating with his hands, Ignatius issued orders.

'Myrine. You follow me. Rollandario, you fall in behind her. Fanisius, you and the Brunkai bring up the rear.'

They set off in that order. Myrine memorised her surroundings whilst listening to Rollandario delivering more machine-gun-bursts of information. Besides being an eidetic, she also possessed echoic memory, and automatically stored away all the information received from Rollandario. Far below them the river fast-flowed between the rock cliff face and a thin strip of riverbank. Beyond the riverbank, dense woods disappeared into the horizon.

On the other side of the bridge, from behind a massive granite stone wall, studded with arrow holes, the turrets of Beldarius' castle spiked into the air. Myrine noticed the stone wall was at least two storeys high, topped with a battlement.

'Before we go in the gate, you need to hide your supernatural powers like before. My mother is capable of turning it against you.'

'I will.'

'Also, hide the information I gave you.'

'Will do.'

Five meters from the entrance to the castle, the bridge abruptly ended in an abyss. A glint of movement in the watchtower at the closed entrance caught her eye. Gears groaned. A sturdy, thick-timbered drawbridge opened. It thumped down in a cloud of swirling dust. More groaning of gears and behind the drawbridge a sharp toothed iron gate slowly rose. It stopped high enough for Ignatius, the tallest of them, to stand upright beneath the sharpened iron teeth. Her back hollowing, Myrine quickly stepped through the gate opening. Her eyes darted here, there, and everywhere.

At the winch, a square faced, neckless guard stood. Permanent frown ridges were carved into his broad forehead. Massive scaly hands on the winch's brake handle, his unblinking lidless lizard-eyes fastened on them as they entered.

'Hide it now, Myrine. Or it will be too late!'

Urged by the hysterical note in Rollandario's voice, Myrine hid her supernatural powers. This time she locked away all memories of the Infinity Charm and Rollandario's information into another back chamber of her mind. She hardly closed the last fail-safe door in her mind when an invasive mental onslaught hit her.

Raising her hands, palms out, she covered her forehead and wobbled one step back. Her neck muscles tightened. She stumbled. Rollandario gripped her by the upper arm, keeping her upright. As suddenly as it arrived, the enquiring tentacles retracted. Gasping for air, bone jarring shakes trembled through Myrine. It was many times stronger than those enquiring tendrils Dr Dreckonium had sent into her mind. If not for Rollandario, she would have been caught flatfooted.

'You must control your thoughts. If mother finds out I want to help you…'

'I will. I locked away the memories of your information as well.'

'What are you two whispering about?'

'Nothing Ignatius. I was checking if Myrine is okay. She looked tired.'

Ignatius stretched up into his full impressive two-meter something height. His face darkened. His eyes narrowed.

'Are you going to walk, or do I carry you? You will soon enough be lying down.'

The thick-necked guard turned around, an evil grin spreading over his face. His spotted tongue flicked, and he licked his fleshy lips.

'I can carry her.'

'I will walk.'

Once again flanked by the Brunkai, Fanisius to the side, thick neck, and Ignatius in front and Rollandario at her back, Myrine was herded across the empty inner courtyard at a brisk pace. But for the armed guards standing sentry on top of the outer wall, there was no sign of life. Passing the grey granite castle building, they entered an alley. Forty meters later, it opened onto a vast courtyard at the back of the castle.

On the far right seemed to be troops' barracks. Barred windows sunk into the ground at the bottom of the barracks gave the impression of a medieval dungeon. The back door to the castle opened and a kitchen maid came out, carrying a basket. They stopped to let her cross. No greeting, no acknowledgment. She hurried along, disappearing through a garden gate next to the barracks. Discomfited, the intestines in Myrine's stomach shifted. *No sign of life in the forecourt, and now this. Something is off-kilter.*

Rollandario sidled up to her and whispered from the corner of his mouth.

'Watch your thoughts. We are close.'

It would be tiresome to guard her every thought, but she felt compelled to at least scrub her mind of thoughts that could land Rollandario in the hot water. She doubted she could escape without his help. With that, she cleared her mind of all thoughts of Rollandario and concentrated on the surroundings, even though she could not commit it to memory without her eidetic power. At least it would be natural for thoughts to appear as she saw things.

Near the far side of the castle, a windowless charcoal coloured building hunkered in the shadows of a cluster of massive trees. Slime green vines, dropping from the trees, crawled over its roof, and dripped off the sides. To the right of it was a garden wall. A chain-locked wrought-iron gate with a skull and bones insignia was set in it.

As they got closer, Myrine felt the building's vile aura pulsating through the air. They stepped onto the tar-black footpath leading to the building's front door. A murder of pitch-black, red-eyed crows swooped from behind the garden wall. Their angry squawks fractured the silence. They circled above the garden wall. One broke away and aimed straight for Myrine. Instinctively, she ducked. A wing brushed her cheek. She felt the warmth on her cheek before registering a burning pain.

She touched the cut on her cheek. Her hand came away bloodied. *Dragonscats! Blades in their wings? Red eyes?* Something made her look over her shoulder. In the distance, the crow had turned and was coming back. She turned to face it and assumed a zenkutsu dachi karate stance. Tensed, her body leaning forward, she waited. *It would be better to kick it. My boots protect my feet.*

Meters before reaching her, the crow's clawed feet lowered. It hop-landed in front of her. Just out of kicking range. Eyeing her, it let out an ear-piercing squawk. Hopping a few times, first to the one side then to the other, it let loose a cackle of squawks and took off. Swooshing over her head, it joined the other crows.

Myrine had the distinct feeling it was jeering at her. She looked at the others around her. Everyone, except Rollandario, who missed the scene as he was walking up to the door of the building, stood watching her. *Bunch of regular Don Juan's.* There were a few words she could add, but their ears might burn.

Thick neck waggled his spotted tongue at her. Nauseated, she turned to Fanisius, whose eyes sparked with laughter. Disgusted, she turned to Ignatius. It seemed as if he was contemplating something. She frowned at him.

'So you really don't have supernatural powers. Pity that. You could have avoided the confrontation with Crontanorius. He likes to test himself against those with supernatural powers. And he loves to show off his power. Only Eugenia can best him.'

Before Myrine could answer him, the front door of the building swung open, emitting a belch of bitter smoke. A tallish chalk faced woman in a black figure-hugging cat suit stepped out. Her black hair, drawn back in a severe bun, showed a line of growth of her natural red hair. *That must be Aunt Eugenia. Those black talons could puncture an eyeball.*

'Quite right. And I have punctured a few eyeballs. Blinding those who do not wish to see the truth.'

A picture emblazoned on the screen of Myrine's mind. The back of her neck tingled. Her back hollowed, and she held her breath. The woman let out a burst of maniacal laughter. Myrine could feel her skin shrinking as goosebumps broke out on every part of her body. For a wild moment, she thought about making a break and running. Before the thought had finished, Eugenia was right in front of her. Grabbed her left arm in a steel grip, pulling her to within an inch of her face. Myrine's eyes were in line with the woman's blood-red lips. But for Eugenia's high-heeled boots, they would have been eyeball to eyeball.

'So. This is Grace's hope for a Light Force Ruler on Earth? What a puny little thing.'

A bark of laughter from Fanisius. Myrine gritted her teeth and ripped her arm free. They stood glaring at each other. The only similarity, showing them to be blood related, is their signature emerald Adelstein eyes.

'Oh my. I see we have a little temper.'

With that, the woman grabbed her by the arm again and frog marched her into the building, whilst shouting orders at the guards and Fanisius over her shoulder. Only Rollandario was allowed to enter the building with them.

Myrine blinked her eyes as they entered from the bright daylight into a windowless room. A tattered curtain of acrid smoke hung from the ceiling. Scattered around the room were various clay pots emitting smoke tendrils. Shadows played on the walls in the flickering candlelight. Myrine's eyes watered and she covered her nose with her right cuff, taking shallow breaths through her mouth. The foul bitterness clogged her throat.

Rollandario had moved ahead on his mother's instructions and opened the solid steel door to a room at the back. He stood aside, and Eugenia pushed Myrine into the room. Rollandario shut the door behind them. Out of sync with the room they entered, banks of computerised machinery covered two of the four walls. In the middle of the room was a dentist-like chair. Pale blue light strobes streamed down from the hidden lights behind the cornices. Myrine's head spun. This must be what it would feel like if you stepped through a time warp. From a medieval world into the sci-fi future.

'The front room is only for the ambience. It is rather soothing for our Universal Ruler, Surneal. Once we have you on the right path, you will realise the value of it.'

'Never!'

Eugenia's reply was to thump her into the chair. Myrine grabbed the arms of the chair and tried to push up. Automated steel manacles clamped around her wrists. She kicked out with her legs. Eugenia neatly sidestepped the kicks and pushed Myrine's legs flat on the chair. An automated steel belt clamped over Myrine's thighs. Her anxiety hit a level she never knew she had before. Helplessly, she watched as two automated manacles encircled her legs just above her ankles. Defeated, she laid her head back. The next moment, there was a steel band around her neck, holding her head in place.

'Rollandario did Dreckonium give her any sporalenium.'

'Yes. But not much.'

'Right. I need her fully present and awake before this session starts. Pass me the scraper.'

Myrine's jaw tightened as Eugenia, none too gently, scraped some of the blood from her wounded cheek. She watched her walk to a cupboard near the door. A sharp light blinked on as the cupboard was opened. Eugenia put the scrap of blood in a vial with some liquid and shook it before holding it up to the light.

'Nope. Not a trace remaining in her bloodstream. Lucky for you Myrine, otherwise I would have had to give you a nasty antidote.'

The cupboard door slammed shut. Myrine's heart did a high jump. Fear blossomed anew as she watched Eugenia walking around the chair. She could hear her fiddling with something behind the chair. Despite expecting something, Myrine's body jerked against its confinement as a set of earphones was placed over her head. A movie screen slid out of the ceiling in front of her.

Hypnotised, Myrine watched happy memory after happy memory from her childhood appear on the screen. She lost track of time as she lost herself in the happiness of each memory. Hovering on the verge of completely giving in to the machine's extraction programme, a memory of her ten-year-old self in the rose garden at Silken Oak appeared. With it came the extraction of the awful moment not long thereafter when she presented her mother with the bunch of roses.

Mother hated me. Never a kind word. Always a snide comment. Myrine sniffed as she remembered her tears that day. It was one of the worst days. The same day, she found the body of her missing pet dog. *I don't want to remember anything anymore. Grandma told me to put those unhappy memories away and try to forget them.*

Thrusting away the memories of her childhood, including the happy ones, Myrine willed herself out of her subconscious state of mind. She felt groggy. After ten minutes of desperately batting away the memories, she surfaced. Around her, the machines emitted a monotonous low hum, and she countered it with repeating the Ho'oponopono prayer. In synchronisation with the prayer, her energies positively lifted.

Turning her head against the backrest of the chair, she managed to move the earphones halfway off her ears. Behind her, two people were talking. She strained and heard Faeyet conversing with Eugenia. They were discussing handing over Myrine to Surneal, for their own benefit and to exclude Beldarius.

On the screen in front of her, reels of her childhood memories carried on playing in an endless recurring loop. Stopping at the rose garden scene before returning to where the memory extraction had begun.

They must have extracted those whilst I was under hypnosis. She supposed the object of the exercise was to lure her into complacency. To escape, she would need to unlock her supernatural powers. She decided to take the chance, but to leave memories of the Infinity Charm and Rollandario locked away. *If they catch me before I get away, they would only come to know about my powers.*

One ear tuned to the conversation behind her, Myrine unlocked her supernatural powers. She brought up her short-term memory of the chair before she ended up in it, and with the aid of her synchronicity supernatural power, manifested pressure on the buttons that unlocked the manacles. Luckily, Eugenia and Faeyet were so intent on their plotting and planning, they missed the minute clicks of the manacles unlocking.

About to sit forward, she heard Eugenia instructing Faeyet to leave the room before Beldarius arrived and take a message to Surneal. Myrine's nerves tightened into painful too tight guitar strings. She obscured the opened manacles from plain sight by dimming it, blending in with the chair. Aiding the obscuration was the fact that Faeyet's mind was occupied with her and Eugenia's plans as she walked past the chair.

The steel door closed behind Faeyet. *I would have to catch Eugenia by surprise.* Footsteps sounded behind the chair. Myrine kept the obscuration of the opened manacles in place. Half closed her eyes. Eugenia appeared on her left-hand side, her attention on the screen. Myrine surged up and delivered a vicious karate chop to her neck, under her ear, shutting off the oxygen to the brain. Unconscious, Eugenia's body ragdoll flopped onto the floor.

Knowing it would be mere seconds before Eugenia regained her consciousness, Myrine rolled her over. Put pressure on her carotid artery on the front side of her neck. Assured that Eugenia will remain unconscious for at least twenty minutes, Myrine left the room in a hurry.

Entering the front room, she heard a noise. To the left, she noticed a door leading into another room. Keeping to the wall, she carefully crept up to the door and peeked around the door jamb. Faeyet was standing at a door, disengaging the last of its three bolts. It opened up to the outside. *I had better stop her from delivering that message to Surneal.*

With a burst of speed, Myrine reached Faeyet as she put a foot on the step outside the door, turning to close it. Swinging a fist at Faeyet's jaw, she missed as Faeyet morphed into her fosterling self and ducked away. Myrine grabbed at the thick mane around Faeyet's neck, managing to hang on despite Faeyet's attempts to wriggle away.

She brought her knee up into Faeyet's chest. A guttural umph from Faeyet and they both tumbled to the ground and rolled down the steps. Ending up on Faeyet's chest, Myrine grabbed her by the throat and punched her in the face. Faeyet's yelp of pain did not deter her. She punched her again and rolled Faeyet onto her stomach. As she grabbed her by the scruff, Faeyet bucked her off, but she maintained her hold on Faeyet's scruff.

After a short furious struggle, Myrine got the upper-hand. Panting and sweating, she dragged Faeyet back to the door, intending to lock her in the chair she was earlier manacled to. *Dragonscats! The little shit is stronger than she looks.*

They reached the steps to the door when Myrine received a kick in the back of her knee joint. Her leg folded. Falling to her knee, she let go of Faeyet. Gravel bit into her knee cap. She collapsed sideways, barely missing the doorstep with her forehead. She rolled over and tried to get up. Her knee refused to carry her weight, and she fell back on her bum. She swiped her hair off her sweaty forehead and looked up.

In front of her, Beldarius stood a meter away. Next to him, Faeyet, who had morphed back into her humanlike figure. Aghast, Myrine listened to Faeyet spinning a tale of how she was trying to stop Myrine from escaping. Beldarius had turned his full attention to Faeyet, listening intently to her.

'I was on my way to see how far you were. Lady Eugenia stayed in the memory room with her. Next thing, she attacked me and tried to kill me.'

From previous experience, Myrine knew she would get nowhere if she tried to tell Beldarius about the plot against him. To her mind, they all deserved each other. Something tickled her left wrist. She looked down and saw the strap of her magical backpack had come off her shoulder and slipped down her arm. It was visible. Quickly, she unzipped the top part of her sleeveless vest, maneuvering it back onto her shoulder.

Before she could zip up her sleeveless vest, Beldarius looked at her.

CHAPTER 12

Myrine put her hands up, intending to throw a firewall between herself and Beldarius. But her energy levels were depleted. A few fire-sparks sputtered. Then died on her fingertips. Beldarius was closing in on her. She waited until his hand shot out before she scrambled out of the way. He missed grabbing her by millimetres.

'Father no! If you kill her, you will never become the Ruler of Betwonium. You need her alive to negotiate with Surneal.'

'Without the Infinity Charm, she may not be as valuable.'

'How do you know that Faeyet? Since when have you become a clairvoyant?'

Myrine's eyes darted to Rollandario, then to Faeyet. Faeyet smirked at her, letting out a snort. Looking back to Beldarius, she did not like the calculating look in his eyes, nor the dark aura that emanated from him. He made a sudden grab for her. Hauling her up by the front of her sleeveless vest with his left hand, he pulled back his right arm. Fisted his right hand. She pulled her shoulders up to her ears. Rollandario rushed forward, grabbed Beldarius' right arm, and hung onto it. Following her inner instinct, Myrine remained motionless.

'Father please. We should treat her like a guest.'

'And then?'

'Then we negotiate with her. And you saw Surneal's message, he wants her alive. You don't want to be on the wrong side of him. Not if you want him to make you the Ruler of Betwonium. Please, Father.' How Rollandario addresses him.

Reluctantly, Beldarius released his hold on Myrine's vest. She stumbled. Hobbled a couple of steps sideways, putting herself out of his immediate reach. Whilst Beldarius' back was turned, Myrine bent down. Found the acupressure point on the side of her uninjured calf and pressed it to relieve the pain at the back of her injured knee. She released the pressure after five seconds and repeated the procedure three more times. Rising, she gingerly straightened her injured leg and tested her weight on it. The pain, reduced to a mere echo memory, her leg held. *I am lucky nothing was broken.*

It dawned on her that Faeyet could read her thoughts. Pulling up her supernatural power that did not require any energy, she cloaked her thoughts. *No use hiding her supernatural powers anymore. They were aware of it after her feeble attempt at throwing a fire wall and if she was lucky, they would not put much stock in it. And once her energy levels have normalised, she could come up with a plan.*

It was time to use her supernatural powers that were not affected by her energy levels. Whilst Beldarius and Rollandario bickered, she engaged her eidetic and echoic abilities and memorised the immediate area she found herself in.

An eight-foot stone wall surrounded what seemed to be an inner gravel strewn courtyard. A gate stood open in the boundary wall, which she assumed led back to the castle's back courtyard. She missed the red-eyed black crow that had attacked her previously, watching her from his perch on a branch, high up in a tree on the other side of the boundary wall.

Her memories of the back courtyard were sketchy at best, but with her supernatural powers now out in the open, she could memorise everything and store it away for later use. She intended to escape at the first opportunity that presented itself. She could only hope that when an opportunity arose, her energy had built up fully, returning her supernatural powers to its normal state. *And using it, it will become stronger and my energy to maintain it will last longer. Oh Grandma, if only I listened to you and Aedric and practiced it more.*

Beldarius' order for her to step forward and join them, pulled her out of her reverie. Although she could still detect anger in his voice, he seemed to have calmed somewhat. She took care to stay out of his reach, circled around him and came to a standstill at Rollandario's side, facing him.

'Where is Eugenia?'

'In the back room with the machines. Un…'

'Faeyet, go and see to your Mistress and tell her to meet us in the castle dining room for lunch.'

He jabbed his index finger at Myrine.

'Rollandario, take her with you to the dining room.'

He glared at Myrine.

'And you, don't try anything. I am right behind you. Do you hear me?'

Myrine nodded, turned, and followed Rollandario's lead. Behind her she could hear Beldarius' heavy crunches on the gravel stones. Once through the gate, Rollandario motioned for her to walk by his side. Aloud he spoke, pointing out various features. With no admonishment from Beldarius, Myrine assumed it was agreed that Rollandario now acts as her tour guide, her new status now elevated to being a guest. She sponged up the information, storing it in her eidetic and echoic memory banks.

This time they walked across the back courtyard, traversed the same alley they used before, and entered the front courtyard. They went to the double front door of the castle. Made of thick solid black planks, backed with diagonal iron bracing, Beldarius' insignia was emblazoned in the wood on both sides. Beldarius pushed past them and touched the insignia on the left side. Noiseless, the door swung open. Beyond it stretched a dim, silent hallway.

Entering, Myrine battled to adjust her sight from the brilliant brightness outside to the near dark inside. Following a long unaired hallway, she followed Beldarius' lead past several closed doors before he opened one, beyond which lay a cavernous dining room. A six-tiered dusty candle chandelier, filmed with cobwebs, hung from the centre of the ceiling. Directly above a thick-legged wooden table. Wooden chairs with leather upholstered backs clumped around it. At the head of the table was a huge wooden chair. The candles, together with the yellow glow from the oil lamps against the walls, barely chased away the shadows which gathered in corners of the room.

Myrine was led to the top end of the twenty-four-seater table, where four places were laid with straw table mats with oval bone-white plates. Pewter cutlery consisting of three-pronged forks and knives next to it. The knife points were sharpened into near needle points. She reached out to touch one.

'Don't even think about it.'

Myrine's head jerked up of its own volition and she looked at Beldarius, standing behind a huge wooden chair at the top of the table, glaring at her. She did not like the threatening edge that had crept back into his voice and clasped her hands in front of her.

'I was only looking,'

'You look with your eyes, not your hands.'

Rollandario pulled out a chair at the furthest setting from Beldarius and motioned for Myrine to sit down. Rollandario settled in the chair next to her, on her left, between her and the chair at the head of the table. His eyes never leaving her, Beldarius sunk his bulk into the chair at the head of the table.

From a closed door to the right came kitchen sounds. Myrine's stomach growled, and she pressed it with both hands. Her left cuff had ridden up, exposing her quantum watch. A quick look at it showed that it was near noon in Betwonium. Despite knowing the days in Betwonium were much longer than twenty-four-hour days on Earth, she felt confused. *I wonder if one would call this time lag instead of jet lag.*

The door to the kitchen opened and the kitchen maid she saw crossing the courtyard earlier entered with a pewter jug in her hand. She went around the table filling the glass bowls on pewter stands in front of their plates with a black-red concoction. An acidic smell rose from it, reminding her of the grape dreck they threw away on Silken Oak after the grapes were parched. She tapped Rollandario's forearm.

'Could I please have a glass of water?'

Rollandario got up, went to a sideboard on the side opposite to the kitchen door, filled a glass bowl from a jug and brought it to Myrine. She sniffed it before emptying it in one slug. Myrine held the empty glass bowl out to him. This time, he filled it and brought the jug back to the table with him. She drank down half of it, before setting it down on the table.

Beldarius engaged Myrine in conversation. At first it was civil enough, but soon it took a turn and became a heated debate about the whereabouts of the Infinity Charm and the events prior to her leaving Earth. Rollandario once again came to the rescue and intervened, steering the conversation in a different direction. Beldarius seemed to make a concerted effort to get his temper under control. A formless plan at the back of her mind, Myrine decided to put forward a proposal.

'I am a bit confused. I have never travelled to another planet. I am really trying to get my memories back together. If you could just allow me to have a bit of breathing space.'

'Breathing space?'

'Like walking in the gardens or around the grounds, so I can feel more settled.'

After a serious debate, Beldarius agreed when Rollandario offered to go with her as a guide / guard. Myrine smiled her gratitude at Beldarius, who flicked her off. He thumped his hand on the table.

'It seems your mother is going to be late. Let's eat.'

Myrine did not mind if she never had to encounter her aunt Eugenia again. She had no wish to find out what her reaction would be to having been knocked out and left on the floor in the memory room. She knew there would be some form of repercussion and it would therefore be preferable that she left with Rollandario before the woman arrived.

Rollandario opened the door to the kitchen and requested that they be served, and a plate put aside for Eugenia. A rotund, jowl-faced man with high colour on his sweaty cheeks entered carrying an oval silver platter. He was garbed in a grey tunic and trousers, a grimy apron around his waist and a sort of kerchief on his head. He set down the plate, sloshing some of the liquid from the platter onto the table in front of Myrine. Behind him followed the kitchen maid with a plate of what seemed to be grilled vegetables.

Myrine looked at the meat platter. Despite looking as if it had been grilled, blood trickled from it, joining the pink-red river of grease in which it rested. A ripe venison smell rose from it. Nausea rose in her throat and she decided to eat vegetables only. Hopefully, there was nothing strange hiding in it. She dished a small helping of vegetables, refused the meat and soon the only sound in the room was the clanking of cutlery.

The vegetables were a bit spicy, but otherwise not too bad, and Myrine had two more helpings before she blotted her mouth with a rough napkin. Rollandario had also finished, but Beldarius was gnawing away. Following Rollandario's example, she remained quiet and waited for Beldarius to finish.

As Beldarius sat back, letting out a stinking belch, Eugenia, Faeyet in her wake, entered the room. One look at Eugenia's face and Myrine knew there was going to be trouble. Faeyet grinned an 'I told you so' grin at Myrine. The food in Myrine's stomach bunched into a clay ball. Eugenia walked around Beldarius' chair and stopped next to Myrine.

'She has supernatural powers. She is a conniving, lying little bitch and should be locked up in the dungeon until Surneal arrives and he can deal with her.'

'Yes, yes, yes. Supernatural powers? Not so much. It is very weak. She could not even use it against me. And are your supernatural powers not supposed to be much stronger? How did she get the better of you?'

Eugenia did not answer. Myrine dared a quick glance up at Eugenia, who stood, arms folded across her chest, glaring daggers at her. She glanced back at Beldarius and scraped back her chair. It would be better if Rollandario and I left before Beldarius changed his mind about allowing her to walk around the castle grounds. The scrape from Myrine's chair shattered the thick silence. Eugenia grabbed her shoulders and slammed her back onto the chair.

'Where do you think you are going?'

'Beldarius agreed I could walk around the castle grounds with ...'

'Well, well, well, my dear husband. How did this upstart manage to fool you?'

'Don't speak to me like that woman. Your son, Rollandario, is going to escort her as a guard cum guide.'

'You mean our son?'

'Whatever.'

On high alert, Myrine kept her eyes on Eugenia, who moved and plonked herself on the table next to Myrine. One leg swinging, tapping her lips with a taloned finger and nodding her head. Her gaze veered between Rollandario and Myrine. Despite the quivering in her innards, Myrine refused to look away from Eugenia's face.

'That is not enough. But I can remedy that. Faeyet, bring me the shutterling.'

Sitting next to Rollandario, Eugenia to her right and the chair blocking her from the back, Myrine knew she could not get out of the room unscathed. And any attempt to run would only have Beldarius retract his grant for her to walk around the castle grounds. She turned her head. Looked at Beldarius. Sitting in his chair scratching between his teeth with a horny fingernail, a glint in his eyes, he watched them. Repulsed, Myrine watched as he freed a piece of meat from between his teeth, flicking it onto the table and leaned forward.

'Put the shutterling on her, my dear wife. I assume I have your guarantee that it would not interfere with her attempts to find her memories of the Infinity Charm?'

Without replying to her husband, Eugenia took the shutterling from Faeyet and clamped it around Myrine's right wrist. With a click, the two dark brown live miniature vipers interlocked their poisonous fangs. Myrine stared at their unusual bleached out green eyes. She lifted her hand.

'I would not do that. They are programmed to disable you and, if necessary, deliver a lethal dose of venom.'

'Why do I need to wear this if Rollandario is going with me?'

'Oh. One of their greatest values is that whilst they are on your arm, your supernatural powers are disabled.'

Myrine pushed back her chair, stood up and squared off to Eugenia. A zap from the shutterlings sent a shock wave of electricity down her right arm's nerve ends, rendering it useless. *Dragonscats. That burns like hell fire.*

'Now go for your walk. I am giving you one hour to return here and tell me where the Infinity Charm is.'

Myrine looked at Beldarius.

'One hour may not be...'

'I said one hour! Rollandario, see that the two of you are back here within the hour.'

Cradling her right arm, Myrine followed Rollandario to the front door. Once outside, Myrine set off towards the main gate. Rollandario rushed up to her side and tried to steer her away. She ripped her left arm out of his hand.

'I need to find out if I can memorise the layout. I am not so stupid that I will try to leave whilst I have this shutterling thing around my wrist.'

'I don't think mother would recognise eidetic or echoic memory as supernatural powers. The grounds are vast. Let's go.'

From the gate, they turned to walk across the front of the castle, along the perimeter wall. A couple of steps into walking the length of the front perimeter wall, a shadow fell over them.

'Cloak your thoughts. Mother has sent Crontanorius and he will send every thought you have to her.'

'They have been cloaked since your father found me after I escaped your mother's clutches.'

'No need to be snippy with me. I am not your enemy.'

'Gmph. Famous last words.'

'Come. The clock is ticking.'

Hand above her brow, Myrine looked up at Crontanorius circling above them before she followed Rollandario. They did not speak much until they got to the thick forest barring their way. At all times, they conversed in low whispers. On Rollandario's advice, they hardly moved their lips. For a moment she wanted to snap at him, asking whether Crontanorius, besides his excellent hearing, was also a lip reader. She literally shook her head.

'Something wrong?'

'Is there a way through the woods to the back of the castle?'

'Yes.'

'Let's go that way. I would like to see the kitchen gardens.'

If Rollandario found her request odd, he said nothing, and she followed him as he led the way. Crontanorius did not follow them into the dense woods. The pathway was narrow and slippery, allowing them only to walk behind each other. They agreed not to speak, as it would slow them from having to stop and whisper every time. The humidity increased and became a suffocating blanket. *Strange. No bugs. This is the perfect breeding ground for them.* On the other hand, it was a blessing. The heat and humidity were enough to contend with.

Whilst they were walking, Myrine tested her eidetic and echoic memories of what she had seen and heard before they entered the woods. It was perfect. It gave her an idea. Without breaking a step, she lifted her wrist to eye level and stared at the shutterling on her wrist.

A flash of memory popped. Black magic practitioners used them to control the powers of those with white magic and could also to track their movements. A paragraph detailing how to get rid of it followed. In her subconscious, she must have known all of it, but it only came to the fore now. *Please let there be a witch's herb garden in the kitchen garden.*

According to Myrine's quantum watch, there was quite a bit of time left before they had to return to the castle. Betwonium hours were way longer than an earth hour. Still, if the herb she needed was not in the kitchen gardens, they are going to have to search elsewhere. She was sure Eugenia had the herb growing somewhere, otherwise she would not be able to control and handle the shutterlings. Going to her building was an absolute last resort and not one Myrine would like to entertain. She patted Rollandario on the back.

'Step it up. We must get to the kitchen gardens.'

'You up for a jog?'

'Yes.'

She liked that he did not waste time asking unnecessary questions. She was, however, still not one hundred percent sure that she trusted him. They reached the kitchen gardens and slipped through the gate.

'Where do they grow the herbs?'

'At the back fence bordering the woods. I will show you.'

'Where are the gardeners?'

'Midday they break because the sun is at its hottest. They would return very late in the afternoon.

'And in winter?'

'We only have one season. Not four like you have on Earth.'

They reached the herb garden, and Myrine methodically searched each row. She refused Rollandario's offer to assist and asked him to rather keep a lookout for anyone or anything that may approach. At the end of the last row, she came up empty-handed and swore under her breath.

'Dragonscats. What is that word?'

'I made it up when I was very young and used it instead of a real swear word.'

An idea hit her. It may be growing behind the garden wall with the skull and crossbones gate. The trees provided the perfect shade canopy, and it was known to grow at the bottom of tree trunks where the sun never reached.

'Does your mother have a special herb garden?'

'What herb do you need?'

Debating whether to take Rollandario into her confidence, Myrine looked up and down the rows of herbs. Some known to her. Others unknown. She had been thorough in her search and had checked and double checked every shady spot. She looked at her quantum watch. They would soon have to get back to the castle.

'Sleeping Sage. Do you know it?'

'That is the herb my mother grows in her private herb garden. Wait a minute. She uses it to unlock the shutterlings and control them.'

And with that, Rollandario smacked his forehead.

'I should have thought of that earlier. Now there is no time left before we have to be back at the castle.'

Myrine's hopes were lifted and slapped down, all in one foul swoop. Dejected, she listened as Rollandario explained how Crontanorius and his murder of crows acted as guards. It seemed that it would be near impossible to get to it. That must have been another reason Crontanorius left them alone when they entered the woods, veering away from that building.

In any event, it was clear she would not get to it before she had to be back at the castle. It would be better for now if she started thinking about a way to convince Beldarius to grant her more time. He was clearly more malleable without Eugenia around.

Near the exit from the kitchen garden to the back courtyard, they were confronted by Faeyet. Myrine reacted by wanting to cloak her thoughts, only to find that she had kept it cloaked. Irritated, Myrine made to move past her, but Faeyet sway-stepped sideways, blocking her. They stared at each other. With some satisfaction, Myrine noted the red raised scratches on Faeyet's neck.

'Don't you think anymore? Or do you think you can hide your thoughts forever?'

Hands fisted at her sides, Myrine stepped the other way. Faeyet, rubbing her puffed up little hands, sway stepped again and blocked her. Myrine forced her rising temper under control. She was sure she could best Faeyet in a fight, even without her supernatural powers. The problem was, she needed to curry favour with Beldarius. Giving in to her urge to beat the living dragonscats out of Faeyet was not a good idea.

Rollandario pushed past Myrine, grabbed Faeyet by the shoulder and kept her in one place.

'What are you doing here?'

Myrine took two steps past Faeyet. She had noticed before the two of them did not get along. She was about to call Rollandario, when Faeyet ducked under his arm and shouted gleefully at the top of her voice.

'Surneal will be here by tomorrow night.'

CHAPTER 13

Wordless, Myrine stared at Faeyet, who looked back at her with a cheek-splitting grin, waggling her left six-fingered hand. Fury rose and rode atop a wave of anxiety, cresting in Myrine's chest. Clenching and unclenching her hands, she gritted her teeth, turned, and walked out the kitchen garden gate. *Better to walk away before I act without thinking and kill that thing.*

Outside the gate, Myrine stopped. Waiting for Rollandario, she rubbed her stomach. A persistent dull ache had set up host in the nether regions of her stomach. She wondered whether Eugenia had sent Faeyet, or if the spiteful fosterling acted of her own accord. Not that it really mattered. Either way, she was glad to have been forewarned.

Her thoughts turned back to her predicament as she looked at the barracks at the far end of the back courtyard, wondering what was at the back of it. She had to escape. She had no wish to come face to face with Surneal. *Not without my supernatural powers.* And to be honest, even with her supernatural powers intact, she knew she would be no match for the age old Universal Dark Force Leader.

The relentless afternoon sun was beating down on the hard, cobblestoned back courtyard. Thankful that her hoodie was an all-weather garment, protecting her skin, Myrine swiped a stray strand of her off her sweaty cheek. *What the dragonscats was keeping Rollandario so long.*

Deciding not to wait for him, she started across the back courtyard towards the double storeyed barracks. Underneath it, the barred windows at ground level she had noticed earlier in the day. *If she could get to the other side of the barracks, there may be a way she could get over the perimeter wall at its back.* Hearing footsteps behind her, she turned. Rollandario had caught up with her. There was no sign of the dastardly Faeyet.

'What are those barred windows underneath the barracks?'

'A dungeon where Father keeps prisoners.'

'Prisoners?'

'Those who disobey him and sometimes, though not very often, infiltrators that do not belong on Betwonium.'

'Infiltrators. Like me?'

Rollandario, a sheepish look on his face, shrugged. Looked away. *Maybe if she were in the dungeon, she would have stood a better chance of escaping. Instead, here she was. Wearing a shutterling bracelet.* There was still a possibility that she could end up there. Deciding to investigate, she walked to the barracks, Rollandario in tow.

'We better hurry. There is not much time left.'

'We can go in through the back door opposite the barracks. I first want to see the barracks.'

Myrine checked her quantum watch. She had twenty Betwonium minutes before she had to be back in the castle. She hoped to be able to calculate how many troops could be housed in the barracks. In case she found a way through to the other side of it and over the boundary wall. She could ask Rollandario, but it would not hurt to keep her plans to herself.

They stopped in front of the barracks. Their backs to the castle. At Myrine's request, Rollandario without using hand gestures, in a low whisper, pointed out the entrance (there was only one) and four exits, one each on the sides, one in front next to the entrance and one at the back (which she could not see). According to Rollandario, there was a

Myrine Goes Through the Quantum Door | 125

huge parade ground and stadium at the back of the barracks, inside the perimeter wall. *If only she could have called up her supernatural penetration vision.* She sighed and gave her full attention to Rollandario and tried her best to picture the scenery as described by Rollandario.

'Father also has an office inside the barracks on the ground floor. Dr Dreckonium has his surgery next door to it and he stays in a room right next to his surgery.'

Dread's cold finger traced slowly down Myrine's spine. Dr Dreckonium's windows were small, with dark blinds drawn across them. She could imagine him experimenting in those rooms with all sorts of unmentionables. She thought him to be as dangerous as her aunt Eugenia.

'There is a guard up in the turret and he has noticed us. We should move.'

Myrine glanced up at the turret that sat on the far-right side corner on top of the barracks. A figure stood motionless at one of the small slits. Perfect for shooting arrows, whilst protecting the archer.

'Is that a bow and arrow he has with him?'

'Yes. And those who do guard duty are precision archers.'

Well, that was something else she would have to remember when she escaped.

From the dungeon below came a plaintive moan. She looked down. They were standing in front of one of the barred glassless openings. A pair of hands, a few coarse black hairs sprouting from the knuckles, appeared, and latched onto the bars. Speechless, Myrine stared at the hands. She blinked slowly and looked again. *Aedric? Could it really be? Here in Betwonium? Locked here in the dungeon?*

Her mouth dry, Myrine sunk to her knees, leaned forward, and peered through the bars. Looked straight into Aedric's bloodied face. One eye swollen shut. A cut across his right cheek. His always neat hair in disarray. His clothes were torn and there were no shoes on his feet. Her brain had difficulty accepting what her eyes saw.

'We have to go to the castle now. If anyone saw you looking into the dungeon, there would be big trouble.'

Myrine flung Rollandario's hand off her shoulder.

'That is Aedric in there. My tutor. My mentor. The closest thing to a real father I have ever had. I could never leave him like that. Look at his face. He had been beaten up.'

'Ooh. I see you found your trusted tutor. Aedric is it?'

A blinding river of fury raced through Myrine, crested in her chest, and threw a red haze over her eyes. She jumped up. Stormed over to where Faeyet was standing a few steps behind them. Stiffened her right hand's fingers and jabbed Faeyet in her sternum. With every step Faeyet took backwards, Myrine stepped forward, delivering another hard jab.

'Who. Did this? To him?!'

Faeyet shapeshifted into her fosterling self, scuttled sideways, putting herself beyond Myrine's reach. Turned and raced away across the courtyard to the castle. Myrine strode back to the barred dungeon window and shoved Rollandario out of the way. Sunk to her knees and gripped the bars. White-knuckled, she poured every ounce of energy into her arms and tried to pry the bars apart.

'You should not do that. There are guards...'

A warning buzz from the shutterling on her wrist. She ignored it. Took a huge breath. Her neck muscles tightened. A snarl marred her face. She re-tightened her grip. Pulled harder. An almighty zap from the shutterling. Useless, her numbed right hand slipped off the bar. Holding onto the bars with her left, she fell sideways. Her head bounced against the bars and she half sat, half laid, in front of the barred window. Her left hand still clinging to one of the bars.

Grabbing Myrine under her armpits, Rollandario heaved her backwards. Her left hand slipped off the bar it clung to. An arrow whizzed past Myrine's front, nicking the top of her right boot. Bounced on the cobblestones and skidded to a stop against the wall to her left, where she had been moments before.

'We got to go. We got to go. We got to go.'

Myrine peered at the turret. The guard had another bow at the ready.

'Okay.'

With Rollandario's help, Myrine managed to get to her feet. Useless, her right arm hung at her side. She looked at the barred window. The hands were no longer clenched at the bars. As much as Myrine did not want to leave Aedric, she realised that without her supernatural powers, there was nothing she could do. Reluctantly, she turned away. She looked at the agitated Rollandario, shifting from one foot to the other as he waited for her to walk with him to the castle's back door.

They hardly took a step when a door slammed behind them. She looked over her shoulder. Two guards had come out of the barracks and were rushing towards them. They pushed Rollandario aside. One on each side, they grabbed Myrine by her upper arms and without a word, drag marched her across the two-hundred-meter distance to the castle's back door. She could hear Rollandario following behind them, but he remained silent as well.

Her mind pin balled between trying to think of how to convince Beldarius to give her more time, to a vision of Aedric's battered face. *If only I had some sleeping sage flowers to get rid of the shutterling.*

They had reached the castle's back door and Myrine had yet to come up with a proper plan to gain more time. The gargoyle-faced guard on her right let go of her arm and reached to open the door, but it opened before he touched it. The kitchen maid, about to step out, stopped and stood with her back to the left door jamb. Beak-nose on her left loosened his grip, and she pulled away from him.

Myrine stepped ahead of the guards and sidled past the kitchen maid standing half in the doorway. Both guards remained at the door, and only Rollandario followed her inside. She could hear voices in the dining room. She snuck up to the interleading door and cocked her head.

It seemed Faeyet was reporting back to Beldarius and Eugenia. Hearing Faeyet's voice, a fresh wave of hatred rushed through her. It very seldom happened that Myrine intensely disliked someone. And from past experience, she had learnt to heed her gut instinct in that regard. The genuine person always showed itself somewhere along the line. She had better go in before the 'story' was further embellished.

With that, Myrine squared her shoulders, stepped through the doorway, walked into the room, stopping midway between the kitchen door and the dining room table. Beldarius was in his chair at the head of the table, Eugenia sitting on his left with her back to the kitchen. Between them stood Faeyet. For a moment, no one noticed her.

'She was very upset when she found that tutor man of hers in the dungeon. Then she saw me and attacked me with no cause.'

Beldarius noticed Myrine first, where she stood halfway between the kitchen entry and the dining room table, and half rose out of his chair. Eugenia swung herself sideways in her chair and glared at Myrine. Faeyet stopped talking halfway through a sentence and moved closer to Eugenia.

'Am I interrupting? Do you want me to wait in the kitchen?'

Beldarius leaned forward and pulled out the chair on his right. She hesitated, then walked around the table at the other end. She reached the chair he had pulled, knowing she did not really have a choice. Stiff-backed, she sat down and fisted her hands in her lap. Rollandario, sitting down in the chair next to her, brought a little relief. Faeyet had moved back and stood between Beldarius and Eugenia. Beldarius' chair groaned out a creak as he sunk back into it and leaned back. She did not like the speculative look he gave her.

'Where is the Infinity Charm?'

Myrine looked away, straight into Eugenia's diamond hard eyes.

'I don't know.'

'Really?'

Myrine looked down at the table before her. Biting down on her lower lip, her hands clenched even tighter. A sting of pain. Her nails had cut into her palms. She unclenched her hands and looked at the four red half-moon crescents in her palms, before rubbing her palms on her thighs.

'My husband had asked you a question. Your answer is unacceptable.'

'I have no idea where the Infinity Charm is.'

'I am sure Grace must have given it to you before you left Earth.'

Annoyed at herself for the squeak in her voice, she cleared her throat and looked from Eugenia to Beldarius.

'I need more time.'

Beldarius leaned into her face and she held her breath to avoid the stench emanating from his open maw. He drummed the fingers of his left hand on the table and scowled at her.

'Time? To try to free your tutor?'

His voice jarred on Myrine's ears. She had the unpleasant feeling he would not give her more time, but she had to try. She cleared her throat again. Swallowed.

'I saw Aedric in the dungeon. He looked badly injured. If I could go to him, he may be able to help me remember.'

Beldarius' right fist slammed onto the table, centimetres from Myrine's chest. Her whole-body marionette jerked.

'GUARDS.'

The two guards who were waiting outside the kitchen door came running into the dining room. Stopped, came to attention, and looked expectantly at Beldarius, who had in the meantime stood up from his chair.

Myrine's chair screeched as Beldarius roughly pulled it back. He grabbed her ponytail. Hauled her up and pushed her in front of him, walking to the guards.

'Take her to the dungeon to meet her tutor. Lock her in the same cell. She needs some time with him. Rollandario you stay right where you are.'

CHAPTER 14

Myrine looked up at Gargoyle Face. He grinned at her. Behind his thick curled back rubber lips, a row of sharp yellowed teeth showed. Beak Nose stepped forward, gripped her left arm, and swung her towards the kitchen.

Outside the kitchen door, he let go of her arm and pushed her in the back, sending her tripping down the steps. Gargoyle Face came up on her right and gave her a slight ankle tap, unbalancing her. Her arms shot out in front of her and she sprawled on all fours at the bottom of the kitchen steps.

Beak Nose clamped his hand under her left armpit and hauled her to her feet. She tried to rip free from Beak Nose's hold. He tightened his grip and gave her arm a twist. Pain raced from her shoulder to her elbow, leaving her left hand's fingers numb.

'Let go of me. I can walk by myself.'

'What is going on here?'

'Dr Dreckonium. We have instructions to take her to the dungeon, and she tried to escape.'

If it was not for the pain in her arm, she would have laughed out loud at the squeak in his high falsetto voice, directly in contrast to his enormous body.

'It is important that she remains unharmed. For the moment.'

'Yes, Dr Dreckonium' the Gargoyle Face and Beak Nose chorused.

'Any serious injury and I will see the two of you in my rooms.'

Myrine liked the way Dr Dreckonium's implied threat wiped the grin of Gargoyle Face's lips. In one smooth motion, she took a step towards the barracks. Stopped and turned. Her voice came out in a low hiss.

'Touch me again and I will scream blue murder and tell whoever wants to listen you are trying to harm me.'

Both guards' eyes widened. The three of them stared at each other. Beak Nose reached for her. Myrine opened her mouth. He immediately dropped his arm to his side.

'Walk to the barracks.'

As if she was going to walk anywhere else, but to where Aedric was held captive. Myrine turned, stiffened her back and set off across the back courtyard towards the barracks at a brisk pace. The thrill of having gotten the better of the two guards, was short-lived. She looked at the shutterling around her right wrist. Emotionless bleached out green eyes stared back at her.

The rest of the walk to the barracks she spent looking at the shutterling whilst trying to remember if there was any way other than using sleeping sage flowers. The shutterling spasmed. *Can they read my mind? Surely not?* The shutterling spasmed again.

Maybe the shutterling could only read her mind when she stared into their bleached out green eyes. She looked away. *Aedric might know how to get rid of the shutterling.* Not a spasm from the shutterling. *So, my gut instinct was right. The shutterling can only hear my thoughts if I look in their eyes.* She knew she could request nothing to do with black magic from her magical backpack. And sleeping sage was used solely for black magic.

Perish the thought. If the shutterling somehow reported to Aunt Eugenia that she had a magical backpack with her, she would be doomed.

There was something else that was important about the backpack. It hovered at the edges of her mind. But, having locked away her memories of the Infinity Charm to safeguard it, Myrine could not remember the reason why. All she knew was she had to keep the backpack hidden at all costs.

They reached the barracks and entered, Gargoyle Face in front, followed by Myrine and Beak Nose bringing up the rear. An unfamiliar scent hung in the air. Somewhere between dirty socks and sour sweat. *Yuck!*

She followed Gargoyle Face down a steep flight of stairs off the entrance. Oil torches flickered against the stone walls, their dim light casting sinister shadows against the walls. At the end of the staircase, they proceeded single file through a narrow passage. Having reached a large office sized room, Gargoyle Face took a ring of iron keys and walked to the second iron barred cell door.

He fumbled until he fitted the right key into the lock, turned it and pulled it open wide enough for Myrine to fit through. The squeal of the iron door dragging over the stone floor grated on Myrine's already raw nerves. A none too gentle push from Beak Nose from behind sent her lurching forward. Grabbing onto the iron bars next of the half open cell door, she stopped herself from falling.

With a sweeping bow, Gargoyle Face stepped aside.

'Welcome to your lodgings, madam.'

Careful to avoid contact with Gargoyle Face, Myrine sidled into the cell and stepped away from the door. Despite noting the motion and realising Gargoyle Face's intent, a freight train rushed from her chest to her stomach at the noise of the cell door slamming shut.

The key turned in the lock with a harsh grating sound. She watched as Gargoyle Face took the key out of the lock and hooked the iron ring of keys back onto a loop of his belt. Beak Nose, picking at a scaly scab on his cheek, stepped forward and stopped next to Gargoyle Face. Both grinned at her. With a glare, she turned her back to them. *If only I had access to my supernatural powers...*

She waited for their footsteps to fade away before inspecting the cell. A bright shaft of sunlight entering through the barred window, shattered and fell, broken onto the straw littered floor. It hardly lifted the cell's gloom. Slow dust motes spider walked up and down the light rays. Deep shadows lurked in the back corners. Myrine sniffed back a sneeze. A faint metallic taste hit the back of her throat. *It must be Aedric's blood. From his injuries.*

Myrine held a hand above her brow and walked to the wall under the barred window, turned around and faced the cell. With the light now in front of her, she could see better. Against the shadowed back wall, she noticed a mattress on the floor. On it was the outline of a body. *What if it was not him and yet another trick played on her?*

She crept closer to it. Found Aedric slumped on his back. His breath ragged. His eyes closed. He looked much worse than when she last saw him on Earth, when her mother's goons loaded him into her car. His face was battered and bruised. His nostrils crusted with blood.

She looked around the cell, walking its perimeter, but could not find a drop of water. She grabbed the bars of the cell door and rattled it.

'Guards!'

Her voice echoed, taunting her. She called until she was hoarse. About to give up hope, she heard approaching footsteps. Beak Nose appeared. *She would much rather have dealt with Gargoyle Face than this slimy one.* She pulled herself together.

'What do you want? Ready to go back to the castle and tell our Ruler where that thing is that you are hiding from him?'

She bit off a retort about 'the thing'.

'Could I please have some water?'

Beak Nose walked out of view and came back with a wooden pail, its panels held together by rusted iron bands. She stepped back from the door. Instead of opening it, he threw the water over her. Dripping wet, she shook with rage. *Dragonscats. When I get out of here, with my powers, he is first.* In the back of her mind, she heard Grandma's advice.

'Never give a man the fight he is looking for. It will frustrate him more and he will make mistakes. That is when you act.'

She turned her back and walked back to Aedric, ignoring the laughing. Her hoodie was sodden. Checking that her sleeveless vest remained intact and covering the backpack, she took off her hoodie and wrung the one sleeve over Aedric's face. He came to as she dabbed away the last of the blood on his upper lip. He gripped her wrist.

'It's me. Myrine.'

'What in the heavens are you doing here? You are supposed to be in Tsaonin.'

'It's a long story and we don't have time. In short, Dad tried to stop me and I fell through the wrong door.'

Wringing out the other sleeve of her hoodie, she dripped some water into Aedric's mouth. They conferred in low whispers. From Aedric she learnt, he took one of her mother's minions with him to the sub-portal in the stable and they tumbled through the only exit portal it had into Betwonium. They concluded that, because of the time delay in the sub-portal, Aedric arrived after Myrine had left and gone down the mountain. Faeyet had found Aedric when she went looking for Myrine's backpack, raised the alarm and he was taken straight to the dungeon. Her mother's minion did not make it, and his body was still in the cave.

'Your injuries seem worse than when mother's Dark Force minions put you in the back seat of her car.'

'It was a rough portal travel and impossible to avoid all the airborne, gliding rocks.'

Myrine lifted her right wrist and showed the shutterling to Aedric.

'Eugenia put a shutterling around my wrist. Do you know how to get rid of it?'

Aedric levered himself into a sitting position and inspected the shutterling without touching it.

'That is black magic. You need sleeping sage.'

'I know, but I could not find any. Is there another way?'

The key rattled in the cell door. Myrine jumped up. Aedric, less mobile because of his injuries, slowly rose from the straw mattress. Together, they turned towards the door. The tension in Myrine's shoulders released. She noted Aedric's combat stance, his feet thirty centimetres apart, his knees half bent.

'Relax. I know him.'

'Do you trust him?'

'Sort of. So far, he has not harmed me.'

'Gmph.'

Aedric remained in combat stance. They watched Rollandario's approach. He had a pail in one hand and a plate heaped with fruit in the other. Gargoyle Face remained at the open door as Rollandario walked towards them. Setting down the pail in front of them, some water sloshed over the side.

'What....'

'We must communicate telepathically. The guards have acute hearing. I have arranged with father to bring fruit from our usual mid-afternoon snack and water. I have to take Aedric to him after you have eaten.'

Aedric, having been taught by Grace how to telepathically communicate, could follow the conversation, but remained silent for the most of it.

Myrine was able to telepathy speak as it was not a supernatural or paranormal power that the shutterling could interfere with.

'Why?'

'Surneal sent a message that Aedric is to be taken back to Earth. They want him to help get information about the Infinity Charm from your grandmother.'

'That will be a stretch. She is in a coma.'

'Apparently your mother has called in a doctor who specialises in releasing self-induced comas.'

'I will protect Grace with all I have against the Dark Forces.'

'What about me?'

'You have a duty to fulfill and a promise to keep. You have to go to Tsaonin.'

'Maybe we should both go to Earth and I can go to Tsaonin when Grandma is able to travel with me.'

'Myrine. Enough. You know there is no time for that if we are to stop the Dark Forces from taking over not just Earth, but the Universe.'

Fireworks of malevolent pictures burst into Myrine's mind. Wrangled bodies. Complete lawlessness and disorder. Wars breaking out. She shuddered with horror and turned to Rollandario.

'There is a small tissue paper packet under the fruit. In it are sleeping sage flowers. I have loosened a few granite blocks over there in the back wall. When taken out, it opens into the kitchen gardens. I will wait there for you. I think I have a way to help you escape.'

Still torn between wanting to escape and go through the exit portal to Tsaonin, versus travelling with Aedric to Earth, she watched Rollandario walking to the back wall marking three of the interlocking granite blocks with a small x. She turned to Aedric.

'Maybe I should go with you and tend to Grandma.'

'That is not an option if we want to save Earth from the Dark Forces. You have to fulfill your destiny or all will be lost. This is not the time to act like a spoiled little child.'

Aedric's words cut her to the core. The gravity of her duty was glaringly clear. Failure was not an option. There was only one way to go. Forward towards Tsaonin at all costs. *And you promised Grandma* a little voice at the back of her mind reminded her.

Turning back to the plate offered by Rollandario, she moved the fruit aside, found the tissue packet, and slipped it off the plate. Careful not to alert the shutterling on her right wrist, she secreted it in her hoodie's left pocket. She ate and swallowed her portion of fruit without tasting it. *I will be no good with an empty stomach. My energy levels will be too low to operate my supernatural powers. As it is, they are not as strong as they should be, but that should get better as I would have no choice but to use them more often.*

Scooping up water with their hands from the pail, Myrine and Aedric slaked their thirst. A noise from the direction of the door. Myrine glanced over her shoulder. Gargoyle Face was shuffling his feet impatiently. Beak Nose appeared from the mouth of the passage with two more guards in tow. One carried iron leg shackles, the other a pair of handcuffs.

'I thought you were going to take Aedric to your father.'

'He said he would send guards to accompany me.'

'With leg-irons and handcuffs?'

Beside Myrine, Aedric had straightened to his full impressive six feet something height. He gave her shoulder a squeeze.

'It will be fine. They need me alive as much as they do you.'

'But the leg-irons and stuff. Really?'

'Well, I had a bit of a scuffle with them before being thrown into this cell. They probably thought it better to be more, shall we say, prepared?'

Side by side, Myrine and Aedric followed behind Rollandario and walked to the cell's gate.

'I will wait for you in the kitchen garden. It will be sunset soon. Surneal will arrive sometime after that and we need to be away from here before he arrives.'

Myrine did not reply to Rollandario's telepathic message. He frowned at her over his shoulder. She gave a slight nod. At the cell's gate, Rollandario stepped through. Before either Myrine or Aedric could move, Gargoyle Face pushed her back into the cell and Beak Nose grabbed Aedric by the front of his tattered shirt, pulling him through the gate. In the blink of an eye, the gate was closed, locking Myrine inside the cell. She watched as Aedric stood, allowing the guards to put on the leg-irons and shackles. Clinging to the cell door bars, she watched as the lot of them disappeared into the passage.

The cell had darkened. The sunshine through the window had started to fade, as the sun had shifted higher into the sky. Myrine pulled on her all weather hoodie. In what little light was left, Myrine turned to the window and fumbled the tissue packet out of her hoodie's pocket. Shooting a quick prayer to the powers that be in the Universe, she rolled the two sleeping sage flowers into cylindrical tubes, then bent them u-shaped. Not a single zap from the shutterling. The slight bitter scent from the crushing of the sleeping sage seemed to calm it.

She sat down cross-legged and rested her right wrist on her right knee. Bending forward, she rolled the cylindrical tubes out of her palm onto the floor. Moving them apart with the fingers of her left hand, she pinched one between her thumb and index finger. She started to shake and dropped the tube. *Dragonscats!*

She took a deep breath through her nose, releasing it through her mouth. Retrieved the dropped sleeping sage tube and inserted it into the right nostrils of the two vipers, forming the shutterling. Then took the second cylindrical tube and inserted it into the shutterlings' two left nostrils.

The shutterling's eyes closed and their bodies relaxed. Their teeth opened but remained slightly latched. Myrine collapsed her right hand's fingers and pushed her thumb inward towards her palm, making her hand as narrow as possible. Taking care not to disturb the cylindrical tubes, she smoothed the loosened shutterling over her hand.

With the slack shutterling in the palm of her left hand, she cast about and saw an iron hook on the side wall near the gate. *There is a tracker in the shutterling alerting Eugenia of my whereabouts every step of the way. I need to make sure it stays in this cell.*

She hooked the limp shutterling over the hook. Powered up her psychokinetic power and bent the hook until it formed a closed ring. Limp, the shutterling hung from it. *What if they became so relaxed that their teeth unlocked? Definitely not a good idea.*

Myrine removed the sleeping sage tubes from the vipers' nostrils. Missing a fingertip by inches, their interlocked teeth snapped shut. Their bleached out green eyes opened. *Was that fury in their eyes?* Stunned, she watched as the vipers contracted back into a shutterling, then carried on contracting until it formed a tight ring around the bent iron hook.

The sleeping sage could not be used a second time; however, it would not be a good idea to leave any evidence behind. She stuck it into her pants pocket and walked to the back wall where Rollandario earlier marked the granite blocks he had loosened from the outside. She bent and picked up the lever he left for her, lying at the bottom of the wall.

After a moment's contemplation, she used the sharp flat end of the lever and cleared the dirt around the granite block in the middle. *That should be big enough for me to crawl through and the two on its side will stop the wall from collapsing.*

Maneuvering the loosened granite block out of the wall was not as hard as she thought it would be. It seemed Rollandario had done most of the hard work from the outside. Before levering it out of the wall completely, she collected some straw and put it directly beneath it. It landed with a thump on the straw. She looked at the cell door, craned her neck and peered at the room leading to the passage beyond it, and waited.

Satisfied no one was alerted, she took off her all-weather hoodie. Rolled the lever in it and pushed it through the hole. *It could come in handy as a weapon if needs be.* A last look at the cell door and what lay beyond it before she turned and kneeled on the floor in front of the hole. On her stomach, she crawled headfirst into the cavity.

Halfway through the hole, head out at the kitchen garden side, the loosened granite block on her right shifted, narrowing the opening. Her hips stuck. She tried to wriggle forward, then backward, but remained stuck. *Too much wriggling and I will only manage to unsettle the granite block more. If Rollandario was here like he said he would be, he could have pulled me free.* As if on cue, Rollandario appeared. He kept glancing over his shoulder as he approached. Myrine could feel waves of anxiety rolling off him, and it did little to quell her own fears of discovery.

'The lever is in my hoodie, lying there on the ground. If you could lift the loosened block on my right-hand side, I can crawl through.'

Rollandario set to work stabilizing the granite block to her right. A slight movement from the granite blocks above Myrine's back had him hesitate.

'Hold it in place with the lever. If I move slowly, I can crawl through.'

Rollandario placed a hand under the brick above Myrine's back. She wriggled forward, using her elbows. The granite block on the right scraped the skin on the side of her hip. Ignoring the burning pain, she kept wriggling forward. Her upper body free of the hole, she grabbed onto Rollandario's legs and hauled the rest of her body through.

Her feet hardly freed from the hole, Rollandario's hand slipped. The granite blocks above the hole shifted and dropped with a loud thud, barring the hole. A cloud of dust rose in its aftermath. Myrine grabbed her hoodie from the ground. She was disoriented in the sudden bright sunshine. Rollandario grabbed her by the hand, the lever in his other hand, and they raced into the kitchen gardens. In the distance, a Crontanorius cawed.

They came to a stop behind a thriving growth of some sort of beans at the far edge of the kitchen garden. A low stone wall separated it from a wooded area. An iron gate hung half open on its rusty hinges.

'There is a seldom used pathway through the woods and on the other side is the perimeter wall. I know of a tree we can use to climb on top of the wall.'

A loud siren blared, tearing through the air, getting louder with each wail. Myrine jumped up and looked towards the barracks, where she escaped from the dungeon a hundred meters away. Troops were milling about in the distance. Rollandario stood up.

'We must hurry. Follow me.'

CHAPTER 15

A platoon of troops had entered the kitchen gardens. One meter apart, they formed a horizontal line and combed the garden. All of them had long wooden clubs which they used to sweep through the bushes. The afternoon shift of garden workers, prevented from entering the kitchen gardens, milled about outside the garden gate.

Keeping behind the hedge of beans, Myrine and Rollandario set off at a half-jog towards the gate opening into the woods. They reached the end of the hedge. The last five meters to the gate provided no cover and they would have to step out into the open. Next to Myrine, Rollandario settled himself into a sprinter start position. Myrine grabbed him by the back of his shirt and pulled him back as he was about to launch himself from behind the hedge.

She put the fingers of her right hand to her lips and motioned with the other hand downwards. Hunkering down herself, Myrine looked at the troops through a gap in the hedge. She judged them to be about seventy odd meters away.

Powering up her kinetic supernatural power, she created a slight disturbance behind the troops. She watched as one turned to look and followed it up with a rustling of bushes. The troop that had turned called the others to a halt. Their wooden clubs at the ready, they all turned. Myrine created more movement in the bushes, just out of their reach. As one, they started stalking the movement.

'Now.'

Myrine rushed through the gate, Rollandario hot on her heels. Rollandario took over the lead, and she followed him up a faint path. They rounded a bend. Out of sight of the kitchen gardens, they stopped. Both of them were breathing hard. Ahead of them, the footpath disappeared into a dark tunnel canopied by age-old trees. Above them, the sun shone brighter than a new penny. Myrine looked at her quantum watch. The length of an hour stretching far longer than that of an Earth hour confused her. *Time moved extremely slowly here.* She noticed Rollandario was moving in one place from one foot to the other and realised that he was on edge. Anxiety rolled off him in waves.

'From here on we are only using telepathic communication. Follow me.'

'Wait. What was the warning sign on the gate for?'

'There are plants in between the trees that are carnivorous, patches of magic mushroom circles, and a few other things to be wary of. That is why no one comes in here. It is dangerous if you don't know which patches in these woods you have to avoid. Up ahead, the path is hardly visible, but as I told you. I know these woods well and I know which way to go.'

'Well, someone has entered here not long before us. There were fresh footsteps in the soft ground heading up the path.'

'There is the odd one that knows the woods who may come in here like Dr Dreckonium and he has trained a few of the troops, so he could send them when he needs a plant from here for his concoctions.'

'My gut says someone is in here now. Maybe we should get off the path.'

'It is too dangerous.'

'But someone is here and if we are on the path, we will be seen. And the chain on the gate was unlocked.'

'Coming to think of it, the gate was open, and it is supposed to be closed and locked.'

'So? Should we then ...'

A branch snapped. Without speaking further, they reverted to telepathy speak and stepped off the path. Myrine waited as Rollandario searched for a safe place to hide. She looked at the dark tunnel leading into the woods, from where footsteps crunched closer.

They had hardly settled into their hiding spot on the side of the path when a whisker faced guard appeared. He had a long handled three-pronged pitchfork and stabbed at the sides of the footpath as he walked along. Now and then, he stopped and added something to the bag that hung across his chest.

Two meters from where they were hiding, the guard stopped and sniffed at the air. The whiskers on his cheeks rose. Elongated and stiffened, it formed a spikey halo around his moon face. One eye enlarged and roved over their hiding spot. Turned away, came back.

'Create a disturbance before he spots us.'

Myrine sent a tiny kinetic energy blast into the dead leaves on the other side of the path. A brown horned beetle got unsettled and scurried from under the leaves. One of moon-face's whiskers shot out of his cheek and impaled it. A blur and he was at the heap of dead leaves, flicking the dead beetle aside, scratching in the dead leaves with his three-pronged pitchfork. Myrine's eyes widened. A new whisker had appeared in place of the one that had shot out.

'Don't move. He can shoot more than one whisker and his accuracy is absolute.'

A sharp finger of fear spiked through Myrine's naval, raked through her intestines, and twisted her large intestine into a painful knot. *Dragonscats. He was faster than lightning.*

Myrine held her breath and together with Rollandario, they watched as moon-face moved towards the gate after having found nothing of interest amongst the leaves. They were about to get up when voices rose from the gate area.

Recognising Gargoyle-Face's voice, she motioned for Rollandario to stay put. Activating her enhanced hearing, Myrine turned her left ear in the direction of the voices and listened in on the conversation.

Despite her intense concentration, she only heard snatches of the conversation before the gate clanged shut. There was the rattle of a chain and the click of a lock being snapped shut. The voices faded. She looked at Rollandario, whose face sported an enquiring frown.

'Some guards asked him if he saw me. I think they are satisfied that I am not here in the woods. They closed the gate and locked it.'

'That is a relief. Let's get going. We need to find a place on the perimeter wall where we can watch the road along which Surneal will be travelling. Once he has entered the castle grounds, everyone's attention will be on him and we can leave and hide at the portal until it opens at sunrise.'

'You said he only travels at night? Should we then not leave before nightfall?'

'The Brunkai would be patrolling until sundown before they go to their hub to recharge. It won't be safe to go outside the castle walls before then. I know of a place where we can hide until then.'

Fresh out of options, Myrine had no choice but to follow Rollandario's lead and hope for the best. One hundred meters later, the path narrowed. The trees were getting thicker, their canopies hiding the sky. Strange firefly type insects clumped together at intervals, hung from the tree branches above the path, bathing it in a weird grey-green light. Myrine eyed the clumps of insects, ducking her head each time she walked under a branch where they hung.

Myrine Goes Through the Quantum Door | 147

'Don't worry about them. They are harmless, if not disturbed. Without their light, we won't see where to go.'

'What happens if they are disturbed?'

'The fluid in their bodies providing the light is released and has a nasty sting that burns for days on end.'

'Sounds like you have had some experience.'

'When I was a little boy, I used to come here and hide, knowing my father would not come looking for me here. Then one day, he sent Dr Dreckonium to fetch me. I tried to run away and bumped into one of the clumps.'

Rollandario abruptly turned away, but not before Myrine saw the blush that spread over his face.

'Let's go.'

Wordless Myrine followed Rollandario, who set off at a stiff pace. Despite his assurances, Myrine instinctively ducked her head as she passed under each clump. Mindful of the species of dangerous plants Rollandario mentioned, she kept an eye out to the sides of the footpath, making sure she did not stray off it. Startled by the loud shrill of a bird, she looked up, failed to see Rollandario had halted and walked smack bang into his back.

In her attempt to keep her balance, she stepped off the path. The plant closest to her opened its branches. The twenty-centimetre stalks that laid close to its stem rose outward. Each stalk was laden with a mixture of bright blue, pink, and white flowers. The stalks bent in her direction and leaned towards her. The flowers' calyxes opened wider. In their centres, between the petals, were tiny purple circles. The circles opened, revealing three layered circles of razor-sharp teeth.

The circles opened and closed. Sucking, clicking, and gnashing. A saccharine vapour filled the air around Myrine. Spellbound, her upper body gradually bent forward. Closer to the flowers.

Rollandario grabbed her from behind around the waist and heaved her back onto the path. The drool from the flowers closest to the footpath fell to the ground where her boot was moments before and burnt a hole through the undergrowth. A pungent rotten fruit odour sprung into the air, extinguishing the saccharine vapour.

'Put your hand over your nose and don't breathe it in!'

Myrine realised Rollandario was raising his voice and no longer telepathically communicating with her. She held her breath. Her body felt lame. With Rollandario's help, she raised her right arm, bent it at the elbow, holding her forearm over her nose. She breathed through her mouth. She could barely walk as Rollandario pulled her further away. They crab-walked sideways until the plant was no longer in sight before stopping near a clearing.

Wheezing. Her throat was burning. Myrine took her water bottle from the side of her magic backpack. She tilted her head back and poured a stream of water down her throat. The bottle emptied, but she was still thirsty. She put it back in its holder, waited for a few seconds for it to automatically refill, and drank more water. The second bottle of water slaked her thirst. She put it back in its holder and left it there and turned to Rollandario, who stood panting beside her.

'Do you want some water?'

'Yes, please.'

Rollandario took the bottle from her, drank half its contents, and handed it back. She half expected him to ask about the water bottle filling itself.

'You ready to go?'

Following Rollandario's example, she responded telepathically. In the affirmative.

'We have reached the end of the path. From here, you need to place your boot in each step as I move in front of you.'

Myrine Goes Through the Quantum Door | 149

'How far are we from the perimeter wall?'

'About fifty meters or so, but it is dangerous and we need to go slow. You must be careful to step into the indents my steps leave behind me.'

Myrine nodded. She did not need another terrible experience like the one she had minutes ago. At least the strange green glow provided enough light for her to follow in Rollandario's footsteps.

They came to a stop. Peeping past Rollandario, Myrine saw a humongous tree trunk. Behind it rose the perimeter wall. To the left of the tree trunk, there was a magic mushroom circle. Clusters of red-black centred mushrooms circled a dead organic patch. A twig dropped into the circle. Its centre mass moved and absorbed it in seconds, settling back, once again motionless.

'Wait here.'

Despite reaching the perimeter wall without incident, Myrine's shoulders remained tight. Only her eyes moved as she followed Rollandario's movements when he stepped up to the tree trunk and put his hand inside a tree knot hole. The tree trunk creaked. Its branches shuddered. Spheres of fungi sprouted out of the bark.

On closer inspection, Myrine noticed grey oyster mushroom fungi resembling an uneven set of stairs, all the way up the tree trunk to the top of the perimeter wall. Rollandario walked back to Myrine and put his hand on her shoulder.

'Follow me up once I reach the top of the wall. Be careful not to step on the thin edges. Watch how I place my feet in the middle, which is the thickest part. You can touch the tree trunk. Use it to balance yourself on the way up.'

'Is the tree trunk safe to touch?'

'Yes. This tree has been my friend since I first came in here. He is one of the Light Force members that remained when the Dark Forces took over.'

'The Dark Forces don't know about him?'

'They don't believe that trees are anything other than trees. They have no idea that trees can communicate across great distances. I have often been comforted by this one when I got into trouble with my father.'

Myrine looked at the tree. Hesitated. Then touched the trunk. A warm sensation pulsed from the tree into her palm. Her shoulders relaxed and dropped away from her neck. Moving her hand away from the tree trunk, she rubbed the back of her neck.

She watched Rollandario going up the fungi steps and kept her eyes on him till he reached the top of the perimeter wall. He beckoned to her. Myrine put her left hand against the tree trunk and her right foot on the first step. Climbing up the steps was not as easy as it looked. Her progress was much slower than that of the experienced Rollandario.

A shout came from below. Myrine looked down. Gargoyle Face was standing at the bottom of the tree. *Dragonscats!* Gargoyle Face stepped onto the first fungi step, gripping the trunk with a clawed hand. The tree shivered, releasing a shower of dead leaves, raining onto Gargoyle Face's head. Myrine grabbed Rollandario's outstretched hand, and he pulled her from the last fungi step to hauling her to the top of the perimeter wall.

Myrine hunkered on all fours at Rollandario's side, who reached towards a knothole in the tree trunk where it leaned against the wall. Gargoyle Face had reached the third fungi step directly above the magic mushroom circle. Rollandario pushed his hand inside the knot hole. The fungi steps retracted into the tree trunk. Screaming at the top of his voice, Gargoyle Face's legs bicycled as he fell straight into the magic mushroom circle.

Myrine leaned forward and looked down. Gargoyle Face's body trampoline flopped a few times before it disappeared from sight. A few bubbles seethed in the magic mushroom circle. Gargoyle Face's head appeared for a second. He let out a strangled cry. A bloodied tentacle appeared, wound itself around his head, and pulled him under. Nausea bubbled up in Myrine and she turned away and dry heaved. Nothing but sour bile dribbled from her mouth.

She straightened and wiped her mouth with the back of her hand. The perimeter wall was wide enough for two people to comfortably walk abreast. Both sides had a two granite block high wall, reaching her hips. She walked to the side, facing the river. Below, a rock-strewn steep embankment abutted the wall.

She heard Rollandario approaching and stiffened her spine. She knew he saved them from sure disaster, but she was wary of the cold detachment with which he acted. It showed a side of him she never suspected.

Standing on the perimeter wall, Myrine looked over the horizon. The sun's head rested on the ridge above the portal. Behind it, dusk's moth-eaten pale-yellow blanket slowly unfurled across the sky. The baby blue patches that were not covered turned a dishwater grey. She realised it would soon be dark. Myrine, who had always loved sunsets and how the sky changed, did not like the look of this one at all.

'We have to hide out until dark. There will be troops stationed in the arrow holes at the front of the castle. There is a point near that turret over there where the wall is not too high off the ground and we can jump.'

Myrine looked at the turret Rollandario had pointed out. They would be out in the open, crossing the wall.

'I think we must wait until it is dark before we cross. How about we climb up the tree and settle on that branch over there? I think it will be thick enough to carry our weight.'

They debated the pros and cons with Rollandario pointing out that at full dark they will be hampered in various ways. Myrine thought she won the argument, when she pointed out that he may have night vision in his brown lizard eye, but she could enhance her night vision and see with both eyes.

'We also need to rest. I need my energy to restore to normal levels so I can activate my supernatural powers. I have a feeling I may well need to use them.'

'Surneal will be coming after dark.'

'I still think it would be better to take our chances after dark. You said earlier everyone's attention will be on him and we can use that diversion to at least get away from the castle and into the woods bordering the path to the portal.'

'What if guards are sent to patrol this wall?'

'We deal with it as it happens. It is no use arguing about something that may or may not happen.'

They reached a truce. Myrine climbed up to the tree limb she had pointed out, with Rollandario following her. They settled down with their backs to the tree trunk and drank more water from Myrine's water bottle, which she surreptitiously took from the side of her magic backpack. Rollandario got up.

'Where are you going? I thought we were going to wait until dark.'

Rollandario pointed to tree branches from a neighbouring tree interlinking with the branches of the tree they were sitting on. Mouth-watering clusters of golden berries hung from the spiny white branches.

'Getting us some Vacinisium berries from that tree over there.'

Myrine's mouth watered as Rollandario came back with a shirt full of the berries. They were full of juice and had a tarty sweet taste. They washed their sticky hands with a bit of water from her magic water bottle before Myrine stood up and secured it back in its holder on the side of her magic backpack. She checked that her sleeveless vest was in place and unzipped her hoodie.

'How do you manage to keep your water bottle full?'

She knew he would notice at some time that the water bottle remained full. She had thought of different explanations, but they all sounded lame. Whilst thinking about how to explain, Myrine had screened her thoughts for a few seconds. Longer and he would know she was blocking him from reading her mind. With only a few seconds, he would read it as a blank mind.

'I use one of my supernatural powers.'

'Really? What supernatural power can fill a bottle with water?'

'The mind is the strongest part of the body. By thinking of something you want and believing you will get it, you make it happen.'

'You have to imagine a full water bottle every time?'

'No. I imagined that I would have a full water bottle at all times whilst travelling.'

Myrine did not drop her eyes from Rollandario, who was the first to look away. She did not like the skeptical frown on his face. She held onto a branch above her head and stepped onto another branch. Facing away from the portal, she sat down looking towards the woods they came through. Before Rollandario could query her action, she spoke.

'I will watch the woods. You watch the road. That way we cover both ends and whoever sees someone approach alerts the other telepathically.'

CHAPTER 16

With no wind blowing, the thick foliage of the tree provided a decent cover for both Myrine and Rollandario. Thinking back to Gargoyle Face following them, Myrine wondered whether his cohort, Beak Nose, would be looking for him.

'Both of them knew the woods and how to avoid its perils.'

Myrine looked at Rollandario, who clearly read her mind and answered her question.

'Does anyone know how to get up the tree to reach the top of this wall?'

'No. That has always been my secret and you are the first one I have shown.'

A medium-sized bird landed on the branch above them and released a series of jarring calls. Myrine was sure she had just been berated for her audacity of sitting in the bird's tree. She locked eyes with the bird.

'That is Caprimulgius. He is harmless.'

'He does not seem to be happy with us in his tree.'

'Probably, but he will soon settle.'

Rollandario whistled soft tweets and soon enough Caprimulgius settled and with a final shudder of his wings. Knowing that some of her supernatural powers were fully developed and did not deplete her energy levels required to use them, Myrine made an instant decision.

'I am going to use one of my supernatural powers and use him as a scout.'

'Don't go near the path. Surneal will immediately note your presence and disable Caprimulgius.'

'Oh. What if I sent him to the castle to see what is happening?'

'As long as you steer clear of my mother. She would notice him too.'

Powering up her avian manipulation superpower, Myrine entered Caprimulgius' mind. She steered him in a circle over the woods. Found no-one present and moved closer to the castle. Crossing the kitchen gardens, a mouse was running about. Fighting Caprimulgius' hunting instinct, it took all her willpower to keep him on course and leave the mouse be.

The encounter with the mouse had tired Myrine, and her hold on Caprimulgius loosened as he glided and circled the courtyard. It was abuzz with preparations for the arrival of Surneal. Pigs were roasting over fire pits and castle staff bustled about. The kitchen door was open and Myrine saw the cook and her staff sweating over various steaming pots. The guards in the courtyard were clearly on a mission as they searched the entire area around the castle. The same went for the barracks and castle.

At the entrance gate, there were now more than a single troop. A whole cadre had set up weapons at the ready inside the gate. Others occupied the arrow holes on both sides of the gates. The two top towers besides the gate were occupied by guards who vigilantly scanned the path and its surrounds leading up to the gate. In the distance, troops were stationed on the other side of the bridge.

Myrine had Caprimulgius circle one final time over the castle and grounds, but before she could steer him back to the tree, Eugenia, with Faeyet in tow, came out of the castle. Her heart lurched as Eugenia, hand above her brow, frowned up at Caprimulgius. An irresistible magnetic pull from Eugenia. Caprimulgius spiraled down. Gritting her teeth, neck muscles straining, Myrine put every inch of her strength into pulling Caprimulgius out of the magnetic pull.

At the last minute, she got control of Caprimulgius, dove over Eugenia's head. She dared not return him to the kitchen gardens and sped over the perimeter wall near the front gate. Behind her, she heard Eugenia scream at the guards to shoot Caprimulgius. Turning Caprimulgius into a sideways dive, an arrow barely missed them. Thanks to the speed of Caprimulgius, there were no further close encounters, and she returned to the tree.

Myrine slammed back into her own body. Her heart hammered irregularly, beating a painful tattoo against its rib cage prison. Her throat tightened. Her mouth opened wide, and she surged upwards. Hands grabbed her shoulders, kept her from falling off the branch. Pulling huge breaths of air into her open mouth, revived her into full consciousness. She allowed herself to slump against Rollandario. If she had fallen off the branch, she would have sustained a nasty injury.

'What happened?'

'I saw Eugenia. She tried to pull me to her. I dove over her head and flew over the perimeter wall towards the river. Troops were sent to search for me at the river. Thank you for keeping my body steady as I came back into it.'

She could feel the tension rise in Rollandario as he let go of her. Responding to it, her body tightened.

'Mother is not so easily fooled. It is nearly full dark. Are you ready to go?'

'In a minute.'

The branch dipped and sprung back. She watched Rollandario step onto the perimeter wall. Throwing a last look in the dimming light at the woods they had earlier travelled through, Myrine got off the branch. Walking to Rollandario, she watched the sun disappear below the horizon, leaving behind a dirty coal dust sky. A night-wind stirred the air. Myrine pulled her hoodie tighter around her and zipped it closed.

'We can move to the turret now, without attracting too much attention.'

'And if they see us.'

'Keep your face averted and they will mistake us for guards patrolling. The light is low enough to fool them.'

They reached the cone-shaped turret that projected over the perimeter wall at the corner, linking the front and side perimeter wall. Rollandario pulled her back.

'Watch out. We are at the corner where the front wall joins this turret. There will be guards along the front perimeter. Keep to the inside wall of the turret, away from the exit onto the front wall.'

Her eyes on the exit to the front wall, Myrine entered the small turret and bumped her head against the wooden corbel jutting out of the stone inside the door. *Dragonscats*. She rubbed her forehead where a bump had formed.

Myrine looked around. On the left was a sturdy wooden door set in the castle wall, standing half open. To the right, a large aperture. Straight ahead of her, set at a ninety-degree angle, was a door sized opening, which she assumed led to the front perimeter wall.

She walked to the aperture and looked out. It opened up to a view on the side of the castle that overlooked the river. A grassed embankment abutted the wall beneath the aperture.

Myrine walked back to the wooden door, kept to the wall next to it, and went to the opening leading to the front perimeter wall. Having reached the opening, she leaned sideways and peeped at the front perimeter wall. There were three guards stationed at arrow holes leading up to the main gate.

She retraced her steps and went back to the aperture. The embankment below was steep. Grassed with boulders dotting it at irregular intervals. Looking back to where they came from, here the wall was at its lowest point. But still at least a two-storey jump. If timed right, one could roll down the grassy area and reach the trees and be undercover in no time. Rollandario, standing beside her, having read her thoughts, nodded his head.

Myrine thought back to her physical training with Aedric.

'It would be easier if we had a rope that we could tie around this hook on the wall.'

'There should be one in the storeroom downstairs that I used when I was younger.'

'When you were younger?'

'About a year ago, Faeyet followed me. I had no time to fetch the rope and climb down. I did not want her to find out how I escaped from the castle. She would have run straight to father, reporting me. I jumped. After that, I always jumped. With time, it became easier.'

'I am not sure I can jump once it is dark. Where is the storeroom?'

'Through that door. Downstairs. No one will see me. I will be quick. Wait here for me.'

Myrine turned back to the aperture. A gust of wind blew into the turret, twirled through the layers of sand on the floor and whipped a cloud of dust into the air. Myrine bit back a sneeze. Squeezing her eyes shut, she pinched her nose closed with her right-hand thumb and index finger and prevented the follow up sneeze that threatened to burst free.

She pushed away from the aperture and turned, coming toe to toe with Faeyet. Rooted to the spot, she watched Faeyet shapeshift from Fosterling into her human form.

'Here you are. We have been looking for you all over. Did Rollandario bring you here, showing you how he escapes from the castle?'

'Does it look like he is here?'

'You know he is a betrayer, right? Betraying his father and mother, refusing to conform to the Betwonium Rules. But then, what could you expect from a halfling.'

'Halfling?'

'Neither a true Betwoniumite nor a true human.'

Myrine tried to pull her arm away as Faeyet made a grab for her wrist. Her elbow glanced off Faeyet's cheek. With a hiss, Faeyet shapeshifted into her Fosterling self. Grabbing for her, Myrine failed to get a proper hold on the loose furry skin. She fell to her knees. Faeyet jumped on her back, curling her limbs tight around Myrine's waist and chest, forcing her to the floor on all fours.

Rolling onto her back, Myrine pinned Faeyet to the floor and tried to loosen the hold on her. Black spots danced before Myrine's eyes as Faeyet's hold tightened, squeezing the air from her lungs. Myrine rocked to and fro and tried to dislodge Faeyet's limbs. Kicking with her legs, her feet found purchase against the side of the turret's wall. She levered herself backwards, dragging Faeyet underneath her across the floor. Faeyet's one set of limbs around Myrine's waist loosened and Myrine grabbed them, stretching them in a split. She rocked her body until the set of limbs around her chest loosened. Keeping the momentum going, crushing Faeyet's body under her, she kept rocking until Faeyet's body went limp.

Inhaling deeply, Myrine rolled off Faeyet and got up. Her head swimming, she looked down. Faeyet's eyes were blinking. Myrine grabbed for her MagLite torch, then remembered she no longer had her utility belt since Beldarius stripped her of it. *Dragonscats. And there are no loose rocks lying around either.*

Movement at the wooden door caught Myrine's attention. Rollandario had come back with the rope.

'Give me that rope. We need to tie her up.'

'Don't just stand there. Give me the rope and help me before she is fully conscious.'

'What happened?'

'I will tell you later.'

With Rollandario's help, Myrine hog-tied Faeyet. A thin wail issued from Faeyet. Rollandario put his hand over her mouth and, with the other hand, fished a rag from his pants pocket and held it out to Myrine. She gagged Faeyet, whilst Rollandario held Faeyet's head.

'We can't leave her here. Someone may come along and find her and she is sure to run straight to father.'

'What about the storeroom?'

'Not safe enough. The staff often fetch provisions from there.'

'Is there a landing behind that door before the steps go down that is big enough?'

Together, they wrangled Faeyet's struggling body to the door. The hinges squealed as Myrine pulled it wider in order for them to fit through, with Faeyet between them. As they thumped Faeyet into a corner, they heard running footsteps. It seemed to come from the front perimeter wall. Faeyet started snorting. Before Myrine could think of how to silence her, Rollandario cuffed Faeyet and her body slumped to the floor.

'Quick. Close the door.'

Myrine shut the door as quietly as she could. Rollandario lowered the drop latch slowly. An all-consuming darkness descended. Myrine activated her night vision. It turned the enveloping dark into sludge grey.

'Don't stress. We should be fine.'

'I can't see.'

'Don't worry. I can see with my lizard eye if needed. Don't move. Don't make a sound. If the guard finds the door locked, he will go away.'

Myrine closed her eyes, folded her hands across her chest, and dropped her chin to her chest. An itch crawled up her left nostril. She pinched her nose shut with her right hand and pressed her left hand's middle finger into the acupuncture point between her eyebrows. Regulating her breath through her mouth, she stood motionless, back against the cold stone wall. She allowed herself a small feeling of comfort in having Rollandario next to her.

She always found it hard to put her trust in someone. In her seventeen nearly eighteen years of life, the only people she could trust to the nth degree were Grandma and Aedric.

The running footsteps entered the turret outside and came to an abrupt halt. She could imagine the guard looking around. Hopefully, he does not notice the disturbance of the dust on the turret floor. The footsteps restarted. It sounded as if the guard was walking to the aperture. Then again, sound could be tricky and he may be right in front of the door. The footsteps restarted. Then halted. This time, she was sure the guard was right in front of the door. She held her breath. Next to her, she felt Rollandario's body stiffen.

A push against the door from the outside had the latch rattling in its hook. It held. The guard on the outside rattled the door harder. It held.

'Anyone in there?'

Myrine's body jerked at the menacing sound in Beak-nose's voice. Of all the guards, it had to be him. She fisted her hands at her sides. A second set of footsteps sounded.

'Found anything?'

'No, but I am sure someone was here. I saw a movement.'

'The stairs in this turret lead to the food storage in the cellar under the castle. Maybe you saw a rat?'

'I suppose it could be that.'

'And the door is latched. I will send someone to go and check the food cellar. Come back to your post. Surneal will be arriving soon.'

The guards' footsteps faded away. She could hear Rollandario counting to thirty in his head before he opened the door a crack. He peeked out and beckoned Myrine forward. They squirrelled to the turret window.

'We can't wait. I will jump first.'

Myrine watched as Rollandario jumped out the window, landed on the slope, and somersaulted to a stop. It sure looked like he had done it before. Her stomach fluttered. She climbed onto the sill. It was a bit different to the jumps she used to do in training with Aedric from the roof of Grandma's house. There was no steep embankment, but flat grass to land on. She knew she had to jump before her nerves overtook her senses.

Climbing onto the sill, Myrine stood up, took a deep breath, and jumped. Landing awkwardly, her ankle twisted under her weight. She fell sideways and rolled down the embankment. If it was not for Rollandario grabbing hold of her, she would have rolled head on into a boulder.

Myrine tried to stand up. Pain shot from her ankle straight up her leg into her hip. Involuntarily, she sat down hard. Her tailbone protested. She prodded the area around her ankle. At least it was not broken. With Rollandario's help, she hobbled down the embankment and sat down against a boulder at the bottom.

'You okay?'

'I think so. My ankle is not broken. Do you have another rag in your pocket?'

'Here.'

Wetting the rag with water from her water bottle, Myrine wrapped it around her ankle. She battled to get her boot back on. Left it unlaced, tucking the untied laces into the sides.

Dark was settling in fast and she did not like that they were close to the path on which Surneal would be travelling. His senses might just alert him to her presence.

'Can you help me up? I think we need to move further away from the path.'

'We would have to travel through the woods. I heard father instructing his troops to guard the path tonight whilst the Brunkai is recharging to take over the morning shift.'

'And the woods? Had he sent any troops there?'

'No. He, after consultation with mother, was of the opinion that you would go straight to the portal along the path that leads to it.'

'And the Brunkai?'

'They go to their tree nest to recharge. Fanisius stays there with them and releases them at daybreak.'

'Well then, from what you are telling me, it seems the best way would be through the woods.'

'I nearly forgot. I got this for you.'

Myrine watched as Rollandario took off his jacket and swung a backpack off his back and unzipped it. She took her utility belt from him and checked it over before fastening it around her waist.

'Thank you. I really appreciate this.'

'No worries. I thought you may have a use for the objects you carry in it.'

Her arm around Rollandario's waist and his arm around her shoulder, they started for the woods. Every step sent a throb through Myrine's ankle. Their progress slow, they reached the entrance to the woods as torches appeared on the road in the distance.

'There is a place about ten steps away where we can sit down and you can rest a bit.'

Having gotten off the path, Myrine slumped down behind the fallen tree trunk in the small clearing Rollandario had led her to. Her hands shaking, she wiped the sweat from her face with the cuff of her hoodie.

'Where are you going?'

'You need something for your ankle. I won't be long.'

Watching Rollandario's disappearing back, Myrine took her Spyderco knife from her utility belt, flicked it open and kept it at the ready in her hand. Exhaustion and sleep fought an intense jerk-dance for control over Myrine. One moment her eyes would close and her chin drop. The next her head would jerk up and she vowed to stay awake.

In the end, exhaustion won. Her head dropped. Her hand relaxed and the Spyderco knife dropped to the ground.

CHAPTER 17

Seized in a nightmare, Myrine tried to run. Her legs were paralysed. Her arms windmilled. She remained in place. Ahead of her, Grandma and Aedric disappeared into the woods. She tried to call for them to wait. Only a wheeze fell from her lips. They disappeared around a bend. She tried to will her body forward. It refused to co-operate. Blackness enveloped her. Her night vision failed. Her throat closed. Something moved behind her. The monster's smell filled her nostrils. A hand touched her shoulder.

Myrine's eyes flew open. She struggled against the hands on her shoulders. Her heart hammered. Her pulse sped up. She tried to scream. A hand clamped over her mouth. She heard Rollandario speaking in her mind.

'Stop fighting me. You seemed to be having a bad dream.'

'Is there someone out there?'

'No. But it is best to be cautious. We are close to the entrance to the woods and a passer-by may hear us. I think we should from now on keep to the habit of speaking telepathically.'

'My ankle is going to slow us down. We better start for the portal now.'

'Wait. I brought you Cynoglosium for your ankle. Let's treat it first.'

Myrine looked at the evergreen velvet leaves and violet flowers lying in the palm of Rollandario's hand. It was similar to the common comfrey growing at Silky Oak. Aedric once used it for his sprained wrist when they were training in the woods.

'I can make you a poultice to tie around your ankle.'

Loosening the rag around her ankle, she took it off and handed it to Rollandario. Under her watchful eyes, he placed the leaves and flowers in it, folded the rag into a poultice, and pounded it with a stone.

'Wet it with some water from your water bottle, then tie it around your ankle. It will dull the pain and the swelling will go down.'

Wetting the handmade poultice, the smell of rotting flesh rose into the air. Maybe it was common comfrey. It certainly smelt like it. Suppressing her gag reflex, Myrine made quick work of tying the poultice around her ankle. She took Rollandario's outstretched hand and levered herself off the ground.

'The smell will help hide your Earthling smell.'

'How wonderful! I always wanted to smell like I was rotten.'

Shame washed over Myrine as Rollandario shrugged his shoulders and looked at his feet.

'Look. I didn't mean it like that. You don't smell bad, nor does your mother. Faeyet has no smell at all. But the rest stinks.'

'You can say it. So does my father. It is the Betwoniomite smell. Mother, your aunt, is originally from Tsaonin. I guess I am lucky to have her genes when it comes to body odour. Let's go.'

Holding with one hand onto Rollandario's arm, and using her uninjured leg, Myrine levered herself around, in the direction of which they were going to travel. Holding onto Rollandario's forearm, she hobble-stepped next to him. Deeper into the woods, the tree canopy above grew denser, keeping the moonlight out. The lanterns from the previous night were absent, and Myrine activated her night vision.

Halfway into the woods, Myrine gladly followed Rollandario's suggestion that they rest for a bit. They sat down on a fallen tree trunk.

She inspected the poultice rag around her ankle. It had loosened and was drying out. She untied it. Her ankle was less tender to her touch. The swelling had gone down considerably. Wetting the rag, she re-tied it and tightened her shoelaces.

'Does your ankle feel better?'

'The swelling has gone down, and it is not so sore anymore.'

Myrine used the tree trunk to lever herself into a standing position. She balanced on one leg. Then lowered the and tested her weight on her injured ankle. It held. She took a few experimental steps by herself. There was a mere twinge, and she was sure she could walk without using Rollandario as a crutch. Despite the Betwonium night being the equivalent of more than an earth day in hours, Myrine did not want to delay going to the exit portal.

The worry knot in her lower stomach remained tight. At the back of her mind, mister nag had set up camp, chipping away at her confidence at every opportunity. For all she knew, there might be more unknown obstacles along the way.

More than ever before, she wished Aedric had come with her. On the other hand, when back on Earth, she knew he would protect Grandma. She knew he would do his utmost to prevent the Dark Forces specialist he told her about from bringing Grandma out of her self-induced coma. She could not waste the two weeks' grace Grandma's unselfish action granted her. It was as if Grandma knew she may miss the correct quantum door opening in Tsaonin. Well, she had a promise to fulfill, and she was going to give it her all.

Squaring her shoulders, she turned to Rollandario, who was still sitting on the fallen tree trunk. Myrine picked up on Rollandario's despondent thoughts. She would have to make up for making him feel rejected. Of all the things, she did not have the will or the energy to deal with his *little boy lost* attitude. She barely had enough energy to keep herself positive. *Dragonscats!*

When Rollandario's head jerked up, she realised she had sworn out loud. She reverted back to telepathy.

'You need to get a hold of yourself if you want to go with me through the exit portal.'

'But you don't really want me to go with you. Despite my best efforts, you still don't trust me.'

Wordless, Myrine contemplated Rollandario's scowling face. He had been useful.

'Yeah. Useful.'

Careful to keep her main thoughts cloaked, Myrine considered her next step. She knew she would be better off with him in tow to the exit portal. After all, this planet was his home and very different from earth. Here the ogres traipsed about undisguised, whereas on Earth they stayed under cover, masquerading as normal beings. Her dilemma was whether or not to keep Rollandario at her side all the way to Tsaonin. Deciding to deal with that issue once they are at the exit portal, she uncloaked her thoughts.

'I have changed my mind. You can go through the portal with me. Trusting you? That will take time. I don't easily trust others. On Earth, the planet I come from, I only trust Grandma and Aedric. Come. Let's go.'

Myrine stepped onto the path. She looked back. Rollandario was still sitting on the fallen tree trunk, drawing circles in the dirt with the toes of his boots. A rush of irritation rose in her. She clamped her teeth and walked back to Rollandario.

'If you want to go with me, we leave now.'

'The night is long and we will be at the portal hours before it opens.'

'Or we will find problems along the way that could delay us. If we get there hours before the portal opens, we can take turns to rest.'

She turned and limp-walked back to the footpath. This time, Rollandario followed her and fell into step next to her. Careful not to over-stress her ankle, Myrine kept to a slow, steady pace. They had little to say to each other. In the surrounding woods, intermittent night sounds came alive.

In telepathic conversation, Rollandario told her what the different night sounds meant or which animal it belonged to. Myrine found it curious that there was not any dangerous sort of animal around. But then again, it was probably because there was neither fosterling nor Betwoniumite around.

'That is not totally correct. There are dangerous animals, but they are controlled by either mother or Dr Dreckonium. So far, none of the controlled animals have been sent after us.'

'How long before they realise we have escaped?'

'I don't know. But it will take longer now that Surneal's nearly here. Father can only use half of his troops to search for us. And there are plenty of hiding places inside the castle walls and castle they would have to check.'

'Once they find Faeyet, though, it would change. She would tell them we left the castle.'

'We left her gagged and bound at the top of the stairs, remember? They will search the storeroom.'

'Won't they go up the stairs?'

'No. It leads to the perimeter wall where there are troops on the outside guarding the wall.'

Myrine was not so sure that Faeyet would not be found. She tested her ankle. It felt stronger. It was time to step up to a faster pace. Rollandario, as before, followed alongside her, allowing her to set the pace. They reached a fork in the path and Myrine stopped.

'Which way?'

'The left hand path. To the right, it goes to the riverbank and only Fanisius can walk across the quicksand covering it, without sinking.'

The memory of her encounter the night before with the quicksand flashed to the fore. Her body broke out in goosebumps. She shivered. Oblivious to her reaction, Rollandario carried on communicating in telepathy. She missed half of it.

'We will come out on the cliff opposite the one where you were taken captive yesterday. It is lower. We can dive into the plunge basin and wait on the rock platform behind the waterfall for the portal to open.'

'It sounds like you have done this before?'

'No. It was what I planned to do before you arrived. Let me show you.'

She watched as Rollandario pulled his sketch pad from the satchel he carried with him. Myrine unclipped her MagLite from her belt and switched it on. The detailed drawings were beautiful. Heads together, he explained to Myrine, his finger tracing the arrowed path he had drawn.

If the details were correct, it was a good plan.

'The details are correct. You will see when we get there. I have been working on this for the past year. I need to get away from Betwonium before I turn twenty-one.'

'What happens when you turn twenty-one?'

'My parents will take me to Dr Dreckonium's surgery for him to change me into a fully-fledged Betwoniumite, removing every trace of my human DNA.'

'Is it possible to do that?'

'Maybe. I don't know. I am the only halfling in Betwonium. What I do know is that I do not want to be changed into a Betwoniumite, nor do I want to be his experiment.'

Myrine Goes Through the Quantum Door | 171

She gave back his sketchpad and waited for him to put it in his satchel, all the while looking around. To the right, where the right-hand path led, a slight disturbance shimmered in the air. Her left-hand index finger to her lips, she grabbed Rollandario's left arm with her right hand. A low static buzz crackled.

'What is that buzzing sound?'

'It is coming from the Brunkai's charging nest.'

'Where is Fanisius when they are charging?'

'With them in the charging nest, resting.'

'And if I understand it correctly, they start patrolling at sunrise as part of keeping the portal inaccessible?'

'Can they be split into different groups?'

'No.'

'So only Fanisius controls them?'

'My mother probably could, but she is too busy. When I helped her to design them…'

'Wait a minute. You helped to design them?'

'Yes. But only the drawings of what they should look like. Then mother and Dr Dreckonium put together the parts and mother created Fanisius from a tree of black magic knowledge, putting him in charge as their keeper.'

This new load of information had Myrine's head spinning. She wondered if there was a way that Fanisius and the Brunkai could be disabled.

'There is. But it is dangerous. We need the seeds from the Tree of Eternal Sleep's fruit.'

'Why?'

'It is the only way to put Fanisius into an eternal sleep and, without his control, the Brunkai would stay in their nests.'

'Where is that tree?'

'It is extremely dangerous. One of us could fall prey to the Tree of Eternal Sleep.'

'How far are we from the exit portal?'

'Another half hour's walk at the pace we have been keeping.'

'And how far back to the Tree of Eternal Sleep?'

'Back the way we came, off the path and deeper into the forest. About twenty minutes.'

Myrine checked the time on her quantum watch. A plan formed. There was more than enough time to go back and get the seeds. Disable Fanisium and the Brunkai and get to the portal before sunrise.

'I think we should go and get the seeds and disable Fanisius and the Brunkai. That way, we will have one less enemy trying to stop us from going through the exit portal.'

After a heated debate, Myrine turned. She ducked around Rollandario, who tried to stop her and stomped back along the path to where he indicated the Tree of Eternal Sleep was located. Irate at Rollandario, trying to stop her again, she waited until his hand landed on her shoulder.

She pushed him simultaneously forward and to the side, pulled him towards her, and drew him onto her hip. She followed it up, sweeping his legs from under him and hung onto his one arm, twisting it as he fell on the ground.

'Ouch. Please. It is too dangerous. We do not have a rope harness…'

'We will deal with how to get the fruit when we get to the Tree of Eternal Sleep. Either you come with me or you can take your yellow-bellied self to the exit portal and wait for me.'

'I will go with you. Now let me up.'

Whilst walking back to where the Tree of Eternal Sleep was located, Myrine listened attentively as Rollandario launched into an explanation of how the fruit was picked by a two-man team. A picker wearing a rope harness. His team member, holding onto a rope fastened to the harness, would drag the picker to safety in the event that the picker accidentally touched the seeds.

They reached the tree. At the bottom of its trunk, there were bodies in various stages of decay. Another dangled from a branch, still in its harness. The putrid stench of death clogged the air. Oddly, neither a single fly nor other insect were buzzing around the bodies.

'Should there not have been flies or something similar that you have on Betwonium, eating away at those corpses?'

'There are, but they would die if they did. I think they know to stay clear of the poisoned corpses.'

Rollandario's words reminded Myrine once again that she was on an unknown, dangerous planet. She took the ointment Rollandario held out to her after he rubbed some on in the groove between his nose and his upper lip. Following his lead, she did the same. Inhaling the strong menthol smell brought her some relief from the stench.

Handing the ointment back to Rollandario, Myrine cloaked her thoughts. She did not want to take off her magical backpack in front of Rollandario, nor did she want him to read about it in her mind. But she would need to take off the backpack sooner or later, as there was nothing in the vicinity which they could use to pick a fruit or two from the tree. The branches were too high to reach. From what Rollandario shared with her, she knew it would be best to have a pair of lead-lined gloves to prevent direct contact with the fruit, which could burst open and expose one to its lethal seeds. *Maybe if they had a long-handled fruit picker with a basket, it could work.*

The sound of Rollandario's voice in her head interrupted her thoughts. Coming to an instant decision, she dropped the cloak covering her thoughts. She contemplated the lowest hanging branch covered in fruit. Some were over ripe and had burst open. There were, however, a few clumps that were ready to be picked.

'If we could find a long enough branch, we could knock some of the fruit off that branch.'

'Maybe, but we would need some type of basket to catch it before it hits the ground and bursts open.'

'We could use some of your rags. I still have the one from my ankle as well. Why don't you go that way and I will go this way and look for a long branch? There must be one out here somewhere.'

Myrine cloaked her thoughts, hustled in the direction she indicated she would search, and slipped behind a tree trunk. Peeking around it, she watched Rollandario's back as he walked in the opposite direction. She waited until he disappeared.

Knowing she could not keep the cloak over her thoughts for too long without alerting Rollandario, Myrine set to work. She took off her hoodie and sleeveless vest. Shrugged off her magic backpack. Set it down on the ground. Closing her eyes, she pictured a branch, fashioned similar to a fruit picking pole, but without the basket, and stuck her hand in her backpack.

Myrine opened her eyes. Pulled her hand out of her backpack, extracting a long thickish tree branch. The one end forked. She laid it on the ground. Zipped closed her backpack and shouldered it. Then donned her sleeveless vest, covering it. Uncloaking her thoughts, she shrugged on her hoodie, picked up the branch and dragged it back to the Tree of Eternal Sleep.

Rollandario had got her telepathic message and was waiting for her. She gave him the branch.

'That was lucky. Pity the forked end is not smaller.'

'The rags you have can be tied to it around it to form a basket.'

Myrine held the branch whilst Rollandario tied two rags around the forked end. She checked it over after Rollandario was done. If they were careful, the fruit would fall and stay in the rags. She looked up at the fruit, wondering how much they would need. Fanisius was large and, as she now knew, created from a black magic tree.

'How many fruits do you think we would need?'

'To be safe at least four.'

'I hate the number four. Make it five.'

'Why do you hate the number four?'

'In Cantonese it sounds the same as the word used for death and many Chinese believe number four is bad, josh.'

'You are not Cantonese, are you?'

A picture of herself with slanted green eyes popped into her head and Myrine nearly laughed at the absurdity of it.

'No, but I have studied the culture and their belief system. I agree with a lot of their cultural beliefs. They are in tune with the flow of energies and a lot of what they believe in makes sense.'

'Oh.'

As Rollandario topped Myrine's one meter six hundred and seventy centimeters by a good two hundred centimeters, they decided Myrine should hold the back end of the pole to stabilise it. Rollandario would hold and lift the middle of the branch and steer the forked end with the makeshift basket to the fruit hanging from the Tree of Eternal sleep's lowest branch. After a few attempts, Myrine called for a break.

Her tired arm muscles tremored and threatened to destabilise Rollandario's hold.

'I think if you balance the middle of the branch on your shoulder instead of holding it up with your hands, I would be able to hold it steadier at the back end on my shoulder.'

'But I need to reach the fruit.'

'First steer it until it is positioned under the fruit, then lift it up and tap the fruit.'

They tried again. Their movements were steadier. From the back Myrine directed Rollandario towards a clump of over four fruits bunched together. They stopped and steadied the basket under the fruit.

'Now lift. I will hold the back steady.'

After a light tap against the branch, the bunch of fruit fell into the makeshift basket, filling it to the brim.

'I am going to lower the branch back onto my shoulder and step backwards. Be ready.'

Three steps backwards, Rollandario stumbled over a stone. Myrine tightened her grip on the back end of the branch, but it turned in her hands. The makeshift basket tilted. One of the fruits rolled out, missing Rollandario by centimeters and burst open on the ground. Grunting, Myrine righted the branch. She ignored the burn in her palms and held on for dear life. In front of her, Rollandario settled the branch on his shoulder.

'Are you ready for me to step further back?'

Myrine took a deep breath in through her nose and blew it out through her mouth.

'Yes.'

They laid the branch on the ground, careful not to tilt the remaining fruit out of the basket. Taking her Spyderco knife from her utility belt, Myrine put her right thumb into the thumbhole and flicked it open. With its blade made of the second hardest steel on Earth, it was easy to saw through the branch where it narrowed. She sat back. The fork holding the makeshift basket with a ruler length handle would be much easier for either one of them to carry. Looking up, she caught a glitter of envy crossing Rollandario's face as he eyed the knife.

'I never thanked you for giving me back my utility belt. The tools I carry in it come in handy.'

'After what I just saw, I am glad I did.'

'You want to carry the basket with the fruit, or do you want me to carry it?'

'Before we go to the Brunkai's charging nest, let's work out a plan of action. Fanisius is a very light sleeper and much more agile than he looks.'

Myrine did her best to envision the layout of the charging nest as Rollandario described it. Rollandario, realising her dilemma, called up photographic pictures in his mind. It made it clearer. Having a better understanding of the layout, she suggested which of her supernatural powers she could use to assist with disabling the Brunkai and Fanisius.

Accepting Rollandario's offer to carry the makeshift basket, they set off for Fanisius and the Brunkai in their charging nest.

CHAPTER 18

Myrine and Rollandario were back at the fork in the path. Despite having made it with no further incident, a feeling of impending doom niggled at the back of Myrine's mind. Rollandario, giving off his own waves of nervous energy, was no help to her. Looking at her Quantum watch, she was satisfied that they had enough time to stop and put their heads together. She tapped Rollandario, who had stepped onto the right-hand path, on his back.

'We have not really discussed how to go about disabling Fanisius and the Brunkai. Let's just slow down. We need to have a proper plan.'

'I suppose you are right. A proper plan.'

Making sure they had time to stop and formulate a plan, Myrine, for the second time, checked the time on her Quantum watch. The feeling that time was ticking faster was a figment of her imagination. There were seven hours left until sunrise, and it was Betwonium hours. She had yet to get the hang of how long a Betwonium hour is in relation to Earth hours.

She wondered what would happen if her Quantum watch was wrong. She clicked her tongue, shook her head inwardly at herself. She should trust the watch Grandma gave her instead of giving in to her own insecurities. At least it was not a person who could betray you. She scanned up and down the empty path.

'We should get off the path, in case someone comes along.'

'Here is a gap we can fit through and I don't see any dangerous plants that could attack us. Follow me.'

Following Rollandario through the gap, a low-hanging branch sprung back in his wake. Myrine ducked and stepped sideways. Her ponytail touched the branch of a thorn bush and became instantly ensnared. Hands behind her head, sweating a river, she worked most of her ponytail free. The last twig snapped, and the tip remained embedded in her ponytail. A few strands of her hair stayed wrapped around one thorny branch.

Sucking the blood from one of her fingers where a thorn had stung her. She pinched her finger. A shiver of goosebumps jostled in her shoulders. She took her finger out of her mouth and rubbed it against the front of her shirt.

Something in it hooked on her shirt, sending a burning pain through her finger. She unclipped her MagLite from her utility belt. Lowering herself on one knee, she switched her night sight to normal, switched on the MagLite and inspected her finger. A piece of thorn had stayed behind in the flesh of her finger pad. She pinched it again and worked the thorn free. The flesh around the puckered hole had turned white. She rubbed some spit on it. It was tender to the touch, but at least there was no longer a thorn in it.

Rollandario's shadow fell over her. She looked up into his frowning face.

'You okay?'

'Had a tangle with a thorn bush after I tried to duck a branch that you let go of without warning me.'

'Sorry. Show me your finger.'

Myrine put her hand behind her back.

'It is fine. I got the thorn out.'

'Which thorn bush was it?

Swinging her MagLite over the thorny bush behind her, Myrine wordlessly showed it to Rollandario. In the torchlight she could make out purple black berries hiding amongst the emerald green leaves. What she thought was a bramble bush seemed to be a type of berry bush. Most berry bushes, being from the rose family, had vicious thorns. No wonder her finger was burning like hell fire.

'You are right. It is a Fruiticocius bush. Here, hold this and I will pick us some. They are tasty and the sour sugar in it is a good source of energy.'

She held the basket with the fruit from the Tree of Eternal Sleep whilst Rollandario filled a side pocket of his satchel crossed over his chest with berries. Her mouth watered in anticipation. Berries were her favourite fruit. *As Grandma always said. Everything for a reason. And she guessed so was her tangle with the berry bush.*

Not far from the Fruiticocius bush, they came across a small clearing. Rollandario took the basket with the Fruit from the Tree of Eternal sleep from Myrine and placed it carefully on the ground. They sat down on the leaf strewn grass. Myrine switched her MagLite to dim and set it down on its torch handle in front of them.

Myrine evenly divided the fruit Rollandario had put down on a large leaf he had cleaned. She waited for Rollandario to eat some of his share before she carefully picked up the smallest one and bit down on it. A burst of sweet and sour exploded in her mouth. Savouring the flavour, she proceeded to eat them one by one. She chewed and swallowed her last one.

Taking out her water bottle, she dribbled a bit on her hands before passing it to Rollandario. She wiped her hands on her pants, took the water bottle from Rollandario, and secured it in its holder on the side of her magical backpack. Facing him, she saw he had retrieved a sketch pad and pencil from his satchel.

'I will quickly draw a rough layout of the charging nest.'

Myrine shuffled closer until she was right next to Rollandario. Taking her MagLite, she shone it on his sketch pad, which he balanced on his left knee. He flipped to a blank page and started drawing. An obstinate gust of wind ruffled the pages of his sketch pad and flicked one page over the one he was drawing on. Myrine flipped it back. Rollandario folded the top pages under the sketch pad, re-settled it on his knee and finished the rough sketch.

Whilst Rollandario was sketching, Myrine flipped her ponytail forward. Taking care not to touch the thorns, she worked the tip of the branch knotted in her hair, free. She re-tied her ponytail and looked at the completed sketch.

'What are those words?'

'Sorry. Habit. I wrote in Betwoniumite.'

'Wait. Don't rewrite it. I assume those words indicate Brunkai, as there is only one different word, that must be Fanisius.'

'Yes. I will write the rest of my notes in English.'

Myrine still battled to make out the words written by Rollandario in a spidery crawl. On top of it, the sketch was different to the picture recollection he called up in his mind and which she looked at earlier. She could not blame him. The mind was a tricky thing. It often remembers things different from reality.

She remembered her discussion with Grandma and her solicitor one night during dinner, when she was sixteen. She now understood what he meant when he said if you have a court case about an accident, call only your best witness and not all of them. They will all paint a different picture of the accident scene.

Realising her predicament, Rollandario took her through the sketch, pointing out the Brunkai charge pods they laid in, Fanisius' usual spot he rested overnight, and the tree hollow in which the controls were stored. Myrine could only hope that the sketch was as close as could be to the real layout of the charging nest.

'Is there a way that we could go around the charging nest? With Fanisius near the back and him being our main target, it might be better if we approach him from behind. The distance from the entrance into the charging nest to where he rests may be a problem. And as you said, he can move fast.'

'I am not sure if we would be able to get in at the back. There are clusters of bamboo around the whole nest and at the back it might be thicker.'

'Maybe we could check it out when we get there. There should be enough time if we hurry along now.'

Myrine switched off her MagLite and, using her night vision, she moved back to the path with Rollandario following in her wake. This time giving the berry bush a wide berth. She stepped through the opening onto the edge of the path. Bright lantern lights glared. Before she could lower her night vision, she was blinded.

Disoriented, she stopped dead in her tracks and closed her eyes. A bump from behind sent her flying. An involuntary squeal escaped her as she landed on all fours in the middle of the path. Neon white stars burst behind her closed eyelids. Disabling her night vision, she opened her eyes. Her vision fuzzy, she noticed something similar to Faeyet's fosterling shape moving in the distance.

Myrine shuffled back into the bush on her hands and knees, pushing against Rollandario's shins, forcing him backwards.

'Hey. What are you doing?'

'The lanterns are on. I think I saw Faeyet.'

'Faeyet?'

'In her fosterling form.'

'There are wild fosterlings around. They are mainly harmless. They come out at night to scrounge for food.'

'And you did not think to mention that to me earlier?'

'With all the activity around Surneal's arrival, I thought they would all stay in hiding before he ordered them to be captured.'

'That does not explain why the lanterns are now on. They were off before we moved off the path.'

Keeping to the shadows of the bushes on the side of the path, they stalked towards the charging nest. The closer they got, the clearer the low buzz from the nest became. They reached the bamboo circle fence within which the nest lay. A low green light shone through the opening to the nest.

'Can Fanisius pick up on our telepathic communication?'

'No. But he is very sensitive to movement.'

One foot in front of the other, then waiting a beat before taking another step, the two of them crept up to the bamboo fence and stopped to the right of the opening. Myrine turned her head, laying an ear against the bamboo fence.

'I can hear voices.'

Rollandario mimicked her and laid his ear against the bamboo fence.

'Yes. There is someone with Fanisius.'

They both leaned their ears against the bamboo fence. Footsteps sounded, then stopped. A voice sounded closer to the opening. Myrine recognised Beak-nose's voice.

'I last saw Grondacius when he went off into the woods next to the kitchen gardens in search of the Earthling. Surneal arrived an hour ago and is in conference with Ruler Beldarius and that black witch Eugenia.'

'Be careful how you refer to Eugenia. Surneal holds her in high regard. And she is very powerful. Your worry about Grondacius may be unfounded. Unlike you, he has been trained to walk safely through those woods.'

'He missed the kneeling ceremony upon our Dark Lord of the Universe's arrival. That is very unlike him. After going into those woods, he has not been seen or heard of. Everyone who was tasked with the search for the Earthling in the castle grounds and the castle had been accounted for and attended the ceremony.'

'That is a bit worrying.'

'I think that Earthling is no longer inside the castle walls.'

'What makes you think that?'

'Our Ruler Beldarius' son has also gone missing. Beldarius and Eugenia were both fuming at his absence at the kneeling ceremony. Rollandario thinks no one knows, but we all know that he wants to change allegiance to the Light Forces. I have a feeling he is with the Earthling.'

Myrine could feel Rollandario stiffen next to her. She gave his hand a squeeze.

'Don't let that bother you. The information Beak-nose is relaying to Fanisius can help us.'

'Beak-nose. How apt.'

Myrine felt Rollandario's body shaking and in response, a nervous giggle threatened to escape from her. She dropped her forehead on her knees and quickly stifled it before it broke free. She bit down on her lower lip, put her left hand's fingers under her nose, and laid her right ear against the bamboo fence.

'The halfling won't be much help to the Earthling. The question though is, why are you out here searching, besides your feeling that the Earthling is no longer within the castle walls? Which, by the way, you have no proof of?'

Myrine could feel Rollandario getting ready to stand up. She gripped his hand and pulled him back down. They missed a part of the ongoing conversation between Fanisius and Beak-nose.

'There has been an offer of promotion from our Ruler, Beldarius, to the one who brings him the Earthling. I intend to find her before Faeyet does.'

'You would have quite the task of beating Faeyet to it. Besides her natural fosterling tracking abilities, she is a highly trained fosterling and Eugenia's pet.'

'More like Beldarius' pet.'

'What do you mean?'

'Grondacius and I saw her with Beldarius. She has no allegiance to anyone but herself. I would not be surprised if she betrays both Beldarius and Eugenia. Anyway, as a true full-blooded Betwoniumite, I am entitled to a promotion.'

'So. You are seeking a promotion then? And here I thought you were worried about Grondacius.'

'I am worried about him. We have been partners since we were accepted into Beldarius' army. We are like brothers.'

'I am tired and need my rest. Is there anything else?'

'There are also rumours by those who support Eugenia, of a different offer.'

'What is Eugenia's offer?'

'Freedom to Faeyet and her siblings if she brings the Earthling to her and not Beldarius. She wants to use the Earthling for her own purposes. It is well known that her relationship with Beldarius is not as it should be and that she has aspirations to join Surneal's inner circle. And now Faeyet is nowhere to be found and I am sure she is tracking down the Earthling.'

'Aaah. I see. Those offers do not extend to me and my Brunkai. Not that I mind. I am happy with my power as the controller of my Brunkai. I now have to rest so I can see to my duties when the sun rises.'

'Blow this whistle if you hear or see the Earthling.'

'Leave before I blow you out of here. I need my rest.'

As one, both Myrine and Rollandario sank down on their haunches, deeper into the shadows at the bottom of the bamboo fence. Myrine held her breath and tried to reign in her fear of Beak-nose as he appeared in the entrance hole. Her insides shrunk as he sniffed at the air. His head turned in their direction. The fosterling Myrine saw earlier slunk through the bushes on the other side. He looked in its direction.

'Be off with you before you are served with dressings for Surneal's dinner.'

The fosterling sloped off. Beak-nose slinked away and without a sound of a footfall, disappeared up the path towards the fork where it split. It was anyone's guess which way he would go, but Myrine decided to not waste any energy on that and rather deal with Fanisius and the Brunkai. Split attention will only hamper her. One thing at a time. She made an attempt to stand up.

'Wait. Don't move yet. Give Fanisius time to settle down.'

Impatient, she removed Rollandario's hand from her shoulder, but stayed down. From inside the charging nest, Myrine could hear wood-creaking sounds. It sounded as if Fanisius was settling down on his resting stump depicted in Rollandario's sketch.

'Wait here for me. I am going to look and see if he is resting.'

Whilst Rollandario went to the entrance to the charging nest, Myrine stood up. Her left calf muscle cramped. She rubbed the rock-hard tennis ball sized lump, but it refused to release. She leaned against the bamboo fence. It was not as sturdy as it looked. It swayed.

'Who's there?'

'It's me. Rollandario. Father sent me.'

'Not another one to disturb my rest. What do you want, boy?'

'We are searching for the Earthling and I wondered if she may have come this way and perhaps you have seen her.'

'And Tachyglosius has just left. He came looking for you. Is the Earthling with you?'

'No. Why would she be?'

'Because you want to be a Light Force member and maybe you hope to travel with her to Tsaonin.'

'That would be impossible. Father would never agree to let me go. I am scheduled for my full inauguration as a member of the Dark Forces with Dr Dreckonium.'

'I am not so sure I can believe you. Come inside so I can see you.'

Myrine picked up the forked basket holder with the fruit from the Tree of Eternal Sleep, which Rollandario had left outside the entrance to the charging nest. She looked at the bamboo encircling the charging nest. It was much too dense to get through. It would most probably be the same at the back.

With a magical spell, she invoked a cloak of invisibility, picked up the basket and stepped into the entryway. The floor of the charging nest was layered with empty nut shells. Ahead of her, Rollandario took a step. The empty nut shells crackle-crunched.

'Go slow. I am behind you and I need to time my steps with yours for it to sound like one.'

'He will see you.'

'He won't. I am invisible.'

She grinned as Rollandario glanced over his shoulder. His searching eyes swiped right over her.

'I can't see you.'

'That's the idea.'

'What are you waiting for, boy? I said come closer.'

'I thought I heard something outside. Give me a moment.'

'I said come closer.'

'I cannot go too close to him. He will sweep me into an entanglement of branches.'

'He cannot hear me if I step in time with you. Why would he entangle you?'

'Are you speaking to someone?'

'No. I was just looking around to see if it was just you, me and the Brunkai.'

'Of course it is only you, me and the Brunkai. Now, are you going to step closer or do I have to fetch you?'

Before Myrine's eyes, Fanisius' branch arms thinned, elongated, and whooshed towards Rollandario, who took a nimble step sideways. Myrine's invisibility cloak fluttered open. She looked down. Her boots, the front of her pants and the basket with the fruit from the Tree of Eternal Sleep had become visible.

CHAPTER 19

Myrine looked towards her left where Rollandario stood, rooted to the spot. Movement in front of her. She swung her gaze to Fanisius. He had retracted his branch arms to his trunk. His eyelids at half-mast over his bloodshot eyes. His twig fingers twitched, drumming against the sides of his trunk. A low thrum emanated from inside Fanisius' trunk. The Brunkai's buzz heightened. Butterflies performed a crazy ballet in Myrine's stomach. She was sure he would not see her if she moved her still cloaked arm and flick her cloak shut.

'Don't do it. You are too close to him. I told you he is very sensitive to movement!'

'No need to shout in my head. I can hear you perfectly well if you speak in normal tones. What is your plan, then? I cannot keep this cloak up for much longer. It takes too much energy.'

'I am going to try to get him to open his mouth. The opening will be large enough for the basket to fit into it. Follow in my steps. Like before.'

Myrine kept her eyes on Fanisius. Rollandario moved. Fanisius' eyes shot open. A tree root, the size of an adult boa constrictor, snaked from under his trunk. Lightning fast, it encircled Rollandario's waist, trapping his arms to his sides, and whipped him forward.

She inwardly cringed as Rollandario's head cracked against Fanisius' trunk. Helpless, she could only look on. The root let go of Rollandario's waist and slithered back under Fanisius' trunk.

Rollandario fell backwards, landing hard on his butt at Fanisius' splayed feet. Empty nut shells flew everywhere. Rollandario curled himself into a foetal ball. Raw fear's sharp fingernails raked through Myrine.

She wanted to rush to Rollandario's side, but knew she dared not move unless she had a plan. She never suspected Fanisius, whom she only ever saw sway-walk, could move that fast. Her energy level was far too low for her to use more of her supernatural powers. She was sorrier than ever before for refusing to perfect her supernatural powers when she had the chance. There was nothing she could do about it now. No use crying over spilt milk, as Grandma would have said.

Rollandario's groan brought her back to the present. His body uncurled. He rolled away from Fanisius' feet and sat up, facing her. There was a goose egg-sized lump on his forehead.

'Are you okay?'

'I have been better.'

'This is not the time for jokes, Rollandario. The plan we had will not work. What are we going to do?'

Before Rollandario could answer her, Fanisius leaned over and grabbed him by the shoulders. Turned him around and pulled him onto his feet. Her head reeled at the speed with which Fanisius had once again moved. She found it next to impossible to relate it to the gnarled stump of a tree man. Swaying limbs, too many toes, too many fingers. She had grossly misjudged him.

Maybe there was still a chance for Rollandario to get Fanisius to open his mouth wide. She sent a telepathic message to Rollandario and readied herself to dash forward at a moment's notice. She would have to drop her invisible cloak if she was going to teleport herself forward fast. Hopefully, despite everything not going according to plan, she would be able to get the timing right. A light sweat broke out on her forehead. In her gut, she knew they were going to get one chance and one chance only.

'You need to get him to open his mouth wide as soon as possible. I am going to drop my invisible cloak before it uses all my energy. I need to save some energy to teleport to your side.'

'He has always threatened to swallow me and make me sit inside his hollow trunk stomach when I was a little boy, and when I angered him. I will do my best. Oh. And you are right. We probably will get one chance only.'

'Make sure he keeps his eyes on you or we will be done for.'

At the same time, Myrine felt her energy waver and dropped the cloak. Her energy stabilised within seconds and started to replenish itself. It felt as if it happened quicker every time she exercised one of her supernatural powers. Hopefully Fanisius remained intent on Rollandario and would not see her.

She turned her concentration back to the conversation between Rollandario and Fanisius. At first, it seemed to go round and round in circles. Then she realised Rollandario's parrying word dance with Fanisius was probably done to give her time to regain her normal energy levels.

She looked at Fanisius. Spittle had gathered in the corners of his jagged edged mouth. It sprayed every time he spoke. Rollandario's show of wiping his face every time before answering Fanisius and it seemed to irritate Fanisius to the extreme. His mouth worked. His sentences became shorter. The words spat out in an ever-increasing staccato tempo.

'I am sure you were talking to someone. Who are you talking to? Where is the Earthling?'

'I am not talking to anyone but you, Fanisius. Do you perhaps see anyone else around I could talk to? The Brunkai, lying at rest in their charging pods, are incapable of speech.'

'You should know better than to cheek me, boy. You know exactly who I am talking about. Don't play dumb. Are you with the Earthling?'

'Does it look like it? You think I am carrying her in my satchel? Hiding her?'

Myrine saw the bark on Fanisius' trunk bristling as Rollandario made a show of opening his satchel and looking inside it.

'Enough! I will swallow you and you can spend some time in the darkness of my trunk and think about telling me the truth.'

Fanisius swiped the open satchel from Rollandario's hands, sending its contents flying. He grabbed at Rollandario, catching him by the arm as Rollandario ducked. He lifted Rollandario off the ground. Stunned, Myrine stared at the huge opening that appeared where Fanisius' mouth was.

'Do it now or I will end up with the basket in his trunk.'

'Dragonscats. Move your head out of the way.'

Myrine catapulted forward on a surge of adrenalin. With both hands, she shoved the basket into Fanisius' open mouth and tilted it. She heard a plop as one fruit dropped out of the basket down Fanisius' throat. She hung onto the handle and tried to tilt the basket, but Fanisius had clamped his jaws on the forked frame. She pushed with all her might. The basket did not budge. She could see the fury in Fanisius' eyes.

The one fruit that dropped in his trunk seemed to be too little to render him manageable. It was as if Fanisius read her mind and he started twisting his trunk from side to side. Slowly at first, she kept up. Then he started to lift his mouth up at the end of every swing, and down on the return swing. Myrine's arms started to tremble.

The swinging motion stopped and Myrine thought the one fruit that had dropped into his trunk had started to work. But then Fanisius started moving his head up and down. Lifting her and trying to slam her to the ground. Her palms burning, she hung onto the handle, willing herself to hold on.

The basket had come halfway out of Fanisius' mouth, when she felt Rollandario's one hand closing over hers. Fanisius tried to raise his head, but Rollandario's added weight made it impossible. With his other hand, Rollandario thumped the back of the handle. Three quarters of the forked end holding the basket in the front inched into Fanisius' mouth.

One of the rags of the homemade basket tore. As one, Myrine and Rollandario tipped the basket into Fanisius' mouth. All the fruit dropped into Fanisius' trunk. Foam bubbled in his mouth. His trunk shuddered. His eyes lost focus. His body began to collapse. An ominous crack came from the midsection of the trunk. Myrine jumped back. Rollandario slipped as he tried to move away.

Myrine made a grab at Rollandario. Before she could drag him to safety, one of Fanisius' branch arms slammed into his chest. He stumbled backwards. Stepped on Myrine's previously injured ankle and it gave way with a twinge. They tumbled to the ground in a heap of limbs.

Adrenaline coursed through Myrine's veins. She pushed Rollandario off her. Jumped to her feet and looked at Fanisius. The spasming fingers of Fanisius' left twig hand were on the ground next to his folded over trunk. It tried to reach them.

'Move back. Move back.'

Ignoring the twinge in her ankle, Myrine gripped Rollandario under his arms and heaved him backwards. Fanisius' twitching hand landed with a thump where Rollandario's feet were moments before and crunched a handful of empty nutshells. Retreating, Myrine held onto Rollandario's right arm and pulled him with her. She dared not take her eyes off the spasming fingers.

A groan pregnant with frustration issued from Fanisius. Eventually, his fingers stopped twitching. Everything stilled. Even the buzz from the Brunkai seemed to have lowered in intensity.

'That was close. Thank you for pulling me away.'

'It seems the Fruit from the Tree of Eternal Sleep has finally put him to sleep.'

'From his reaction, it seems to affect him differently than those who died at the tree. I think because he was created from a black magic tree, he may sleep for a while.'

'My gut says you are right. He will wake up at some stage. One cannot fight black magic with black magic. We should take the remote control as originally planned and destroy it. That way, if he wakes up, he cannot send the Brunkai to the exit portal at sunrise.'

The hollow where Fanisius kept the Brunkai's control at night in a charging pod was now hidden behind his sleeping mass. Favouring her twinging ankle, Myrine limped to the left, stretched her neck forward and tried to locate the tree hollow that held the Brunkai's control.

'Why are you limping again?'

'When you stumbled into me, you stood on my foot.'

'Sorry.'

'I know you did not mean to. Let's just get on with removing the Brunkai's control. It looks like we have to get behind Fanisius' body. His body is covering it.'

'Wait. Let me check if he is fully asleep.'

Taking the weight off her injured ankle, Myrine stood on high alert and watched as Rollandario crept towards Fanisius. He knocked Fanisius' twig hand with the tip of his boot.

'He is not moving. I am sure he is in a deep sleep. Let me get the controls so we can get out of here.'

'Be careful.'

'His trunk is half covering the hollow. Maybe I can get to it if I can push my arm through the gap that is left.

Myrine took her Spyderco knife from her utility belt. Thumbed it open and held it at the ready. The hum from the Brunkai took on a different cadence. Myrine looked around at them. They had started to vibrate in their pods, rattling the tree branches in which their pods lay. She wondered if they were sending a message out to Eugenia.

A snore rumbled. Her eyes zipped back to Fanisius. His mouth was slightly open. Green, red speckled drool ran from the corner of his mouth. A drop fell from his chin. It scorched the empty nut shells lying around his trunk.

'My hand is too big. Could you come and try? Your hands are smaller.'

Myrine noted that when Rollandario retracted his hand from behind Fanisius' trunk, the Brunkai's hum returned to their normal buzz. She limped to Rollandario and followed his gestures as he explained where in the hollow the Brunkai control was. She closed her Spyderco knife and clipped it back on her utility belt. She looked down at her feet and wondered whether her injured ankle would hold.

'Here. I will hold you steady.'

With Rollandario's hands on her waist, she leaned forward, craning her neck, and spotted the hollow. Inside it was something black. Relaying a description of what she saw to Rollandario, he confirmed that it was the control.

Myrine had to lean forward. Her fingertips touched the edge of the hollow. She put her right hand on Fanisius' trunk, angling further forward. Her left hand touched the control. A faint beat pulsed under her right hand. She waited for a beat. Confident that Fanisius was still sleeping, she withdrew the control. The Brunkai's buzz verged on the note of hysteria. Under her right hand, Fanisius' trunk shivered.

Myrine teased the control with her fingers into the palm of her hand. She closed her hand and ripped the control out of the hollow. The Brunkai let out keening wails. Fanisius' trunk rippled with shudders. She let go of his trunk. Fanisius' eyelids moved. She swung her left hand, holding the control sideways.

'Take the control. He is waking up.'

Myrine hobble skipped after Rollandario to the bamboo entry. Behind her, she heard an angry grunt and looked over her shoulder. Fanisius' body was rocking from side to side. The floor of the enclosure rippled. Empty nut shells rattled. She stepped into the doorway of the entry. Her feet suddenly refused to move.

'I can't move my feet.'

Rollandario turned back, grabbed her, and dragged her out. Behind her, tree roots criss-crossed, closing off the entry.

'Here, hold the control and get on my back.'

Seventy meters away from the Brunkai and Fanisius' bamboo enclosure, Rollandario set Myrine down. She slid off his back. She became aware of a pulsing sensation in the palm of her hand holding the control. Looking at it, she noticed a pulsing green light. She turned to where the bamboo enclosure lay behind them. Green circles of light pulsed above it. She looked back at the control.

'I think it is sending out signals to the Brunkai and Fanisius. See. This green light is pulsing. Now look at the Brunkai nest.'

'Give it here. I will disable it.'

'Do you know how?'

'No. I am going to open it and break the fine wires of the circuit board inside. That should work. Could you shine the light of your torch on it, please?'

Myrine watched as Rollandario turned over the control in his hand, moved a slide button from close to open and removed the top of the control. Inside it there were strands of tiny herringboned silver wires. The middle formed a thick ridge from which the wires spread, connecting to the side. Rollandario prodded the herringboned mat with his right index finger. A green flame zapped his finger. He dropped it. Lopsided, it started moving, dragging the opened top half with it.

Myrine stomped on it with her uninjured foot. Her injured ankle threatened to give way. She teetered back onto both feet. Black goo oozed out of the control. Still, it moved. Pushing her aside, Rollandario jumped on it with both feet. Its shell cracked. It spun around and around in a crazed circle. A loud wail rose from the bamboo enclosure. Myrine grabbed her water bottle and poured water on it. Sparks flew and died in mid-air. The water sizzled and boiled on the silver wires. The wires blackened. A noxious smell hit her nose. She turned her head away and coughed into her elbow.

The smell wafted away on a slight breeze. Quiet descended. Not a single buzz from the Brunkai. The pulsing light circles above the bamboo enclosure had disappeared. Before she could say anything to Rollandario, an unearthly scream of rage shattered the quiet. She was sure it was Fanisius coming awake.

'I think you are right. Time to move and hide in the place by the exit portal I told you about.'

CHAPTER 20

Myrine took a few steps, testing her sore ankle. It was not too badly hurt. Rollandario gave her a suitable stick to use as a walking stick, which he had found at the side of the path. Within minutes, they were back at the fork in the path. Weariness washed over Myrine.

'It is not much further and we will be able to rest. It is about four bentums to sunrise. I will take watch the first two and you can take over from me and keep watch the last two.'

She assumed correctly that bentums must be what hours were called in Betwonium.

'How long before we reach your hiding spot?'

'Give or take, I would say five parts of a bentum if we keep up at this pace. The path from here is very narrow. I will go first.'

From past experience, Myrine knew that if she rested now, she would have a hard time getting herself going again. She lifted her head and squared her shoulders.

'Lead the way.'

The twisting and turning path had narrowed considerably. At least the low growth on the sides did not contain any thorny bushes. The trees were thinning as they proceeded further along the path. Her stomach remained drum tight with worry. A few times she thought she saw movements in the bushes, but it was merely her imagination playing tricks on her overwrought mind. Soon Myrine heard the thunder of the waterfall. The sound gave her renewed energy, and she urged Rollandario to walk faster.

They came to the end of the path and stopped, remaining under cover of the now sparse trees. Before them lay a sloping grassy bank. Myrine stepped to Rollandario's side and looked about.

'It seems clear, but you never know if someone is lurking around.'

'I thought you said no one knows about your hiding place.'

'I did, yes. But, we have to cross the grass bank to get to it, leaving us out in the open and sometimes there are some of father's guards about.'

'Oh.'

'Why don't I go first? When I stop, you run to me as fast as you can. You think you can do that with your sore ankle?'

'How far is it?'

'See where the river flows over the ridge?'

'Yes.'

'To that side of it.'

It did not seem that far and Myrine decided to up her pain threshold, keeping the twinge in her foot at bay. That way, she would be able to run without feeling any twinge. Hopefully, it won't exaggerate her injury. But if it did, she will have to deal with it afterwards. She dropped the walking stick. Then thought better of it and picked it up again. She may need it later. Taking a deep breath, she suppressed her brain's pathway to her thalamus where its pain centre was located. Immediately, the twinge in her ankle became non-existent.

'I am ready.'

'Okay. I will lift my hand when I have reached my hiding spot. Give it ten beats before you follow. And if any movement…'

'Yeah, yeah. Don't follow. I know.'

'What's up with you now?'

'I don't know how long I can suppress the pain in my ankle. So, the sooner you get going, the sooner I know whether I can follow. I need to rest my ankle so it can get better before going through the portal.'

'Be careful near the edge. The grass is wet from the waterfall's spray and it is quite slippery.'

Myrine's eyes darted back and forth over the grassy bank as Rollandario loped across it. He stopped at the cliff's ridge at the far end and, after ten beats, lifted his hand in the air. All the while waiting for him to lift his hand, Myrine walked in place. Her eyes scanning the surroundings, she counted ten beats. Finding no sign of anything untoward, she took off and sprinted to Rollandario. He caught her as she skidded to a stop on the wet grass next to him. They were very close to the edge of the cliff. Two steps and she would have tumbled over it.

The deafening thunder of the close by waterfall extinguished all other sounds. Not even her extended hearing worked. A damp cloud hung around them and soon her fringe dripped water over her face. Looking around, she failed to see any sort of hiding spot. Rollandario grinned at her.

'Let me show you.'

Myrine could not believe her eyes when Rollandario picked up a large boulder that lay against the cliff's edge. Behind it was a burrow and when she looked into it, it was big enough to lie stretched out in it.

'You can rest there whilst I keep watch. I will put the boulder back, leaving a little edge open through which you will be able to see out.'

'But if something happens to you, how will I get out?'

'You will be able to roll it away with one hand like this.'

Astonished, she looked at the boulder as Rollandario moved it with one hand.

'I did not know you had supernatural powers?'

'Not really.'

Amazed, she listened to him explaining how he used waterproof glue, mortar-mache, waterproof exterior paint and some type of glue he had fashioned from a fir tree. At the edge of the burrow, she saw the groove he said he dug and when rolled into it, the boulder remained in place. It was weatherproof and if she had to believe Rollandario, had been in place for more than a Betwonium year. Touching the boulder's rough surface, she exerted some pressure, and it moved under her hand.

'The burrow was already there. All I had to do was clean it out, make it comfortable and find a way to close it. I made the boulder in a clearing in the woods over there, hiding it in plain sight amongst the few real boulders. When it was finished, I rolled it here one night.'

'Why would you do that?'

'I was working on a plan to go through the exit portal at sunrise and find my way through the other planets to Tsaonin. I needed a hiding place no one would easily find.'

'Do you know the other planets between here and Tsaonin? Have you ever been to any of them?'

'No, but there were rumours that uprisings started against the Dark Forces on all the planets of the Universe where they are ruling.'

'So. You were hoping to find a friendly that could help you along your way?'

'Something like that. Anything would be better than staying here with this lot. Mother hates me for my Adelstein looks and makes me dye my hair black like she does with hers. Father hates me for not being the son that he wants to follow in his footsteps as the next Ruler of the Army. And then there is Dr Dreckonium, who has been instructed to change me into a Betwoniumite by removing all of my Adelstein DNA I inherited from my mother. Some of his experiments have gone disastrously wrong. Anyway, you need to rest. Get in and I will roll the boulder in front of the burrow.'

'Okay. Call me for the second watch. We both could do with some rest.'

There was a thick sleeping bag in the burrow. Myrine unfolded it and laid down, curling onto her left side and faced the opening. Despite its comfort, Myrine shifted and re-shifted on the sleeping bag. Everything felt unsettled. From the strange earthy smell of the burrow to the thunder of the waterfall. She had never been able to fall asleep easily in strange surroundings. The more she tried to get comfortable, the more she shifted and re-shifted, to no avail.

It had darkened considerably when Rollandario had rolled the boulder back in place, leaving a slight opening as discussed. Her overwrought mind became active. Jumped around on a merry-go-round of irrational thoughts about past, present and future scenarios. She blinked her dry eyes. They burnt. She closed them and rubbed her eyelids. It did not help. If anything, the burn increased. She opened them again and tried to unsee the pictures that kept popping into her mind's eye.

Turning on her back, she stretched out her legs and stared unseeing at the ceiling of the burrow. A steel headband entrapped her head, creating a dull ache in her temples. The more her body cried for sleep and rest, the wider awake her mind became. On top of it, a voice at the back of her mind nagged at her. There was something she had forgotten about. The harder she tried to remember what it was, the more elusive it became.

A shadow fell over the opening to the burrow. The boulder shifted.

'Are you okay?'

'Just an overactive mind. It always happens when I am overtired.'

'You have to try and sleep now. This is your last chance to rest before we go through the portal. I know a calming herb that grows nearby. Do you want me to get you some Valerianius root?'

'No thanks.'

'It won't harm you. The juice from the root is calming. I have often chewed on it when I was anxious. I think I will go and get some. We could take it with us.'

'Must I keep watch whilst you go and get some of it?'

'No. It grows along the edge of the woods we travelled through. I will have sight of the entire area all the time. Try to sleep. I will come wake you when it is your turn to keep watch.'

The boulder rolled back, leaving a slight enough opening for Myrine's hand to fit through. Activating her enhanced hearing, all she heard was the thunder of the waterfall.

On the spur of the moment, she slowly insinuated a block between her and Rollandario's thoughts and the telepathic communication link between them. Slowly, she blanked her mind so he would not be alerted to what she was about to do. He had to be kept under the impression she had gone to sleep. If anything happened on his watch, though, she knew he would be unable to warn her. It was worrisome, but she could not take the chance of him listening in on her conversation with Aedric.

Aedric should be on Earth by now. Maybe he was with Grandma. Myrine sent an enquiring telepathic whisper to Aedric. Surprised by the immediate response from Aedric, Myrine sat up and started babbling.

'Where are you? Are you with Grandma? Is she okay? Did they hurt her?'

'I am in the secret passage of the wall in her bedroom.'

'How did you get there? What are you doing there?'

'Calm down Myrine. Give me a chance to talk and I will tell you.'

'Is Grandma in her bedroom? How did she get there? She was in her herb cellar when I left.'

'Myrine. I said, give me a chance to talk.'

Myrine heard the note of irritation in Aedric's voice and bit her tongue.

'Sorry.'

'That's better. Let me fill you in on what happened here.'

Attentive, Myrine listened to Aedric's rendition of how he got rid of the guard that took him back to Earth. His cunning instincts amazed her. She always knew he was good, but changing into the guard's clothes and wearing his shoes to avoid detection from Inspector Teivel and the dogs was thinking way outside the box.

'But would they not have noticed that the dead body was not you?'

Her skin crawled a bit when Aedric explained he did a good job of disfiguring the guard's face. What had to be done had to be done for the sake of Aedric getting to Grandma and keeping her safe. What was apparently in Aedric's favour was the fact that the guard was the same size as him, but the shoes were a bit tight, so he had left them in the mudroom before entering the main passage into the wall.

'I know that you may feel a bit squeamish about what I have done. Remember though, they would not think twice of doing the same or worse to you, me, or Grace. You only have a value to them whilst you are in possession of the Infinity Charm. Grace's value ends the moment she tells them where it is and my life won't be worth much when they find out I cannot bring Grace out of her self-induced coma.'

Put like that, it made sense to Myrine. She then remembered the nagging thought that was bothering her earlier. The fact that she had locked away her memories of the hidden Infinity Charm in her magical backpack resurfaced when Aedric mentioned it.

'You must be careful when you lock away memories. You won't be accepted in Tsaonin if you cannot produce the Infinity Charm upon entry.'

'Eugenia was going to extract the memory of its whereabouts from me. I had to hide it.'

'Then follow what Grace and I taught you and leave a little trapdoor you can spring to bring it back when you need to access it.'

'Yes. In my panic, I have completely forgotten to do that.'

'That's okay. No harm done. You have the memory back now. Keep it safe and put the trapdoor in place now.'

Myrine put the memories of the Infinity Charm in the locked compartment at the back of her mind and fashioned a trapdoor before sealing the door to the locked compartment. Now, every time the thought of having forgotten something would come to the fore, the string would dangle and, upon pulling it, would bring back the memories. She would have to rely on her instinct to not pull the string if the Infinity Charm was in danger of being discovered by a Dark Force member.

'Done?'

'Yes. And tested like I was taught to do. It would be better to keep it locked away now that I have to travel through four more planets to get to Tsaonin after I leave Betwonium.'

Aedric made Myrine re-test the safety trapdoor to satisfy him that she had done it correctly. Satisfied, he answered Myrine's questions about her Grandma and why he was in the secret passage behind Grace's bedroom wall.

'Surneal summoned your mother to attend a meeting with him and your aunt Eugenia in Betwonium. She left a few minutes ago with your father. Serilda is inside the bedroom watching over Grace, waiting for the Doctor that is coming to take her out of her induced coma.'

When Myrine heard about the Doctor, a highly qualified Dark Force member, her anxiety levels climbed to new heights. It seemed there was someone similar to Dr Dreckonium on Earth.

'So that is why I am waiting here. When the Doctor comes, Serilda would have to leave the room. I intend to move Grace from her bedroom into a room only she and I know about. We had installed it in the event of anything like this ever happening.'

'But Dad knows about the passages behind the walls. He used to tell me how he played hide and seek with Grandma when he was little.'

'That is why Grace and I made changes to it. We suspected he started to support your mother and the Dark Forces some time ago.'

'What if he notices the changes?'

'We did it in a way that does not interfere with the old passages. Those have remained the way he would remember it. Grace made a potion we painted over the door to the new area, rendering it invisible.'

Myrine now understood the worried look she caught every now and then on Grandma's face when she thought no one would notice. Since Myrine's disastrous sixteenth birthday dinner and the court case that followed, she had started to frown more often. The merriness in her sparkling emerald eyes was not always there.

If only she she could turn the clock back to her sixteenth birthday. Knowing what she knows now, she would never have told her mother she was destined to follow in Grandma's steps and take over as the next Light Force Ruler on Earth. She was sure things would have been different then.

'Don't blame yourself, child. It was bound to happen. Grace had picked up on her first meeting with your mother that there was a hidden agenda. We think she thought your father would become the next Ruler on Earth, following in Grace's footsteps. Stephanie obviously did not do her homework. Only the eldest female in the Adelstein line could be a Ruler. Another reason why Grace never took her husband's surname and why your father carries her surname. You were the blessing Grace wished for.'

'And now mother is on her way here to Betwonium. Do you think Surneal might think she could influence me?'

'No. But your father will be with her and you do have a soft spot for him. That could come in useful for them.'

Anger at her father's allegiance with the Dark Forces flared through her. The last straw was when he stole her key and Grandma was attacked the day she left Earth. Despite her anger, she knew she would not like seeing him come to any harm. It was clear from what Aedric said and what she had experienced over the years that her father was merely a means to an end for her mother. How blind love could make one.

'One more thing. Things have changed on Betwonium and not everything in our history on it is up to date.'

'Some of our Light Force spies bringing through the information from the other planets had probably been waylaid. Is it huge changes.'

'Not that huge. But it was unexpected.'

'The front doorbell went and Serilda was leaving the room. I have to go. Keep safe and we will talk from time to time. Update me later on the changes on Betwonium.'

'Give Grandma a hug from me and please look after her.'

After talking to Aedric and being satisfied that Grandma will no longer be in immediate danger, Myrine settled down somewhat. Forgetting to remove the block she put in place between her and Rollandario's telepathic link, she fell into a deep, dreamless sleep.

CHAPTER 21

Myrine's eyelids fluttered as her mind awoke from its deep sleep. Close eyed, she reached for Bunny on the pillow next to her, to give him his usual morning hug. There was no pillow. No Bunny. Her eyes flew open. The events of the past two days came flooding back. It tilted the start of her morning upside down.

She opened her eyes. The burrow was semi-dark. *Dragonscats. It should not have been that light already?* In one motion, she rolled onto her side and sat up, bumping her head hard against the side of the burrow. Lightly palpitating the tender spot on the side of her head above her ear, she contemplated the boulder covering the burrow.

The light coming through the slight opening on the side was early morning pearl grey. Bending forward, she moved her left wrist closer to the light coming through the slight opening at the side of the boulder. Myrine squinted at her Quantum watch.

Dragonscats. It was half a bentum to sunrise. She shot off a telepathic communication to Rollandario. It bounced back. Realising the block she had put between them was still in place, she hastened to remove it.

'Hey there. Why did you not wake me up for my turn to keep watch?'

Silence. Wondering if he found out about the block and might be upset, she let the silence stretch for a few beats. She could not see how he could have been aware of the block, though. She had taken care to make sure that any telepathic communication from him would not bounce back to him, ensuring that he would think she was asleep.

'Where are you?'

Silence. She rubbed the back of her neck. It might be that he had fallen asleep, and she decided to give him a mental nudge. Myrine pictured herself giving Rollandario a thump on his shoulder.

'Hey. Rollandario. Time to wake up.'

The thump on his shoulder should have met with her, feeling it in her hand. But her fist moved through fresh air, meeting nothing solid as it should have done. A wave of unease ebbed through her. Myrine did not know whether Rollandario was sulking and, if so, how long he would take to come out of it. She tried again to connect telepathically with Rollandario.

'Where are you? Please. We need to get going now. The portal will be opening soon!'

She activated her enhanced hearing, but the sound of the thundering waterfall nearby drowned out any other sounds that there may have been. Still. Rollandario should have heard her in his mind. As far as Myrine knew, no outside sound could ever interfere with telepathic communications. And until she went to sleep, they communicated quite well right here at the waterfall. A creepy feeling trawled through her. With a shudder, she pushed aside the unwanted pictures that came along with it. She decided to come clean, in case she was mistaken, and Rollandario found out that she blocked him.

'Please answer me, Rollandario. I needed to speak to Aedric privately. I didn't mean to block you off from communicating with me any longer than I needed to speak to him. I will explain when I see you. After I spoke to him, I was so tired I fell asleep without removing the block from our telepathic communication. Please answer me.'

Silence. The only sound, her thundering heartbeat competing with the sound of the waterfall outside. A cold sweat dampened her face and neck. She got to her feet and stepped up to the slight opening. Unable to see anything but that which lay directly in front of it outside, she shifted the boulder open wide enough for her head to fit through. Straight in front of her, there was no movement on the grassed bank. Craning her neck, she peered around the boulder's edge.

Moving her head right to left and back, she detected no movement. She sniffed at the air. River water, wet grass, nothing else. Above the ridge where the waterfall dropped into the plunge basin, hung a cloud of boiling white mist.

She stepped back into the burrow. Checked her utility belt and shuffled her magical backpack into place. Picking up the walking stick she had kept with her from the night before, she sent another telepathic message to Rollandario.

'I am going to the portal now. I cannot wait any longer.'

Still no response. Myrine shrugged inwardly. He might have decided he no longer wanted to travel with her. Well, so be it. It would be foolhardy for her to wait longer.

After a final check over of the grassy bank, she rolled the boulder away from the edge of the burrow. Wide enough to fit through. After she wriggled through the opening, she rolled it back into place. Satisfied that it covered the burrow and blended in with the surroundings, she stood in front of it, doing yet another scan of the grassy bank. Despite nothing seemingly out of place, the creepy feeling remained with her. Maybe Rollandario was watching her to see what she was going to do.

'Rollandario. I am leaving now. It was nice meeting you. Thank you for everything you have done for me. I hope whichever decision you have made works out to be the best for you.'

The grass was wetter than the night before. The result of morning dew mixed in with the mist from the waterfall. Whilst her boots were sturdy enough to minimize the risk of slipping, it was still a treacherous walk along the ridge. Glad for having the walking stick, she used it to stabilise herself.

Stopping every second step to check behind and to the sides of her, it took a while before she reached the spot to the right of the waterfall where Rollandario showed her they could dive from into the plunge basin.

The shiny bald head of the sun popped up on the horizon opposite the waterfall, playing rays of light over the cascading water. A beautiful rainbow of colours she had never seen before in a rainbow on Earth had sprung to life. The ridge had lowered to thigh high at this point. She leaned forward. On the rock platform behind the curtain of water at the bottom of the waterfall, the portal had started opening. A feather of excitement mixed with a tingle of fear tickled her navel as she watched it and wondered what awaited her on the next planet.

Myrine pushed her anxiety to the back of her mind and put the walking stick against the ridge. She climbed on top of it. Below her, ten meters to the right, five meters down, she spotted a wide overhang. The rock face over there seemed dryer. She could climb down to the overhang and be closer to the plunge basin. It would be an easier dive into the plunge basin.

She judged the drop from the overhang to the plunge basin to be about three to four meters high. Not knowing how deep the plunge basin was, it would be less risky than diving from the slippery ridge where she was standing. If she dropped down from there, it would be no more than a few extra strokes to reach the rock platform. She looked at the exit portal, which was now halfway open. The sooner she got moving, the better.

On the opposite ridge, the sun was now three quarters of the way out of its night-time hidey hole. Myrine zipped her hoodie closed up to under her chin and tied the string from the cap in a double bow. She gave it a tug. Shoving stray strands of her hair into the hoodie's cap, she rechecked her utility belt, picked up the walking stick and walked towards where she had spotted the overhang.

The going was downhill, the ridge dropping lower, and she took extra care not to slip. Reaching a spot above the overhang, she leaned the walking stick against the ridge and climbed onto it. The rocks were much dryer here. She lifted the right side of her hoodie and sleeveless vest. With her left hand, she opened a zippered side pocket in her backpack and pulled out a pair of strong leather gloves and put them on.

She swung herself over the ridge, gripping onto it with an open-handed grip, supporting her weight with her feet against the rock wall beneath it. Suspended by her arms, feet against the rock-face, she composed her mind and readied her body for the climb.

Keeping a steady grip on the irregular spaced natural jug grips in the ridge, she did a praying mantis swaying sideways walk along it, moving one limb at a time. After every move, she made sure she found new grip spots for her hands and feet. Her years of free climbing with Aedric had paid off. Every so often, she glanced at the overhang to make sure she did not go past it.

She reached the overhang and paused. She would have to drop down to it, free falling a good two to three meters. Making sure she had a decent grip on the ridge with her hands, she took her boots off the side of the ridge, one at a time. Closing her eyes, she willed herself to remain unmoving and waited for her body to stop its slight swinging motion.

A rough sandpaper hand closed around her wrist. Before Myrine could react, she was hauled onto the top of the ridge and thrown onto the grassy bank on the other side. A gigantic shadow loomed over her, blocking the sun. A blur of movement. She rolled out of the way. The kick intended for her, missed. The wind following in its wake lifted her loosened hair tendrils from her forehead.

Adrenalin surged through Myrine. She rolled away, using the downhill trajectory of the grassed bank to speed up. Judging that she was far enough away to avoid being kicked, she rolled onto her back, lifted her torso from the grass, and sat up in one motion. All the spittle in her mouth dried. Her tongue became a blotting paper blob, sticking to her palate. Facing her was a fearsome apparition, straight out of her last nightmare she had on Earth.

The top part of the goanna-like creature was unclothed and covered in scales. The lower part was covered with a dirty loin cloth. Its thick tail thumped the ground as it came closer. If it was not for the eyes and the stench that came from his mouth with every hiss, she would not have recognised him for who he was. Beldarius in his true form.

Anger contorted his hideous features. He glowered at her. Her sphincter muscles contracted. Hysteria bubbled, threatening to rob her of her sanity. Her only thought was to get away. And fast. She dug in her heels, and with her hands behind her, scrambled backwards. With lightning speed, Beldarius rushed at her and grabbed her by the front of her hoodie, lifting her until they were eyeball to eyeball.

Paralysis stole through Myrine's body as she was drawn into the hypnotic rhythm of Beldarius' vertical orange pupils expanding and contracting. The brown of his eyeballs, once a slurry mud colour, had darkened to black-brown clay mud. She slowly got sucked in. Her ribcage tightened, throttling her heart. Her pulse hammered an erratic tattoo under her jawline. Her mind started to dissolve into a catatonic state. Sentences dissolved into a meaningless jumble of incomprehensible words. She struggled and failed, holding onto a single coherent thought.

Unable to break her fall, Myrine ragdoll flopped onto the grassy bank when Beldarius released her from his grip. Somewhere at the back of her mind, a shooting pain in her tailbone briefly registered. Movement at the corner of her vision. It was too hard to turn her head.

Faeyet, in her human form, appeared next to Beldarius. Beldarius returned to the form in which Myrine first met him.

'Did you bring it?'

'Yes, my Ruler.'

'Give it here.'

The eye contact with Beldarius having been broken, the hypnotic fog started lifting from Myrine's mind. Her body's mobility, however, had to yet follow her mind. Helpless, she watched him, taking a set of steel manacles from Faeyet. Myrine tried to stand up, but her jellified legs refused to obey.

She tried to struggle as Beldarius flipped her onto her stomach. Myrine's hoodie and sleeveless vest got damaged at the back by Beldarius' claw-hands as he grappled with her. The cold manacles clicked shut around her wrists. She felt a tug at the sleeveless vest and heard it tearing open. She swallowed the moan that jumped into her mouth. *Dragonscats. This was the worst thing to happen right now. The backpack was going to become visible.*

Myrine tried to roll onto her back, but Beldarius gripped her behind the neck and held her in place. She felt a tug on the shoulder straps of the backpack.

'What is this?'

'Look. It is the backpack she told us was in the cave by the incoming portal. She must have had it with her all the time.'

Instinctively, Myrine avoided the string she inserted at the trapdoor of her memories, hiding all thoughts of the Infinity Charm. Remembering her instructions about the backpack from Grandma, she knew that there was still a chance to avoid them finding out that the backpack was magical and carried an object of importance. She remained statue still.

Myrine also did not want them to know she had fully recovered from the hypnotic trance Beldarius had covered her with. It was unlikely that he would be aware, even though she struggled when he manacled her. She picked up Beldarius' scrutiny and inserted a thought in his mind, making him believe she was still under his spell and her struggle with him was merely an automatic reflex. It took all her effort not to react when Faeyet loosened the buckles of the two shoulder straps and pulled the backpack through the tears in her hoodie and sleeveless vest off her back.

Her torn hoodie's sleeves had sagged down to her elbows, and together with her manacled wrists, thwarted Myrine's chances of any quick action. She could almost hear Aedric's voice in her mind. And even if she broke out of the manacles, she was unsure whether she could defend herself against Beldarius. *'Patience Myrine. Patience.'*

Beldarius rolled her onto her back. Standing over, her backpack swinging from one of his thick claw-fingers.

'What is this?'

Another thing that was drilled into her by both Grandma and Aedric was to never offer more information than that which was asked in a question. It could alert the questioner to things he or she may never have thought of.

'A backpack.'

'Anyone with eyes on their heads can see it is a backpack. What is in it?'

Knowing that the backpack would only show what Myrine would have thought to be in it, she envisioned dried jerky, apples, and a bottle of water.

'Food and water.'

Hatred lit through her like wildfire as Faeyet stepped forward and took the backpack from Beldarius and unzipped it. Myrine froze her feelings about Faeyet, arranged her features into a non-committal expression, and waited. Coming up with a packet of dried jerky, two apples and a bottle of water, Faeyet turned the backpack upside down and shook it, before throwing it aside.

Raising her right shoulder to her mouth, Myrine covered the slow release of her pent-up breath.

'Put all that stuff back in that backpack and bring it with you. There may be something in those items. I am sure her mother or Eugenia would be able to figure it out.'

Myrine did not like the way Faeyet inspected every item closely before putting it into the backpack. She hated it even more when Faeyet put the backpack onto her own back. Faeyet looked at Myrine, a sly grin spreading over her face.

'I can read your thoughts. Your hatred means nothing to me. I like the colour of this backpack. I think it goes nicely with my dress. I will ask Eugenia to gift it to me.'

'We shall see.'

'Very, very cheeky for one standing there with her hands manacled behind her back.'

In response, Myrine blocked Faeyet from her mind, leaving herself open to receive other telepathic communication. At least she knew Faeyet could only read her thoughts when she concentrated her attention on it. Otherwise, she would have picked up about the food and water, and that would have been a fiasco of epic proportions. She needed to find a way to escape with the backpack.

'Beldarius, Beldarius!'

'Yes.'

'You know your hypnotic spell you had cast over her did not last?'

'What?'

'Oh yes. Her mind is fully back and active.'

'Well, she is manacled now. With the special glaze from Dr Dreckonium on the manacles, and her hands behind her back, I don't see her escaping this time. Not before I hand her over to Surneal's guards. They were waiting for us at the beginning of the road back to the castle.'

Myrine picked up the worried thought by Faeyet, who instantly realised that she had brought Beldarius the wrong set of manacles. At least it was one thing less to worry about when the opportunity to escape presented itself. Getting out the manacles was not the problem. It was the when. She would have to stay on high alert. As Grandma would have said, opportunity knocks only once.

With Beldarius in front of her and Faeyet at her back, they set off towards the ridge on the other side of the waterfall, where she was captured previously. Myrine purposely slowed her walk, playing for time.

'She is slowing us down on purpose.'

Beldarius turned around and glared at Myrine. She met his gaze square on.

'The grass is slippery and I cannot balance with my hands manacled behind my back.'

Before she could duck, Beldarius clubbed her on the side of her head, threw her over his shoulder. Her head kept banging against his back. She wanted to give him a vicious bite on the back, but her teeth would never break through the scales that she knew lay under his clothes.

The constant tittering in Faeyet's head about what lay ahead, Myrine was sure, was done on purpose. The stupid creature did not know that the information she gave out could come in handy. That is to say if it was true and not a bunch of lies. However, she knew that somewhere amongst all that tittering lay some truths. Myrine listened and absorbed, storing it away for future reference.

Having reached the other side of the cliff where the road started, Beldarius set Myrine down none too gently. Her eyes took in the horse-drawn wagon on which was set a windowless prison cage, fashioned from thick sturdy wooden sleepers. The corners and door were cast iron. There were two guards standing beside it. Another was holding the lead-line tethered to the horses' heads.

Behind Myrine, Beldarius and Faeyet conferred in whispers. Myrine, intent on the prison cage, trying to work out how she was going to escape, missed the content of the whispered conversation behind her.

She did not hear Faeyet coming up behind her and stumbled as she was pushed forward. One of the guards gripped her top left arm, steadied her, and marched her to a set of steps next to the wagon. Faeyet pushed past them, climbed onto the wagon, and unlocked the door of the prison cage.

Numbed to the bone, Myrine got forced up the stairs. The prison cage door shut, blocking off all light. A key crunched in the lock.

Sightless, Myrine fell to her knees as the wagon pulled off.

CHAPTER 22

Myrine sat back on her heels. She picked up the sound of someone wheezing somewhere behind her. Then her nose detected Rollandario's smell. Ensuring that the block between her thoughts and Faeyet was in place, she sent him a telepathic message. This time, when he did not answer, she thought he must be unconscious. That would be the only time he could not hear her.

Somewhat relieved at having found Rollandario, she turned her attention to the steel manacles clamped around her wrists behind her back. Until her hands were free, she could not check on him.

The wagon under the prison cart rocked in time with the clop-clop of the walking horses pulling it. Myrine struggled up, one leg at a time. Her knees slightly bent; she braced her feet a ruler's length apart. Leaning her forehead against the door of the prison cart, she gathered her thoughts. She knew she would have no choice but to spend her energy and use one of supernatural magical abilities to get rid of the manacles around her wrists.

Checking on her energy levels, she found them to be fully recovered, and she was sure it felt stronger than before. That would mean it held out longer. How much longer, she did not know. She was loath to drain too much of her energy. It was a given that she was going to need the use of more of them to get out of the prison cart and past Faeyet and the three guards.

Surneal is at the castle. Beldarius must have told him they caught and imprisoned me. With that in mind, Myrine dismissed having to deal with him as well and concentrated her thoughts on the guards and Faeyet. Ideas flitted through her mind. She dismissed them. None fit, getting rid of them, and getting to the portal.

A groan pulled her from her reverie. She turned around and nearly lost her footing as the wagon hit a dip in the road. Steadying her body, she looked in the direction of where the groan came from. Clothes rustled.

'Maihrheen?'

'Yes. It is me. I am with you in the prison wagon. Why are you slurring?'

More rustle of clothing. Another groan. To Myrine, it sounded as if he was drunk rather than concussed, and she wondered what type of potion he had been given.

'Fathherr. Argh. They hit me.'

'Oh. Don't move. I have to get rid of the manacles tying my hands behind my back before I can check on you.'

'Yesh.'

'And don't speak out loud. Only use telepathic communication. I blocked Faeyet and I don't believe the guards can follow our conversation that way.'

Another groan. Then a sigh. Myrine received his telepathic confirmation that he understood her. She repeated her request for him to remain where he was. Not that the prison cart was that big, however, she did not want to be near him when she used a supernatural power, in case her past of nearly burning Grandma's house down repeated itself.

The rocking of the wagon underneath the prison cart had settled and was moving forward at a steady pace. Not much faster than the pace Beldarius' guards walked Myrine to the castle the previous day. She judged it gave her about half a bentum to get out of the prison wagon before it would be within sight of the castle.

Once within sight of the castle, her chances of escaping would be zero if Surneal was waiting and watching for her arrival. From what Grandma had told her and what she read in Grandma's history books; his powers were legendary. Myrine knew powers were not developed enough to face him. It was time to concentrate on an escape plan.

Myrine had never used her telekinetic power for anything else but moving herself over a short distance. From her studies, she knew it could be used to move inanimate objects as well. To move the levers in the lock of the manacles from lock to unlock, may or may not take more power than moving herself across a distance. But it was the only power she was sure would work.

Myrine called up the image of the manacles as she had seen it before it was fastened around her wrist. Holding the picture in place, she gave her kinetic superpower a tap. Her energy levels were full and seemed stronger than before. Concentrating, to the exclusion of everything else, she set to work on unlocking the six levers of the manacles. The first three unlocked easily. By the fourth lever, she felt a slight waver in her energy levels. Clamping her jaw tight, she forced the fourth lever open. Immediately moving onto the fifth lever. It opened.

Determined to unlock the sixth and last lever, Myrine ignored the flutter of fatigue and intensified her concentration. The sixth lever was open halfway. Myrine's concentration slipped. The sixth lever sprung back to its fully locked position. Without letting go of the image of the partially unlocked manacles, she took a deep breath and, with a superhuman effort of will, she pressed the sixth lever. The manacles fell off her wrist with a loud thump.

'What are you doing in there? Trying to escape?'

The raucous laughter from the guards and Faeyet following pushed a red wave of anger through Myrine. She did not know yet how, but she sure as dragonscats are going to deal with all of them. She stilled as she heard Faeyet's footsteps coming to the prison cart's door. The handle of the locked door turned. Faeyet's footsteps moved away. Myrine waited a beat.

Satisfied the immediate danger of Faeyet coming inside the prison wagon had passed, Myrine took her MagLite from her utility belt. She was immensely grateful that they forgot to take it away from her this time. Switching the MagLite's beam on dim, she looked down at the manacles.

The wrist bands were open and the four interlocking pins locking it together in the middle were separated, leaving it in two separate pieces. She should keep it. It could come in handy. Careful to keep the wrist bands unlatched, she put one in each side pocket of her pants.

Keeping the MagLite's beam to the floor, Myrine walked to the corner, where she thought she had heard Rollandario's voice. When she saw his outstretched legs, she crouched down and moved the MagLite's beam upward. His rope-tied hands rested on his lap. His eyes were closed, nose crusted with blood, and a duck's egg sized swelling marred his jaw. Myrine tapped him lightly on the knee. His eyes flickered open.

'Hold your head still. I want to check your eyes. Look straight ahead and do not blink.'

Getting onto her knees, Myrine shambled forward. She lifted the flashlight's low beam and swung it from the outer edge of Rollandario's human eye inward. The pupil contracted. Doing the same with his lizard eye, the pupil narrowed to a horizontal slit.

'It seems like you don't have a concussion. I am going to untie your hands. When I am done, I want you to stand up. Hold on to the wall for support. We have very little time to get out of here.'

Rollandario nodded. Myrine laid down the MagLite between Rollandario's thighs to keep the light steady on the knotted rope. She tried to untie his hands. The knot was extremely tight. It was going to take too long. She took her Spyderco knife from her utility belt. Rollandario flinched. The MagLite started rolling and Myrine caught it as it was going to hit the floor.

She hastened to tell him she needed to cut the rope. Careful not to cut him, she sawed the knot until the strands all fell away. Closing the Spyderco knife, she put it back on her utility belt and picked up the torch. She motioned for Rollandario to get up.

Myrine stood at the ready to assist as Rollandario slowly climbed to his feet, supporting himself against the side of the prison cage. She breathed a sigh of relief as he stood erect without falling down and placed his feet apart like she did to counter the swaying of the prison wagon.

In the meantime, a plan had taken form at the back of her mind. Her energy levels after using her telekinetic supernatural power had returned to normal. Her powers were definitely growing and using some of her supernatural powers has improved the recovery of her energy levels. *Aedric was right. My energy levels will become increasingly more stable and my supernatural powers more powerful.* Hopefully, soon, her energy levels will not become depleted.

'Stay here for a moment. I want to check something.'

Myrine walked the circumference of their prison, step-measuring each wall. She calculated that if she blew out the wall directly behind the horses with a fireball and created a firewall, it would cut them off from the guards. That left only Faeyet to be dealt with. The trick would be to get off the wagon before the horses bolted. She also needed to get her backpack from Faeyet.

Rethinking her plan, Myrine walked to the back of the prison wagon, where Faeyet had sat down before she was locked up. She sniffed at a tiny crack in the wall. Faeyet was not there. *Maybe that thump I heard was when she got off the wagon.*

'I am going to remove the block between me and Faeyet. Then put a block between our thoughts.'

'Why?'

'I need to find out where Faeyet is. She is no longer sitting on the wagon and she has my backpack. We cannot go through the portal without it.'

'Okay.'

'I want you to walk to me and stand here at the back of the wagon.'

Myrine, keeping the MagLite's beam to the floor, lit a pathway for Rollandario to follow. She waited until he stood next to her. She noticed he was steadier than before as he walked along the wall to where she was. At least that was one good sign. She did not need an extra burden.

'Now I am a burden?'

'Dragonscats. I simply meant that I do not have to worry about carrying you out of here to the portal. I am putting the block between our thoughts now. It will also block Faeyet from reading your thoughts. Watch me. And follow me when I cut a hole in the front wall behind the harnessed horses. You have to be right behind me every step of the way. Can you do that?'

'But we are standing at the back wall.'

'Where we are out of harm's way if I have to blow out a wall. I am going to get Faeyet to come and unlock the door, but it may not work.'

'Oh.'

'Make sure you stay with me.'

Myrine activated the block between her and Rollandario. Hoping it would work, she changed the block on Faeyet's mind, blocking her ability to read anyone's thoughts. *That should keep her from reading Rollandario's mind.* She pinched her brow. Maybe she should play Faeyet's game and taunt her. Sure that Faeyet would be unable to resist responding, she cleared her throat.

'Hey Faeyet! What do you think will happen to you when I escape because you gave Beldarius the wrong manacles?'

'I did not give him the wrong manacles. You are lying.'

'Oh yes. You did. I read your mind as you handed it to him. I already got them off my wrists.'

'You are lying!'

'How do you know? You cannot see through walls, now can you?'

Faeyet uttered a few expletives that would make Aedric's ears burn and ordered the guards to stop the wagon. Myrine whispered in Rollandario's ear and gave his hand a reassuring squeeze. By the time Myrine heard Faeyet's approaching footsteps, she had finished. Using her pyrokinetic supernatural power, she lasered a football sized hole at the bottom of the front wall. She again whispered in Rollandario's ear before she switched off the MagLite and secured it on her utility belt.

The light streaming in through the hole in the bottom of the front wall made the floor of the prison cart visible. Myrine could see the bottom of the door without having to adjust her eyesight. With Rollandario in tow, she walked to the door. A key scratched in the lock. The door opened. Myrine waited for Faeyet to come inside. As planned, Rollandario grabbed Faeyet and knocked her out.

Myrine closed the door and took her MagLite from her utility belt. She played the low beam over Faeyet. *Dragonscats. No backpack.* Faeyet started moving and Myrine clocked her over the head with the baton-handle of the MagLite. She removed the block between her and Rollandario.

'We only speak telepathically. As I throw the fireball through the hole, I made in the front wall. You open the door and we jump. My backpack must be on the wagon somewhere. The horses should bolt trying to get away from the fire, so we have to jump fast.'

'What about her?'

'We leave her right there where she is lying.'

'Maybe we should tie her up first.'

'There is no time.'

Myrine stepped to the hole in the front wall. The three guards were standing by the horses' heads. One of them turned and looked at the prison cage. She heard him wondering what was taking so long. She threw a massive fireball through the hole in the wall as he stepped away from the other two. In her haste, her aim was off and a spark caught the one horse on its rump. It reared. The wagon jerked sideways.

Stumbling through the door which Rollandario had opened, she moved to the side of the wagon and jumped off. She looked at the guards, but they had their hands full trying to calm the horses. Rollandario landed next to her. Myrine saw the wagon, left hand side back wheel stuck in a deep ditch, had blocked off the path to the cliff.

'Hey, hey. Where do you two think you are going?'

Leaving the two guards to hold on to the horses, the third one, who had previously stepped towards the wagon, came running. Stunned, Myrine saw Rollandario throw a little fireball at the guard. It hit him square in the chest, before bouncing off his breastplate to the ground where it lay, sputtering. The guard stopped, looked at it. He stomped on it.

Using the diversion to her advantage, Myrine had straightened her arms in front of her, open palms turned towards the guards. Before the approaching guard could move towards them, she raised a curtain of hell fire between, cutting them off from the guards. The horses went wild. The wagon lurched. The wheel stuck in the ditch broke clean off its axle. The wagon slid forward, leaving an opening to the path beyond it that led to the cliff.

The fire latched onto the front of the wagon and it started burning by itself. Myrine loved animals and could not bear to think the horses might come to serious harm. On the other hand, she dared not douse the fire. It kept the guards at bay. Imagining her Spyderco knife in her hand, using her telekinetic supernatural power, and cutting through the leather harnesses attached to the shaft. The horses took off with a thunder of hooves.

Myrine heard a massive thump as the front shafts of the burning wagon dropped. Sparks flew above the wall of fire she held in place. One of the embers landed in dry underbrush and, with a little push, Myrine helped it turn into a roaring fire. She turned to Rollandario.

'That should buy them some time to find the backpack and get to the portal.'

'What is so important about your backpack?'

'I will tell you later. We should move before the guards find a way around the fire.'

The door of the prison cage opened. Faeyet, in her fosterling form with a teeth-baring snarl on her lips, appeared. Blindsided, Myrine was slow to react as Faeyet launched herself in the air and crash landed into her. Winded, she rolled over, but Faeyet would have none of it and rolled her back onto her back, closing her six-fingered hands around Myrine's throat.

Myrine gripped Faeyet's wrists. Faeyet squeezed harder and starbursts popped behind Myrine's eyelids. Her lungs burnt and her arms started to tremble. She closed her eyes as Rollandario appeared behind Faeyet with a thick stick and clobbered her on the head.

Gulping huge mouthfuls of air as Faeyet let go of her and turned on Rollandario, Myrine sat up. Her throat was raw. The smoke from the fire in the underbrush made it worse. She coughed and spluttered, not taking much notice of Faeyet and Rollandario. Automatically, she reached for her water bottle in the side of her backpack that was not there. Standing up, she wiped her runny nose with her hoodie's one cuff before wiping her watering eyes with the other.

She looked around. There was no sign of either Rollandario or Faeyet. Still gathering herself, she heard footsteps coming from the side where the ridge was above the river. It sounded like Rollandario, but at this stage Myrine was not taking anything for granted and shifted into a fighting stance.

Myrine sighed and relaxed as Rollandario stepped back onto the path.

'Where is Faeyet?'

'Attending a meeting with Aquaserpiuns.'

The hungry wail of the creature she encountered in the river on her first night in Betwonium sounded. Myrine did not need to ask who or what Aquaserpiuns was. That fearsome wail was answer enough. She shuddered to think of Faeyet's fate, then put it from her mind. She knew that if the shoe was on the other foot, Faeyet would not have thought twice.

'Let's go.'

Side by side, Myrine and Rollandario stepped through the gap on the side of the wagon and came face to face with Beldarius.

She faltered and glanced at Rollandario, who cowered beside her and knew there would be no help coming from him.

Dragonscats. I never thought he would stay with the wagon.

CHAPTER 23

Myrine could see Beldarius was as startled at her and Rollandario's appearance as she was at his. They were not far apart, but thankfully not close enough for him to reach out and grab her. The dilemma was that her backpack, lying midway between them, against a rock on the side of the road, was within his reach.

She was not going to repeat her previous mistake and try to fight him physically. And she had to avoid being hypnotised at all costs. She powered up her energy. Ready to be used for her supernatural powers. If she created a firewall, it could damage the backpack.

'He can walk through fire.'

'Not going to create a firewall. I cannot afford my backpack to come to any harm.'

She could stun him with a fireball. It should give her enough time to grab her backpack. Avoiding direct eye contact with Beldarius, her eyes darted between him and her backpack. She noticed Beldarius had caught her looking at her backpack. As he made to move towards it, she threw a fireball. It burnt a hole in his left shirtsleeve. A malodorous stink rose in the air. Next to her, Rollandario gagged.

Myrine wanted to look at Rollandario to see why he was in distress, but she dared not take her eyes off Beldarius.

'Calm yourself. Take shallow breaths through your mouth.'

'I cannot. I am allergic. To the gas he is emitting. I am suffocating.'

Wanting to reassure him, Myrine, whilst keeping her eyes on Beldarius at chest level, reached a hand out to Rollandario. She found and squeezed his forearm. He shrugged her hand off his arm and turned tail. From his running footsteps, she assumed he had gone back through the gap beside the wagon. But for her backpack, she would have followed him.

'Now it is just you and me. My useless son ...'

'I don't need your son or anyone else.'

'Tough are we? Well, little girl. You have not once been able to get away from me. How do you think you are going to get your backpack and get away now? So why don't you give up and follow my orders?'

'You are not my Ruler.'

'Whilst you are in Betwonium. I, as Ruler of the Betwonium Army, give the orders.'

Maybe if she moved towards him, slowly, until she got in line with her backpack. He would think she intended to comply. Simultaneously, she manifested a magic net. She got to the spot where her backpack was lying on the side. In one smooth motion she bent her knees, gathered the net. Reared up and cast it. Beldarius stepped out of the way and the net landed at his feet and faded into nothingness.

Dragonscats. He is faster than a cat with its tail on fire.

'I see the little girl wants to fight. Well. Let's fight. You think you can win this time?'

I could use one or more of my supernatural powers and combine it with my physical skills like Aedric taught me. The problem, though, despite Aedric's best efforts to fully train her, she had resisted and only used her supernatural powers when she was forced to. Myrine did remember, though, as her eidetic memory never allowed her to forget anything, how it could be done.

'No answer? You scared little girl?'

Myrine barely contained a shiver at hearing the evil invitation to battle. She reached for her utility belt with her right hand, closed it around her Spyderco knife's handle, and slipped it out of its pouch.

'You think you can hurt me with that little toothpick?'

She ignored Beldarius derisive laughter. Her mind veered between using her kinetic supernatural power to pull her backpack to her or using another supernatural power and attacking Beldarius.

A stone crunched. She jumped back. Her head shot up. Beldarius had closed the distance between them and they were now a mere three meters apart. They made eye contact. His pupils started contracting, then expanding, then contracting, then expanding. She squinted her eyes, blurring her vision. The hypnotic pull released. Myrine felt a tiny jolt of satisfaction as Beldarius released a frustrated grunt. She opened her eyes, taking care not to look directly into his eyes.

'You may as well give up. You are no match for me.'

'We shall see.'

She waited for Beldarius to make his next move and readied herself to use whatever supernatural power instinctively came to the fore.

'There is a soft spot directly under his bottom jaw.'

'Where are you?'

'Hunkering down behind the rear of the wagon.'

'When he attacks me, can you get to my backpack and wait somewhere behind him with it for me?'

'I will try, but if he sees me, his anger will increase tenfold, and that is dangerous.'

'Then make sure he does not see you.'

Beldarius' shout interrupted their conversation. Myrine declined his invitation to surrender. Something about the ripple that shimmered under his facial skin, set her on high alert. She would have to lure him away from her backpack. Myrine took two steps to the left. Away from the backpack. Beldarius swiftly followed up, stepping to his right. Thinking it worked, Myrine took another step to her left.

She saw Beldarius' mouth open as he took a step closer. A thick purple spotted tongue shot out of his mouth, unrolled, and shot out over the distance between them at warp speed. It thumped her in the chest. She stumbled backwards. The tongue was glued to the front of her tear-resistant, all-weather hoodie. The next moment Myrine was lifted off her feet. The sleeves of her hoodie cinched painfully under her arms. Chameleon-style she was reeled towards Beldarius.

Myrine got a fireball ready in the palm of her left hand. The reeling movement stopped about ten centimeters from his open maw. She did not know what his plan was, but it was the right time for her to make her move. Bringing up her feet, she planted the soles of her boots against his chest. Threw the fireball into his wide-open maw, simultaneously slicing through his tongue with her Spyderco knife.

Jumping out of the way as Beldarius fell to his knees, she wrestled the weakening tongue tip off her chest and threw it on the ground. It spasmed towards Beldarius, who was now on all fours, clothes ripping as he changed into his real Betwoniumite form. Thick yellow strands of drool hung from his open mouth. His tongue tip was still wriggling towards him. She kicked it away from Beldarius.

It tried to move towards Beldarius again. She launched a goal worthy kick and launched it into the bushes on the other side of the path. It landed on a thorn bush branch. Pierced by one of the thorns, it gave a final wriggle. That obstacle out of the way, Myrine turned her attention back to Beldarius. Still on all fours. Head hanging. His clothes hanging in strips off his body. There was no chance of getting to the spot under his bottom jaw, Rollandario had pointed out.

Not wanting to risk getting too close to his mouth, she moved closer to his rump and peered at the back of his neck. The scales covering it were impenetrable. With him having leant forward, the scales in the middle of his back had lifted. She tried to punch a hole with her knife between two scales, but her Spyderco knife's tip bounced off a scale as Beldarius' body heaved. His side jolted against her thighs. She fell. Scrambled up and moved back.

Now that she was not as close to him, Myrine saw he had his one claw in his mouth trying to dislodge the fireball from his throat. She knew she had to find a way to incapacitate him whilst his attention was not on her. There was an old scar that had left a bald patch on his right calf. Beldarius coughed. Myrine jumped. *Dragonscats!*

Digging deep, Myrine gathered all her strength. Grabbed the handle of her Spyderco knife with both hands and lunged. She ripped open the old scar on Beldarius' calf. He jowled. Tar-black acidic goo leaked from the cut. Bubbled and hissed, raising blisters on Beldarius' calf. The scales around it melted. Black acidic goo pooled on the ground. With a life of its own, it carried on bubbling. Gooey fingers formed and crept towards Myrine. It left acidic puddles wherever it found hollows in the ground. The pools got bigger, the fingers thicker.

Beldarius' body had dropped onto his left rump. His head was resting against a massive boulder. His pupils having enlarged, his eyes had become pitiless black holes. She could almost feel the heat of his hatred as they stared at each other. His jaw worked. He uttered a smoke-filled hiss. She had to finish it whilst she had the upper hand.

Using the last of her energy, Myrine let loose a blast of kinetic energy. Full force, it hit the boulder and cracked it, burying Beldarius' head and torso. She stepped past the puddles and fingers of acid, to the broken boulder.

'Rollandario! I need your help. Your father is disabled and won't be able to harm you.'

'You sure.'

'Oh, for goodness' sake. Yes. I am sure. Now get yourself over here.'

Myrine and Rollandario, working together and using their combined physical strength, toppled a large boulder piece, causing an avalanche of other boulder pieces to rain down on Beldarius. Satisfied that the boulder pieces completely buried Beldarius' body, Myrine slapped her hands against the side of her pants. She grimaced and looked at her palms. They were red and slightly swollen.

After dusting her hands as best she could, she looked around. More acid-fingers had crept over the path. Avoiding them, she walked to her backpack. She shrugged out of her torn hoodie and new sleeveless vest. Opening her backpack envisioning a new all weather hoodie and sleeveless vest, she took it out. Put on her backpack, covered it with her sleeveless vest. Making sure it was no longer visible, she donned her hoodie.

Getting back to Rollandario, waiting for her on the path, was trickier. In her haste, she nearly stepped into one of the puddles. She stopped. Scanned the ground ahead. The acid pools had started to join, forming a small river between her and safety on the other side of it. Unsure that she could make it with her nearly depleted energy levels, she looked at Rollandario, who was jiggling from one foot to the other in one place.

'I have to get over this muck without stepping in it and it is too wide for me to step over. If you stretch your arm over to me, I will grab onto it. Can you swing me over to you?'

He frowned at her, then looked at the ground. His head jerked up. He held out his arm. Myrine gripped onto his forearm with both hands.

'Wait. When I say now, you swing me to yourself.'

Myrine waited until Rollandario stopped shuffling his feet. She bent her knees slightly. Tightened her grip on his arm.

'Now.'

Cartwheeling her legs sideways, she gave extra momentum to the swing as Rollandario hauled her over. She crash landed into

Rollandario's chest and winded him. They tumbled backwards, falling into a heap. Thankfully, their tumble took them backwards and further away from the acidic river of black goo.

Myrine sat up first. After taking a long drink from her water bottle, she passed it to Rollandario. Their thirst quenched, Myrine poured some water on her palms and rubbed them before putting it back in its pouch on the side of her backpack. Rollandario stood in front of her, holding out his hand. She grabbed it and he pulled her up.

'Never thought I would see someone do that to my father.'

Myrine looked at the mound of boulder pieces. She wondered whether her eyes betrayed her. She looked again. Saw a slight movement in the heap. Unblinking, she stared at it and waited. Loose gravel cascaded where she saw the movement.

'Let's go. We can still make it back to the place where we hid last night.'

'Wait. I think I saw... There it is.'

Myrine pointed to the mound of boulders. Rollandario turned to look at it. They both watched as one of Beldarius' claw-fingers appeared on the mound's side. *Dragonscats. Any normal being would have been either dead or beyond recovery.*

'There is more to him than you can see. He can procreate himself from within himself.'

'What there is more than one Beldarius and they are all inside of each other. Like a Russian nesting doll?'

'Russian nesting doll?'

Myrine realised Rollandario, not being an Earthling and never having travelled outside of his own planet, Betwonium, did not know what she was talking about. Creating a video in her mind, she showed him a Russian nesting doll opening up.

'Something like that, yes. Except every time after an injury, he revives himself, and he becomes bigger and stronger.'

'How many times can he do that?'

'I am not sure. According to legend, it could happen as many as ten times before he cannot revive himself.'

'How many times has he been injured badly enough to have to revive himself?'

'I believe there was one time when he was younger, but that was before I was born. This is the first time I see him injured badly enough to have to revive a new one of himself.'

'Well. Then we better hurry before something like that Beldarius thing gets out from under the mound of rubble. I do not have the energy to activate my supernatural powers in full force for another bout with him. And you don't seem to have any defence against him?'

Myrine felt sorry for Rollandario as he dropped his head and stared at his boots. There was a reddish tint colouring his face.

'Don't worry. I know the feeling. It is how I feel about my mother. I would rather avoid her than face her. The last time I had a quarrel with her, her actions caused my anger at her to make my supernatural powers go haywire. I nearly killed my Grandma.'

'Really?'

'Really. Now come on. Let's go before Beldarius finds his way out from under those boulder pieces.'

They reached the cliff above the portal where Myrine was captured on her first attempt to reach the portal.

CHAPTER 24

Myrine looked at the place where she had previously tried climbing down the cliff's rock face. She was sure that if she was not captured, she would have reached the exit portal. She opened and closed her hands. They felt stiff. She inspected her palms. They were red and puffy. She would have to find another way. A climb down the cliff's side to the portal was out of the question. She walked to the lowest point above the plunge basin near the rock platform, with Rollandario following her. She peered down at the water's surface.

'How deep is the plunge basin?'

'Three of you standing on each other's shoulders.'

'How do you know that?'

'Before the closure of the portal was ordered, we could swim there.'

She did a quick calculation, multiplying her length, 1.7 and a bit meters by three. Just over five meters. It could be done if there were no big rocks on the bottom.

'The bottom is sand. The rocks are between the cliff's edge and the rock platform onto which the waterfall is falling.'

Myrine looked to where Rollandario was pointing. It was nearly in line with where they were standing. To avoid the rocks, she had to find another spot to dive from. She guesstimated the plunge basin to be about thirty meters long. There was a slight decline in the cliff face towards the middle of the plunge basin and what looked like a flat rock bed.

'If we dove from that spot over there, we would have to swim about fifteen meters to the rock platform behind the waterfall. We would reach it before our boots became waterlogged.'

'Why don't we take off our boots? I can put mine in the front of my shirt.'

'It would be better to keep them on to protect our feet. Both in the water and whilst exiting the portal. Besides, we may not have time to put them back on before going through the exit portal.'

Walking along the cliff, she looked down into the plunge basin. It bothered her that she could not see through the milky green water of the plunge basin. She would have felt better if she could gauge whether there were any rocky outcrops or other obstacles lurking.

'I told you the bottom was sand.'

'I know. You also told me you were very young back then. Your memory might not be absolute. Anyway. Any other creatures?'

'I cannot remember.'

Myrine hovered. If only she had the energy to use her laser detection sight. Her energy level felt fine. But. It would be foolhardy, though, to waste energy that she might need later.

'I will go first, then. And if it is safe, you can follow.'

'Wait. Over there, near the middle of the plunge basin, is a flat rock embedded in the cliff. We could launch ourselves from it. I think the middle would be safest.'

A roaring grunt sounded from the direction where they had left Beldarius, covered under a mound of rubble. It was too far to see what was happening. Another grunt. The noise of shifting rubble. If this version of him, as per Rollandario, was bigger than the one she knew, he could get out from under the boulder rubble. Time to move.

Myrine looked at Rollandario. He was retreating backwards. His odd-eyed gaze riveted in the direction of the mound. She grabbed him by the wrist. Pulled him away from the cliff's edge.

'Don't look at it. Turn around and look where you are going before you fall over the cliff.'

Facing each other, Myrine eventually got Rollandario's attention. She could see the fear in his eyes. She could commiserate with him, even though not to the same extent as her fear of her mother, which was different. Whatever his father did to him in the past had a lasting impact. At least she escaped her mother and had lived with Grandma since the age of three.

'Turn around and walk to that flat rock. I will cover your back.'

Without a further invitation, Rollandario turned his back to the mound of rubble and sprinted for the flat rock. Thankful that there were no loose shales on the rock, Myrine did a quick measure of its top. Five steps. Enough for a running start.

'You ready.'

Before Myrine could tell Rollandario to use a running start, he took one step and jumped over the edge. *At least he had the presence of mind to pull up his legs and curl his arms around them.*

Standing on the edge, she waited for the towering water splash where Rollandario disappeared into the plunge basin, to calm down. Two beats ticked by. From the direction of the boulder mound, footsteps thundered. Rollandario's head appeared. He waved at her with one hand.

Myrine took five steps back. Took off and leapt over the edge, pointing her hands and feet to the water, forming a 'U' formation with her body. Entering the surface of the plunge basin, she straightened herself into a vertical formation.

Rollandario was already climbing onto the rock platform. The noise of scattering gravel from the cliff's ridge above had her look up. Beldarius, twice the size he was before, in full Betwoniumite form, stood on the ledge. She could read murder in his eyes as he glared at her. Then he climbed over the edge and started to lizard-scaled down the cliff's rock face. *Dragonscats.* Energised by her adrenaline, Myrine swam for the rock platform, using a fast crawl swim style.

Grabbing onto the edge of the rock platform, Myrine's foot slipped on one of the underwater rocks at its base. She fell back into the water. Righting herself, she stood in the waist deep water. Took a careful step forward and grabbed onto the edge again, this time managing to keep her hold on it.

There was a massive splash on the other side of the rock platform. A wave of water knocked her into the rock platform. Her knee connected with one of the rocks. A shock of pain sparked through her right leg. Above her, Rollandario appeared. Gripped her wrist and lifted her onto the platform.

'This way. The portal is open.'

The thunder of the waterfall was deafening. Myrine was grateful they could communicate telepathically. She followed Rollandario to an opening in the rock platform. The coloured rainbow she admired earlier shimmer danced against the waterfall curtain, painting hues of swirling colours around the portal entry.

A shadow stretched over the entry. Obliterating a third of the swirling colours. Before Rollandario noticed his father climbing onto the other side of the rock platform, Myrine pushed him towards the opening.

'Go. Wait on the other end for me.'

'I...'

'Just go. This is not the time for an argument, Rollandario.'

Rollandario saw his father, slid into the portal exit, and disappeared. One eye on Beldarius, and one eye on the portal opening, Myrine sidled closer to the portal's opening. She could not jump in. Beldarius would definitely follow. She checked her energy levels. There was enough to use one of her supernatural magical powers. At the back of her mind, she could hear Grandma's voice during one of her lessons.

There is energy all around us. The yin and the yang. The positive and the negative. To create an electrical storm, you need to create an imbalance. Separate the energies and they would want to restore balance. Released, they crash back together. Then you guide the lightning storm you have just created.

With her back to the portal opening, she faced Beldarius. She raised both hands, holding them next to each other, palms out towards Beldarius. She ignored his warning growl. Imagining separating the positive and negative energies in the surrounding air, she pushed her arms outwards.

The air got heavier. It became harder to keep her arms apart, palms facing Beldarius' oncoming figure. She waited a beat. He rose onto his back legs. His lizard form towered and shadowed the rock platform. He thumped his tail on the rock platform and took a step forward. The rock platform shuddered. He opened his mouth. Myrine brought her hands back next to each other. The positive and negative energy crashed back together.

Electricity frizzed. Shafts of fluorescent lightning crackled. She circled her palms. The fiery beams circled around Beldarius, zapping his wet body. Blue tipped fluorescent white sparks danced across his body. He tried to grab at it with spasming movements. He stumbled. Righted himself. Grunted. Hissed at her.

'You better run, little girl. I am coming for you.'

Myrine pushed a stronger wave of electricity at him. He fell backwards into the plunge basin. The water sizzled as he went under. The flames died. She jumped into the portal exit. A fervent search for something to close the portal opening left her empty-handed. There was not a single item she could use to close it from the inside.

Looking down it, she could not see the exit at the other end, only a haze of light showing that there must be an opening at the other end. Maybe she could close it at that end. There were iron rings embedded at regular intervals in the sides of the portal tunnel. Slight contractions issued from the sides of the portal tunnel. Its energy hummed through the air.

Scarcely twenty steps down, the rock platform above shuddered. Fine sand-dust rained down. She stopped. Hand above her eyes, she looked up. Mentally checked her own energy levels. To her surprise, her energy levels had fully replenished. A plan came to mind.

Myrine readied her telekinetic supernatural power. She looked down. In the distance, she could just about make out the portal's opening at the other end. With her telekinetic supernatural power at the ready, she simultaneously readied her mind to use teleportation to exit the portal at the other end. Motionless, she waited.

Beldarius' feet appeared on the first iron rung. Combining her telekinetic supernatural power with the portal's power, she increased the contractions in the tunnel's sides at the top. Beldarius tried to kick free of the constriction. Myrine increased the contractions, and with a blast of energy, he was pushed out. Above, the portal opening had minimised dramatically. The portal was too unstable to close it completely. She froze the top in place.

She tried to normalise the portal's energy. Despite removing her energy from it, it did not decrease and remained destabilised. Myrine's feet slipped off the vibrating rung she stood on. The portal's hum became a host of sinister whispers. Hanging by her hands from the iron rung above the one she stood on moments ago; she closed her eyes. Calmed her mind and teleported herself through the exit at the bottom.

Reconstructing her body's particles into its normal form, she found herself on a sand dune. Behind her, there was a belch. A wave of energy shoved her in the back. She fell to her knees in the hot sand and crawled away until she could no longer feel the energy blasts coming from the portal's exit.

Everywhere she looked, there was sand. Searching through her eidetic memory banks, she confirmed she was on the third plane. Triberia. One step closer to Tsaonin. She looked around for Rollandario. Saw his boot sticking out of the sand near the portal's exit.

No longer feeling energy blasts coming out of the portal exit, Myrine went to Rollandario. He lay on his back, head lolling to one side. She tapped his boot with her toe. No response. Bending over him, she saw his chest was moving. Not dead then. Only out cold. The hum from the portal increased in intensity. She looked at the exit. It started pulsing faster.

Myrine stepped around Rollandario's inert form. From behind him, she hooked her arms under his armpits and dragged him away from the portal exit. A blast of energy from the portal missed them by centimeters.

She dragged Rollandario another few meters before stopping at a dead tree trunk. She laid Rollandario's back against it. His body sagged to the side. Taking her water bottle from the side of her backpack, she splashed some water on his face. He came to moaning and spluttering.

'What happened? I feel as if a boulder rolled over me.'

'I had to use the portal's energy combined with mine, to stop your father from coming through. It became destabilised and dangerous. We need to move further away from it. I think it wants my energy.'

'Dangerous?'

'Like it wants all of my energy and it tried to suck me back in.'

Rollandario used the tree trunk and wobbled onto his feet. Myrine grabbed his one arm and flung it around her shoulder, encircling his waist with the other.

'Come. We have to get away from the portal exit.'

They reached the end of the peak of the dune they had landed on and stopped. Ahead of them lay a dune field. Myrine's spirit plummeted to the bottom of her boots. Portal entrances are always situated at a water source.

'Let's sit down for a bit. I need to go through my eidetic memories of what I have studied about Triberia.'

'I could do with the rest. I brought some cynoglosium with me, and I want to put some on my sprained ankle.'

'I am going to shut off the telepathic link between us for now. I need to concentrate.'

Myrine sank down next to Rollandario, crossed her legs, and rested her hands, palms up. She closed her eyes, and silently chanted the Ho'oppono prayer five times. Her anxiety having calmed down, Myrine turned her attention to the memories of the book on Triberia she had studied with Grandma.

Finding the picture describing the settings of Triberia, she enlarged it and mentally traced the route from where they were to where the portal entrance to the next plane is situated.

She opened her eyes. A wind gust twirled and snaked through the sand. Myrine stared at it. Realised it was headed for them and turned her head into her shoulder in time to avoid the spray of sand. The wind died down. Looking up at Rollandario, she was amazed that it completely missed him.

'How is your ankle?'

She stood up and held out a hand to Rollandario.

'Good. I can hardly feel the sprain.'

'We have to cross the dune field and go to the castle on the other side of it. The portal is underneath it.'

'I think we need to find a place to hide first.'

Myrine looked at where Rollandario was pointing. At the peak of the furthest dune, black dots appeared. It grew larger as it sped towards them. At the base of her skull, her lizard brain reacted. She looked around for somewhere to hide. Only sand and sand and more sand.

Unease turned to dread, threatening to render her immobile.

ABOUT THE AUTHOR

Amouré Kleu was born in Graaff-Reinet, a small town in South Africa's Karoo region. She attended the University of the Free State from 1977 to 1979 and, during her university vacations, worked as a junior reporter at Die Volksblad (an Afrikaans newspaper). Toward the end of 1979, she obtained employment with Bowman Gilfillan Blacklock Inc, focussing on Labour Law. In 1992 and 1993, she was articled to Mervyn Smith Attorneys and was solely in charge of all High Court litigation.

In 1998, she started her own paralegal practice and specialised in litigation focused on engineering matters from steel engineering to PLC programming. In 2007, she left South Africa, moving to the Gold Coast of Australia, but still travelled to South Africa in order to complete legal matters. In early 2019, after finalising a legal matter for a client, she retired. Only, by special request, does she do some legal consulting for certain firms in South Africa.

First published at age 15 in August 1974, Amouré in 2018 decided to study creative writing. She did the Unlocking Creativity course with The Writers' studio in Sydney and found a spark that ignited her dream to write into a goal that she would write and publish a novel.

Having always had a very vivid imagination, she now finds herself in the enviable position of being able to pursue her endless passion for creative writing. She loves taking long beach walks at sunrise. She loves cooking and finds that it alleviates stress when she experiments creatively with different flavours, cuisines, textures.

Manufactured by Amazon.com.au
Sydney, New South Wales, Australia